The Prairie Shrine

**Center Point
Large Print**

**This Large Print Book carries the
Seal of Approval of N.A.V.H.**

The Prairie Shrine

ROBERT J. HORTON

CENTER POINT PUBLISHING
THORNDIKE, MAINE

Library of Congress Cataloging-in-Publication Data

Horton, Robert J., d. 1934.
   The prairie shrine / Robert J. Horton.--Center Point large print ed.
      p. cm.
   ISBN 1-58547-486-X (lib. bdg. : alk. paper)
   1. Large type books. I. Title.

PS3515.O745P73 2004
813'.52--dc22

2004006252

To My Sister
MARION ELIZABETH HORTON

CONTENTS

CHAPTER I
THE WEB

In all that vast, far-reaching vista of open country there was not a head of stock, not a semblance of human habitation, not a moving thing visible to the eye except a solitary figure in the lee of a rise of ground above a shallow coulee, the red banks of which made a vivid scar in the rolling green of the plain.

Mark Neeland shifted about warily in the shelter of the low ridge and peered with alert eyes across the intervening space of prairie between the coulee and a line of stately cottonwoods which marked the course of a stream in the south. This line of tall cottonwoods was the only break in the undulating plain, except for a low-lying series of isolated buttes to eastward. Some forty miles in the west the foothills ranged up to the mountains, and midway this distance a faint streamer of smoke suggested a town.

It was on the cottonwoods in the south that Neeland focused his gaze. He squinted in the dying sun of the late spring afternoon, and his blue eyes glowed speculatively.

"Looks like it's all straight that the Caprons have moved all their stock from north of the river," he said aloud; "an' I guess they're down in the Falls on business, all right. Well, this is as good a chance as any."

He walked down the coulee and out on the plain below. It was a fertile plain, rich in grass, nearly level. Neeland's eyes sparkled as he walked over it. He was a portly man, and he puffed under the exertion. Now he began to look closely at the ground, measuring off distances with his eyes.

"Ought to be just south of the coulee," he muttered, frowning. He walked slowly back and forth, looking downward with frequent quick glances in the direction of the cottonwoods.

Suddenly he gave vent to a smothered exclamation and kicked at a square stone with his foot. With another look southward he dropped on his knees, brushed off the stone, and looked at it closely.

"That's her, sure as shooting," he grunted in a satisfied tone. "With that corner stone located, I can find every quarter section in here."

He took out a small notebook and jotted down some figures which he copied from inscriptions on the sides of the square stone. Then he rose, put the book away, and wiped his forehead with a large bandanna handkerchief.

"More web," he murmured with a grin. "If I don't run out of land I'll put enough in the bank to buy old Capron out, hoof an' horn, if he gets too mean."

He hurried back up the coulee and across the rise of ground above it. A short distance beyond the rise a small, battered car was standing. Neeland walked down to it, cranked it with much puffing, took his place behind the wheel, and drove off westward across the plain. There was no road, but he proceeded unerringly, following the imprint of tires in the grass and soft earth, straight toward the thin streamer of smoke, and, after traveling a score of miles, came in sight of a little town.

"Brant will grow like a mushroom!" Neeland exclaimed gleefully in a voice which carried above the staccato of the little motor. He looked at the ribbon of steel extending north and south from the town.

"They'll be coming in like sheep!"

He glanced back nervously, shrugged his shoulders, sighed with something like relief, bent over the wheel, and sent the small car scuttling into town.

Brant was in the nature of being a nondescript town. The weathered false fronts and drab clapboards of the old buildings contrasted incongruously with the newer structures of wood and brick, brightly painted, and displaying ample windows. There was a new lumber yard, too, and the shed of a rival concern was being built. The depot had been enlarged and painted and a wide cinder platform installed before it.

As might be expected, the old and the new in Brant did not adjoin. The old part of town was west of the railroad tracks, and the newer section was east of the tracks. This division of the town was symbolic of the great change which the country was undergoing.

Millions of acres which had formerly been stock range had been thrown open to homestead entry by the government. Railroads serving the Northwest had carried the message of "Free Land!" to every nook and corner of the Middle West and far into the East. The lure had proved sufficient to start thousands on their way to Montana to file on quarter sections.

The cattle barons had seen the handwriting on the wall and had either sold their herds or moved them southward across the Missouri to a last stand in the wind-swept ranges of the Musselshell. The sheepmen were dying harder. There still were several large sheep outfits operating, and some of them had leased thousands of acres of State school sections in an effort to hold on.

Lawton Capron was one of those who refused to budge before the influx of the potential dry-land farmers. He owned thousands of acres along the Teton River, north of the Missouri, and ran both cattle and sheep.

"It'll go hard with them that tries to string a fence along my range," he had said grimly, when the vanguard of the homesteaders made its appearance in Brant.

Meanwhile, those that filed had six months' grace in which to take up actual residence on their claims. Most of them had filed and gone away, intending to return at the end of the six months. Not a few of them were taking up the land as a speculation with a view to improving it as little as possible, paying a dollar and a quarter an acre at the end of fourteen months, and taking title. They expected land worth five dollars an acre for grazing to be valued at thirty to fifty dollars an acre as farming land when deeded. Perhaps twenty-five per cent of those filing, actually intended to till the soil to make a real farm home and live there.

The newcomers were unfamiliar with the land. They did not know what had been taken up and what was left open to entry. Most of them could not find a given quarter section, for open prairie and government plats were different propositions. Many of them could not understand the markings on the stones at section corners even when they found them! Consequently they had to depend upon professional locators such as Mark Neeland, who charged what they could get as fees for locating homeseekers on quarter sections. The filing was done at the land office in Great Falls.

The long twilight of the semialtitudes was spreading over the land when Neeland stopped his car before the New West billiard and refreshment parlor in the newer section of town.

"How's the web?" called a tall, angular individual with blond hair and sallow cheeks as the locator entered.

Neeland grinned and looked about with blinking eyes before answering: "There's plenty of web left to catch more flies," he said in a thin voice which was out of keeping with his bulk. "You call the land the web an' the homesteaders the flies, Andy; now what do you call me behind my back, I wonder?"

The tall man's blue eyes took on a dreamy luster. He recited: "Where there's a web and flies, sir, there's likely to be a spi-der."

"Ha!" chirped Neeland. "That ain't as good a rhyme as usual for the 'Prairie Poet,' Andy Sawtelle. An' in this case there's got to be spiders, or how would these poor devils get located on nice, choice bits of land?"

"Choice bits!" exclaimed Sawtelle. "I'd like to have *you* picking me out a choice bit. Why, you haven't been in this country only three years, and I was the same as born here!"

"I got a line on some choice bits to-day, just the

13

same," said Neeland, edging up to the bar and nodding to the bartender to serve them with drinks.

Sawtelle lifted his thin brows and spread his angular arms on the bar. "I suppose I'll have to listen as payment for this drink," he said, pouring out some of the liquor.

"Oh, I know you think this country can't be farmed," said Neeland with a scowl. "Maybe you're right, although you've got the prejudiced view of the old-timer. But there's parts that's got a better show than others, an' one of those places is north of the Capron place on the Teton."

Sawtelle put down his glass with a bang. "You been out there?"

Neeland nodded as he drained his potion. "This afternoon. Got a line on the corners. I'm the first that's dared to go out there after all the threats old Capron's been making. But he can't get away with it. This thing's too big. An' the government's behind it. The old fool ought to know it had to come."

Sawtelle hummed softly, looking at the locator. "Fools ride in where angels fear to tread; the which is why so many fools are dead," he said with amusement in his eyes.

Neeland bristled. "He don't own that land," he said hotly. "I'm going to locate folks on every quarter section out there!"

"You mean you are if Capron and his foreman, Jake Gruger, stay down in the Falls long enough," said the poet dryly. "The government in Washington is one thing, and Jake Gruger on the ground with his six-gun

14

is another. You must think your hide is bullet proof, Neeland."

"They won't be coming on the land to live for six months anyway," said the locator nervously, "an' by that time—"

"You'll be gone with your wad, eh?" Sawtelle broke in with a hollow laugh. "I thought sheep was bad, Neeland; but this web and the flies and the—spiders!"

The poet shook his head thoughtfully as Neeland hurriedly ordered another drink.

"You're a dreamer!" snapped Neeland. "A dreamer an' a would-be songster. You ain't practical!"

"But I know what I can see with my own eyes," Sawtelle retorted wistfully. "It isn't going to be easily done—this thing. You can't change a big country like this overnight. This is my third drink this evening, Mark Neeland. I warn you not to coax me too far into my likker this early, or I'm liable to sing about you and your new section of web, and some friend of the Caprons might think there was more of a point to my rhyming than you suspect."

Neeland held up a hand. "I won't coax you," he promised.

"Seven forty-two is whistling," announced the bartender.

Most of the men in the place, including Sawtelle and Neeland, moved quickly out the door. Already, in the little street, there was a procession bound for the depot. In the north the half light was streaked with smoke. By the time the train whistled for the stop at Brant, the cinder platform was jammed.

"She whistles and toots and brings 'em in—the flies to the spiders' web so thin," mused Sawtelle.

"Shut up!" Neeland barked in his ear.

The train came to a stop with a grinding of brakes.

"All out for Brant!" the brakeman was shouting.

"Free bus to the Thompson House," came the call of the hotel runner as the train began to disgorge passengers.

Neeland busied himself passing out cards. "Homesteads located," he cried shrilly. "Relinquishments cheap. Best quarter sections—"

He paused as he saw a woman and a girl alighting. The girl was carrying her hat in her hand with other baggage. The station lights gleaming on her hair turned it to burnished gold. Her face was flushed, her gray eyes were sparkling. As she stepped from the box below the coach steps, she took the arm of the older woman who appeared tired and worn.

"Mother, dear, we're here," she said in a vibrant voice, sweetly reassuring. "Can't you just *taste* the air?"

"Room for all at the Thompson House," shrilled the hotel runner. "Free bus, an' baggage carried."

Neeland recovered his senses and pushed forward, reaching for the two suit cases the brakeman had deposited on the platform.

But he was brushed aside by another.

"I'll help you, ma'am—flowers are rare in the prairie country."

It was Sawtelle's voice, and the poet gathered up the luggage, nodded to the girl and her companion to accompany him, and made a path for them to the hotel bus.

"Thank you so much," said the girl.

"And ample payment, ma'am," said the poet gallantly.

"My card," offered Neeland, reaching over Sawtelle's shoulder and handing the girl one of his pasteboards.

"Likewise his challenge!" mocked the poet.

The girl looked puzzled. Then she laughed and turned her attention to the older woman.

"You see the West isn't so uncouth, mother," she said cheerfully. The rest of her speech was drowned in the clang of the engine bell and the noisy turmoil on the station platform as the train moved away.

The bus driver cracked his whip, and the unwieldy vehicle rattled over the track toward the hotel.

CHAPTER II
THE REMNANT

The girl wrote their names in fine Spencerian on the register while the clerk beamed his admiration and hurriedly clutched at his red necktie.

Mrs. J. C. Bronson, Coltersport, Pennsylvania.
Annalee Bronson, Coltersport, Pennsylvania.

"Have you something with a bath?" she inquired with a twinkle in her eyes.

The clerk came as near blushing as possible through

his tan. "We ain't got quite that far yet, ma'am," he apologized. "This town's just started, you might say. But there's a good bath on the second floor, an' I'll give you a nice outside room close to it."

"That's all right," replied the girl. "I didn't expect room with private bath here—yet, as you say. Some time maybe we'll have them, don't you think?"

"Why—er—sure, of course. Are you goin' to *live* here, ma'am?"

"We expect to make our home here—mother and I. That's what we came West for. I suppose there's some land left?"

"Oh, plenty. Yes, ma'am, there's land enough left for everybody, I guess. Ah—Lem, oh, *Lem!*"

The clerk glared at a sleepy individual in overalls who slouched up to the desk at his call.

"Take these ladies' baggage an' things up to twenty-six an' be right smart about it. An' see that they have some ice water an' anything else they want."

Then, turning to the Bronsons, he said: "I'll see that some bath towels is sent up there right away. There's only one lamp in your room, but I'll have another sent up so you'll have plenty of light. If there's anything else you want, just send down for it—that's what we're here for."

The porter in overalls slouched toward the stairway with the luggage.

"Where do we eat?" asked the girl, smiling.

"Right in the dining room, miss. There's the door in the back there. This other big door leads into the bar, so don't make a mistake."

The clerk laughed at his own joke and Annalee Bronson joined him. Mrs. Bronson looked worried and hurried after the porter. The girl joined her, and they went up the stairs.

"Redheaded!" said the clerk, looking after the girl in undisguised admiration.

"Which is an indication of the extent of your knowledge and education," said Sawtelle, who came up and leaned on the desk. "The hair you mention, my dear man, is not red, but auburn.

> "The glow of the sunset's in her hair,
> The blush of the rose in her cheeks so fair."

"Wonder you wouldn't get a steady job, you know so much," advised the clerk.

"I have a steady job," replied the poet absently.

"So? Since when?"

"Ever since I can remember," sighed Sawtelle. "Trying to sell some verse."

"Of course," said the clerk. "An' you could make money at it at that if you'd stick to those barroom poems the boys understand. You're tryin' to make rhymes over your own head an' everybody else's!"

"Maybe you are right," said Sawtelle dreamily; "but that's got nothing to do with the color of Miss Bronson's hair."

"She's some looker," mused the clerk. "Acts like she had spunk, too. Them girls with that sort of hair ain't ordinarily timid. Going to live here."

"Homestead?" asked Sawtelle.

The clerk nodded.

"Then she's *one* thing we can thank the government and the Great Northern railroad for," said the poet. "They baited her and brought her here. Man, she matches our skies!"

"Say," said the clerk, lowering his voice, "there's somebody else in town."

A burst of hilarity drifted in from the big barroom.

Sawtelle scowled. "That bunch in there is getting wild. Wonder they wouldn't stay over in the old town where such stuff goes wide, free, and handsome. It'll make a bad impression over here with guests like the Bronsons coming in."

"The boss figures their money's as good as anybody's," said the clerk. "They're spending; you've got to hand it to 'em for that. It's that bright, new bar with its big lookin' glass that brings 'em. You didn't ask me who was in town, Andy?"

"Why should I? I've only got to listen, and you'll tell me sooner or later."

"Well, then, it's 'Silent' Fred Scott," whispered the clerk.

Sawtelle slowly faced about, looking keenly at the man behind the desk. "You're *sure,* I take it?"

"Saw him myself," declared the other. "Caught a glimpse of him goin' into the Green Front over in the old town this afternoon. He's here, all right."

"Now, I wonder," Sawtelle pondered. "What can Silent be hanging around here for?"

The clerk shrugged. "He's been here before," he observed. "This used to be a hangout of his once. Shot

20

a man here, I believe. These are tricky days for a man that's greased lightnin' with his gun."

"Silent never went looking for trouble," said Sawtelle.

"But trouble usually follers him like a coyote'll track a lame deer. He might as well pack a chip on his shoulder even if he doesn't."

"Oh, I don't look for any trouble here," said Sawtelle. "The boys have learned to lay off Silent. This bunch around here has been tamed somewhat."

"There's one left down the river that ain't been tamed none," the clerk hinted.

"An' he's in the Falls," said Sawtelle, frowning. "Anyway, Gruger's got too much sense to deliberately stir up anything. He hasn't much to gain any more— *that* way. And I notice he's steered clear of this Scott gent so far."

Another great burst of hilarity, mingled shouts and song, came from the bar as Sawtelle looked up to see Annalee Bronson and her mother coming down the stairway.

The girl saw him. She smiled and nodded.

The poet's hat nearly swept the floor as he stepped to the bottom of the stairs.

The girl appeared strangely beautiful in the light of the lamps hung in the little lobby. She was of medium height, not slender, nor stout, with a trim figure molded on perfect curves. She looked healthy and happy—and excited.

Her mother's face was gray and drawn. The eyes looked tired and a bit frightened. Her hair was nearly white. But she carried herself with a bearing which indicated gentle birth and breeding—a quiet dignity which bordered closely upon the aristocratic.

"If I can be of service at any time, please ask for Andy Sawtelle," the poet was saying.

"You make me think of a cavalier, Mr. Sawtelle," replied the girl. "I'm Annalee Bronson, and this is my mother."

Mrs. Bronson held out a white hand which Sawtelle took with hesitation, held a moment, and bowed again.

"We're going in to eat," said the girl. "I'm starved."

"Right through those double doors," Sawtelle pointed and walked with them toward the dining room.

Opposite the door leading into the barroom the girl paused, struck by the animated scene within. Men in khaki and chaps, overalls and riding breeches, boots and spurs, caps and great, wide-brimmed hats with scarfs variously attired about their necks, were crowding at the bar. Glasses sparkled in the light from the hanging lamps. Smoke drifted like a thin, blue veil above the heads of the patrons. Above the clinking of glasses, the jingle of spurs, the talk, the gruff laughter, the rattle of chips at the poker table, a player piano tinkled bravely.

The girl's eyes were wide, and she stared with startled interest.

Then, as if at the wave of some supreme magician's wand, the talk at the bar—was suddenly stilled.

The girl saw a tall, blond, boyish-looking man walking slowly from the outer entrance. His big, gray hat was pinched in at its high crown. A tobacco tag

22

hung from the breast pocket of his dark, soft shirt. A blue scarf was knotted low under his shirt collar, open at the throat. His trousers were stuffed into the tops of black riding boots which glistened with their brilliant polish. About his waist was a cartridge belt, and tied to his right thigh was a worn, black leather holster from which protruded the black butt of a gun.

All this the girl saw in a hurried, curious glance. Then he looked straight into her eyes. Something in the clear quality of his gaze held her breathless and wondering. Yet she noted his clean-cut features, the high, arching brows, the blond hair, wavy where his hat was pushed back, the tan on his face and neck, the straight mouth which seemed on the point of smiling.

He looked away and stepped up to the bar, the crowd silently making way for him.

She saw him say something to the man in the white apron in a low voice; saw the man hurry to carry out his orders; saw the surreptitious glances directed at the newcomer; saw him look calmly up and down the length of the bar coolly and a bit disdainfully.

"Let us go, Annalee," Mrs. Bronson was saying when the girl again came to herself.

"Who—who was that?" the girl asked Sawtelle.

"That is Silent Fred Scott."

"But why did they all stop their noise so quickly?" the girl insisted. "Oh—he wore a pistol! I see. He is an officer?"

"On the contrary, he is just the opposite," said the poet dryly, as they paused at the dining-room entrance. "They stopped their chatter because they are afraid of him.

Maybe they was scared their small talk might annoy him. Silent takes his drinks and conversation separate."

"Oh," said the girl, still mystified.

Sawtelle bowed, not ungracefully, as the women went on in to dinner.

CHAPTER III
THE LAND

During the meal Annalee thought much. She was amused at the quaint character Andy Sawtelle presented. He was indubitably of the country, and yet, in some inexplicable way, he did not seem to belong in the hectic setting of the boom prairie town. There was a subtlety to his speech, too, that intrigued her interest; he gave her the impression of being a happy-go-lucky nature who knew much. He seemed to pity as well as admire her. There was no question but that his desire to be of assistance to them was honestly and gallantly sincere.

But the girl could not help remembering the eyes of the man Sawtelle had said was Silent Fred Scott. She found herself breathing more rapidly as she recalled the quality of his look—surprise, swift interest, and quick appraisal were in his gaze. It was as if he read her very mind, read her through and through, in the instant that their eyes met. She wondered what he thought of her and instantly chided herself for her feeling of interest in him.

And yet—she could not convince herself that there was not a logical, excusable reason for this interest.

The man was a genuine outdoor type; a perfectly molded figure set off the clean-cut, tanned features; he was picturesque but not obtrusive in his manner of dress. She decided, too, that his eyes were good eyes—and hastily concentrated her attention on her meal.

"I'm inclined to believe we'll meet some new types of men in this country, mother," she said.

"Anna, have you noticed the tablecloth?" her mother asked.

The girl nodded. "It isn't very clean, but I suppose they've fed a lot of people to-night. And we must excuse a great many things in this new country, mother. Anyway, we can have a clean cloth on our own table."

"I wonder if the things have come by freight all right," said Mrs. Bronson in a worried voice.

"They must have, mother. It is almost a month since we sent them. Of course they are here. Mother, darling, you promised me not to worry when we came out here. Just leave everything to me. It is going to be a great lark. And you see how nice everybody is? Did you notice how that Mr. Sawtelle was quick to help us, and how the clerk here in the hotel couldn't do enough for us? That is the hospitality of the West, mumsy; we will find they are wonderful people out here even if they are a little rough."

Mrs. Bronson smiled wanly at her daughter. "You always were an impetuous girl, Anna," she said with a weak gesture of resignation. "You got your wonderful hair from your father, and much of his temperament along with it. I don't see how this settling on raw land ever can be anything like a lark."

"But, mother, we will soon have a little house, and it's spring, and we can have flowers and a garden, and think—we are getting a farm for nothing! A big farm of level land! It won't be like the steep, rocky hillsides in our part of Pennsylvania where about all they can grow is buckwheat. You know what the man who sold us our tickets said, mumsy: 'Every year a harvest of gold.' The wheat will make us rich, mumsy."

"If it gets us a respectable living I shall be satisfied," said Mrs. Bronson, cheered by her daughter's enthusiastic speech. "That, and my health, and seeing you provided for, is all I want." She smiled at the girl.

Mark Neeland was waiting for them when they came out of the dining room. He doffed his hat and immediately plunged into the business which brought him there.

"The clerk tells me you are intending to settle here, Mrs. Bronson," he said affably, his small eyes shining.

The older woman gestured toward her daughter.

"That's what we came here for," said the girl cheerfully. She had looked into the barroom—which again was in a turmoil—without catching a glimpse of Silent Scott. "I believe I left your card in our room Mr.—Mr.—"

"Neeland," the locator supplied. "I can put you next to the best homestead land around here, Miss Bronson. There's still some good land left, but everybody doesn't know where it's at," he added with a significant lift of his thin brows.

"Why, I thought all the land was good," said the girl in surprise.

Neeland shrugged. "You would want the best," he countered. "Some's better than others. And a lot of the best has been taken up. But I can locate you—won't you sit down and talk it over, Miss Bronson? I'm sure you will want my services when you understand the—er—conditions."

"Let us go upstairs to that little front parlor I saw," said the girl. "I suppose we might as well find out about things now, mother?"

"You attend to it, daughter," said Mrs. Bronson; "and I'll go to the room and rest. The long ride on the train was very tiresome. And you are more familiar with what we—or you—want to do."

In the little front parlor, Neeland spread a plat out on the table under the shaded oil lamp and placed a thick forefinger on a square of the print.

"That's where you want to locate, Miss Bronson," he remarked with a note of superior knowledge in his tone.

"But isn't that rather far from town?" asked the girl.

"Only about twenty-two miles. That isn't far in this level country, ma'am. You see it's easy to make roads in the prairie—they make themselves, you might say. And there are no hills or tough hauls. Twenty-two miles out here is about the same as eight or ten miles back where you came from. Besides, there's no real good land left close in—unless you want to buy a relinquishment."

"And what is that, Mr. Neeland?"

"A relinquishment is a homestead that somebody's filed on and changed his mind and is ready to let it go for a consideration," explained the locator. "I could get you two nice relinquishments for about five hundred dollars apiece, Miss Bronson."

"But, I don't understand," said the girl, winking her brows in perplexity. "Why should they want to file on a homestead and let it go right away? Didn't they come here to find homes? Or can they let it go and file on another piece? I thought this land was all free."

"Oh, it's all free, Miss Bronson," said Neeland suavely. "You see you have six months after filing before you have to start living on your land. Some of these people have filed and then have found out that they can't go through with their plans. And some of them—well, it's a speculation with some, Miss Bronson. This land will all be worth big money when it's needed. No, they can't relinquish and then file on another piece—not without a lot of red tape, even if they can make it stick. When you've used your right, you've used your right, that's all. That's why these people want to be paid for relinquishing."

"Is this a relinquishment you have pointed out on the map?" the girl asked.

Neeland hesitated. There *had* been cases where unsuspecting land seekers had been sold locations as relinquishments at a big advance over the usual location fee and had never known the difference. He noted, however, the intelligent bearing and look of his fair prospect.

"No," he said at length; "no, I'm showing you on the plat land that is still open to entry. It's the best land left around here, miss. In fact, there's none better. It has springs on it that are wet until way into the summer, and water's close there for a well. It lies in a good place north of the river and will be right in line for the first ditches of the irrigation project that's planned for this district. I'm showing you the best, Miss Bronson."

"This is very kind of you, Mr. Neeland," said the girl, who was visibly impressed. "I suppose you are connected with the government in some capacity. You should know."

Neeland smiled wryly. "No, I'm not connected with the government, Miss Bronson; I'm a locator. You see," and his tone became unctuous and confidential sort, "the people who come here for land can't very well find it themselves. They don't know how to read section corners on the stones and all that. It's pretty hard work sometimes, even for me, because this country was surveyed on horseback, and there's corners unmarked and all that."

He paused and nodded impressively. "Then there's the thing of knowing what's left and what's already taken up. I keep track of that and save my—er—customers a lot of trouble and expense. No, it's necessary for land seekers to have help in getting located, ma'am, and that's my business. I've located more people than anybody else that's working in here. I guarantee satisfaction. I take you right out and show you the land, and if you don't like one piece I show you another, or a lot of 'em, until you find a quarter section that suits you. But I can't show you anything better than this I've told you about, and that's the positive truth, Miss Bronson."

"If that's the case there is a charge for your services," the girl observed.

"Of course," Neeland admitted with a smirk. "I spend money keeping a record of all filings and for gasoline and tires; and I had to study the country for a long time, miss, so's to be sure I wouldn't be making any mistakes. But it's the best policy to get located right and the value of the land I locate you on will more than make up for—my fee."

"What will you charge to locate my mother and myself?"

"Let's see, let's see," said Neeland, exhibiting some measure of excitement. "That's quite a ways out—that is, quite a ways out for *locating,* ma'am—an' it's an especial good section. That land will be worth a lot of money, Miss Bronson; I wouldn't be surprised if it was worth fifty dollars an acre by the time you get your patent from the government. It's as good wheat land as there is around here. Why, let's see—I'll locate you on the two choicest quarter sections out there for a hundred dollars apiece, Miss Bronson, an' that's a bargain price considering what you'll be getting."

He leaned back, smiling benevolently, while the girl stared at him.

"A hundred dollars apiece!" she gasped out. "Two hundred dollars! Why, I thought this was government land and that it was free!"

"It is, it is," said Neeland hastily. "All you've got to pay the government is a sixteen-dollar filing fee on each quarter section, live on the land, cultivate some of it, an' in five years you get your patent, unless you want to prove up in fourteen months. If you want to get title in fourteen months you can get it by paying a dollar an' a quarter an acre then and get your deed. But, as I explained, it's necessary to get located right, and us locators have to charge for our services."

Annalee Bronson looked a bit skeptical. "How long would it take you to locate us, Mr. Neeland?"

"Oh, I can locate you in less'n half a day!" Neeland ejaculated eagerly.

"It seems to me that two hundred dollars is pretty high pay for such a small amount of time and trouble," the girl commented, pressing her lips firmly together.

"But I had to go out there and locate those corners," said Neeland in a complaining voice. "It ain't all just taking folks out and putting them on the land. But, I'll tell you what I'll do, Miss Bronson; I'll make it an even hundred and fifty and you can't find another man in town that'll locate you out there for that!"

Annalee considered. It was true that it would be utterly impossible for her to go out and find a given homestead from a plat; it was true, too, that she had no way of knowing what was open to entry, even if she could find it. It was expense which she, like hundreds of others, hadn't counted on, but there seemed to be no way to avoid it. And it probably *would* be worth the expense to get a good piece of land. Yes, there was undoubtedly a difference in the land—that stood to reason.

"Are there any farms already established in that neighborhood, Mr. Neeland?" she inquired.

"Not yet, but in six months there'll be houses and

fences all over this country," Neeland replied convincingly. "This'll be another Iowa and Minnesota combined! Oh, there's one ranch near you," he added. "But that's a stock place right on the river. It'll all be cut up into farms some day, too."

"Well, we'll see, Mr. Neeland," said the girl thoughtfully. "I guess mother will be sufficiently rested to go out in a few days—"

"Oh, Miss Bronson," Neeland interrupted, "you can't wait *that* long! Every train is bringing in land seekers; they're coming in droves. That land will be taken up in no time a-tall. You want to go out right away and get yours. To-morrow morning, bright and early, would be best. It isn't necessary for your mother to go along, for you can see just what it is yourself, and I'll give you the description to file on for both of you."

"So this is what they mean by the homestead rush," observed the girl.

"It *is* a rush, miss—first come, first served. That's how all the land close to town went in a twinkling this spring. And they'll be coming in all summer and fall. You better take my advice and come out in the morning so's nobody will get ahead of you."

"Very well—if mother is agreeable," decided the girl. "By the way, who lives on the stock ranch out there? I suppose we might as well know the name of our prospective neighbors."

"Some folks by the name of Capron," Neeland replied. "I'll call for you about eight or half past in the morning," he added hurriedly.

32

CHAPTER IV
LOCATED

When Annalee and her mother went down to breakfast next morning, the girl took advantage of the opportunity to ask the hotel clerk if it was customary to employ the services of a locator, and if Mark Neeland was reliable and his charge reasonable.

"It's customary, all right, ma'am," the clerk assured her. "Anyway, it's the safest way when you don't know the country, and Neeland's as reliable as any of 'em—er—I guess. Some of 'em locate for fifty dollars a quarter, but I guess seventy-five ain't too high."

The girl explained everything to her mother and Mrs. Bronson's only comment was that they "might as well get the foolish business over with as soon as possible."

Neeland was waiting for them when they came out from breakfast.

"Got my car right outside, Miss Bronson," he said. "Won't take us no time. Beautiful morning for a ride, anyway."

Annalee found it was, indeed a beautiful morning for a ride. The eastern horizon was bathed in gold, the skies were cloudless and of a delicate blue; everywhere the prairie stretched like a series of great, rolling green lawns; the cottonwoods along the river in the south reared their stately shapes in quiet majesty; the low buttes were pink buttons of color in the sea of green, and to westward the high mountains were bathed in purple with gleaming minarets marking their summits against the sky line.

The girl drew a deep breath. "It is wonderful!" she murmured in a tone of awe.

"Ain't it?" said Neeland, grinning. "Level as a board, just waiting for seed to sprout dollars!"

"Oh, I wasn't thinking of *that*," said the girl with a shake of her head. "I referred to—to all this." She made a sweeping gesture which included all the landscape.

Neeland looked at her, puzzled. Then he brightened. "You mean the scenery. Of course. It's great. You'll have a fine view where I'm takin' you."

But his speech had had the effect of bringing her thoughts around to their undertaking. She gazed critically at the long sweeps of prairie. Not a road, not a fence, not a building, not a living thing in sight; it was a great, empty, silent land which seemed to brood, to pulsate with some former life, and suddenly she felt a vague sense of misgiving.

She pictured the hills, the fertile valleys, the flowers and streams of her native State. Could this land—this "raw land," as her mother called it—be made into farms? Could it be made to blossom? She recalled what she had heard of dry farming, or what was called dry farming. She did not know what it was; but she knew it was a form of agriculture made necessary because of a lack of rainfall. Could crops be made to grow without rain? She looked again at the skies and could see no hint of rain in them—no hint anywhere that rain ever fell, except in the green of the grass on the prairie; and she had been told this was due to the fact that there had been lots of snow the winter before and that there had been a "late" spring.

"How do they know grain will grow here?" she asked Neeland.

"Why, ma'am, that's the richest soil on earth," shouted the locator above the noise of the motor. "It'll grow anything. It's richer than the Red River Valley in Dakota ever thought of being, an' they grow wheat there."

"But—has anybody tried it?" the girl persisted. "I've seen no fields."

"Course not—but you will see 'em soon. They've tried it in spots, an' always got crops. But it was done on a small scale. You see this was cattle country, an' the stockmen didn't want—didn't need wheat. But they grew oats higher than your head in the river bottoms."

Annalee felt convinced. She recalled the endless grain fields she had seen in the Dakotas. Doubtless Neeland was right. But as she looked about at the great, virgin land she realized fully, for the first time, the enormity of her undertaking to make a farm home for herself and her mother. True, there would certainly be men who could be hired to work, and they had a modest capital, but it would require a strain of moral courage of tougher fiber than any she had been called upon to exhibit in the twenty—nearly twenty-one years of her lifetime spent in the peaceful Pennsylvania hills.

She pressed her lips in renewed determination and shook off the insidious feeling of doubt. Even if they did not make a big thing of it, if it brought back her mother's health—

She felt a glow of gladness. The cool, dry, stimulating

air of the simialtitudes had made her blood bound in her veins; caused her to feel bubbling with energy which she hadn't known she could possess in such a degree. Surely it would have some effect upon her mother. The dryness of the air would be healing, aided by the sunshine; the altitude of thirty-three hundred feet would prove a stimulus to fagged nerves and heart. Yes, she felt it in her heart with a thrill of joy—her mother would become well here.

The little car came to a rattling stop at the bottom of a rise of ground.

"Want you to get out here, miss, so you can see what a fine piece I've got in store for you at one glance," Neeland explained, although he appeared slightly nervous. "Just walk up with me."

He led her to the top of the rise and seemed to breathe a sigh of relief as he looked down toward the river at the vacant space of prairie between the rise and the nodding cottonwoods.

"There!" he exclaimed, wiping his brow, although it was not warm. "There's the best strip of land open to entry left in northern Montana! Look at it! Ain't it perfect?"

It did look good to Annalee. It was a long, gently sloping prairie, rich in grass, more green, she thought, than any she had seen on the ride out.

"There's springs down there, Miss Bronson," Neeland went on. "They don't go dry till way in August, usually. If it happens to be a good, wet year they don't go dry a-tall. Look! You can see where there's some willows 'bout halfway to the river. See 'em? Well, the

36

two quarters I had in mind for you an' your mother are right there. Nor'east an' sou'east quarters of section twelve—I'll give you the descriptions for filing. There's the place. It ain't necessary for us to go down there; you can see 'em from here. There's just what I tell you, Miss Bronson; the best pair of homesteads left hereabouts."

"How does it come no one has taken them up, then?" asked the girl.

Neeland was nervously watching the line of trees to southward. He started at the question; then smiled complacently.

"Everybody's been wanting to get close to town, miss. Seems like that's all they've got in their heads— close to town. I expect they figure land will be worth a whole lot close to town. Well, it *will* be; but land five miles from town that's only average won't be worth a cent more than land that's unusually good farming land this far out. You want farming land, don't you, Miss Bronson?"

"Yes," replied the girl shortly.

"Well, there it is," replied Neeland, beaming. "There's as good as I can show you, and if you take my advice you'll hustle right down and file on those two quarters in a hurry before somebody else gets a crack at 'em. You saw all we passed over; did you see any that looked better than this?"

Annalee shook her head. The land the locator indicated did look favorable. It did look well watered. She visioned a farmhouse, a garden, ripening fields, trees—

"Will trees grow here, Mr. Neeland?" she asked anxiously.

"Ab-so-lutely," affirmed the locator. "All you've got to do is plant 'em. There's a fine place below the springs there. You can have a garden in there, too—" He bit off his speech with a sharp intake of breath.

"I believe I see a horse down there," he said in some excitement. "Maybe somebody lookin' the piece over right now. I think we better be gettin' back as quick as we can, Miss Bronson, so you can get your filings in. You know, in this rush, you can't be sure of anything till you've got your land-office receipt."

"Well, I guess this is as good as any," the girl speculated. "Anyway, it is a kind of a gamble; and I like to see those trees below there—"

"The river's there, ma'am," Neeland put in hastily. "You're right in line for the irrigation project which will be put through sometime. I'm showin' you the best I've got, Miss Bronson—the very best."

"Then I believe we will take it," said Annalee in decision.

"Good!" exclaimed Neeland, turning back down the slope toward the car. "We'll hurry back an' make sure that it's yours."

They drove back to Brant as fast as the car would go, and there Neeland delivered to Annalee a slip of paper upon which was written the description of the two quarter sections he had so strongly recommended.

"Just hand that in at the land office in Great Falls," he explained, "and tell them you and your mother want to locate on those two quarter sections. Now there's a train for the Falls about eleven o'clock, and you and your mother better go right down to-day—this morning. You can come back by suppertime."

The girl's face had clouded. "Do we *have* to go down there, Mr. Neeland?"

"Yes. The land office is there. You can do as you like, Miss Bronson, of course, but you're taking a chance on waiting if you want that piece I showed you. Of course, if it's gone, I can locate you on another—"

"No," said Annalee, stamping her foot. "We'll go down to-day."

She had visualized the farm home that was to be in that spot near the weaving cottonwoods and the river. She felt the presence of the springs made sure the garden—and the trees and flowers. She had no desire to go again seeking a location. She longed to get started on the big task which confronted her.

"My mother *has* to go, Mr. Neeland?"

"That's the way it is, miss," said Neeland. "Everybody has to file in person. But it's an easy trip and you can rest in the Falls before starting back, and then that part of it will be all tended to."

"Very well," said the girl briskly. "Now I'll pay you in traveler checks, and our business will be settled?"

"Everything fine, ma'am."

Annalee paid him and went upstairs to her mother whom she found on the little balcony over the porch out from the small front parlor.

Mrs. Bronson looked up at her daughter with a smile. "Why, mumsy! You're looking better and feeling better already!" crooned the girl, kissing her mother on the cheeks.

"It's—a lonesome-looking place, isn't it, deary?" said her mother. "But it *is* wonderful air."

Annalee warmed to her description of the country as she had seen it on her morning ride and described the land which Neeland had shown her and which she had decided to file on. Then she explained why it would be necessary for them to take the train down to Great Falls to attend to their business in the land office, and Mrs. Bronson, although she objected at first, finally agreed with the laconic statement that she "wanted it all over with as soon as possible."

As they turned to go in, Annalee looked down into the street and drew back, startled. A man was dismounting from a horse in front of one of the buildings across the street. He was covered with dust, and the sides of the magnificent black horse he had ridden were also matted with dust through which the sweat had coursed, leaving unsightly streaks. As the man had slammed his big hat against his thigh he had looked up through the resulting dust cloud at the moment the girl had looked down. Their eyes met, and Annalee recognized Silent Scott. The wistful, questioning, direct quality of his gaze remained with her as she followed her mother to their room.

It irritated her to think that she should wonder about this man. Different? Perhaps he *was* different, in a way, from most of the men she had known; but were not different men to be encountered in this new country? More than likely she would see many of them. She dismissed Silent Scott from her mind.

She and her mother took the train for Great Falls where they visited the land office, found the quarter sections they had selected open to entry, and filed upon them. They returned by the afternoon train.

Andy Sawtelle saw them again that evening as they were taking a walk through the little town in the twilight. He nodded.

"We're residents now," Annalee called to him gayly.

He stopped with his hat in his hand. "You've— filed?" he asked.

The girl nodded, and her eyes sparkled as she told him of the day's work, described the location of their homesteads, and recited what they planned to do in an enthusiastic voice.

The poet whistled softly. "Quick work," he observed, looking at her queerly. "Well, don't forget what I said about being at your service." He passed on with a smile and a bow to Mrs. Bronson.

An hour later he met Neeland in the New West resort. "Neeland, you're a rat!" he said shortly.

"What—why—" But the locator read the poet's look. "They wanted a good piece of land, and I saw that they got it," he said in a mitigating tone. "Capron wouldn't fight with a woman for—"

"Do you know what they figure on doing?" asked Sawtelle scornfully. "They're going to move on to that land right away—*this week!*"

"The devil!" exclaimed Neeland, his jaw drooping.

Sawtelle walked away with a disdainful shrug.

CHAPTER V
ANOTHER SIDE

A nnalee and her mother walked to the western end of the town, through the old section, staring wonderingly at the buildings with their flamboyant signs and false fronts.

It was rapidly becoming dark as they turned back. As they reached the Green Front resort the half doors in the entrance burst open and a man came hurtling through, falling in the street almost at their feet.

Mrs. Bronson drew back with a scream.

Before Annalee could recover from her astonishment, the doors burst open again and another man came running out. This man was followed by three others, all dressed in khaki who were striving to get away from the place as quickly as possible.

Four of the men were running, and the one who had fallen to the ground was picking himself up when there came a crash and one of the small doors was smashed loose from its hinges and sent flying into the street.

A bulky form loomed in the half light, filling the space before the door. Then there were streaks of red at the man's hip and sharp reports which crashed upon the still air with the force of thunderbolts.

The fleeing men darted in behind other buildings and in less than half a minute the street was deserted save for Annalee and her mother.

A roaring voice boomed out. "I'm serving notice on you damned land grabbers to stay on the east side of the tracks while *I'm* in town!"

This speech was punctuated by two more shots, and then the big man thrust his smoking weapon into the holster on his right side and stood leering at Annalee, who was holding her mother. He seemed to enjoy her fright.

"Hello, redhead!" he called out. "Stranger round here?"

Annalee's face was white, but her eyes were blazing. "You—you ruffian!" she cried in a choking voice.

It did not occur to her to be afraid of the gun, or the man. She looked up angrily into the swarthy features and black, slightly bloodshot eyes of the big man who stood, with legs braced well apart, towering above her.

"You've frightened my mother into a faint," she accused. "I suppose you think you are brave—you bully."

The man scowled. "You've got a lot of spunk for a pale-faced Easterner," he said growlingly.

Mrs. Bronson moaned in her daughter's arms.

"Get away!" cried the girl. "Get away from here, you brute!"

Mrs. Bronson came to with a vacant look in her eyes which was followed in a moment by a terrified stare at the man before them.

Annalee soothed her with reassuring words. "Just a big, overgrown bully such as could be found in any part of the country," she told the older woman. "Thinks he's having a good time scaring people with a pistol and frightening women. He's probably drunk, and they'll have him in the jail before morning."

The man's bloodshot eyes were blazing wrathfully. "You talk like a school-teacher," he said sneeringly. "Your kind's been trained out here before. I've a good notion to box your ears or kiss you, one or t'other."

Annalee's face went white as chalk. "You're not only a bully and a brute, you're a beast!" she said with contempt and loathing in her tone.

A younger man had appeared at the other man's side. "Be easy with the kid, Jake," he said; "she's new here and you ain't in the best shape—"

"Who says I ain't?" roared the big man, throwing the other from him.

Annalee was drawing away with her mother. She could not understand why some of the men who must be near did not take a hand and check the bully who had accosted her. And were men allowed to shoot promiscuously like that? Guns!

Silent Scott! She almost wished he would appear, for she believed he was of entirely different caliber from this man who had warned the homesteaders away from the old town.

The younger man was again talking earnestly to the other, and as the girl and her mother moved over to the other side of the street, Annalee saw the big man turn back into the resort, leaving a trail of curses which carried to her ears and made her gasp with mortification and resentment.

Then the younger man came hurrying toward them, doffing his big hat. "I'm sorry, miss," he said in what was evidently intended as a tone of apology. "Jake's just got back from the Falls, and it always starts him on the rampage when he goes down there. Too many dumps down there layin' for stockmen."

Annalee didn't like the look in the young man's shifty brown eyes. He appeared too confident—too much at ease.

"He wouldn't have done what he did if he'd been right," the youth went on. "He don't get this way often, an' when he does, here lately, he takes it out on the homesteaders. He's just naturally sore at 'em, being an old cow hand. You—living round here?"

"You had better go back and look after your friend," said the girl coldly. "Fortunately I know he is not a true example of the manners of men in the West, and I hope you will help me to retain my first impressions."

The young man laughed softly as she took her mother by the arm and walked away.

"Anna, I told you," complained Mrs. Bronson. "This is a wild, rough country; it isn't the country for us. Oh, deary, we never should have come. I know—I *know!*"

"We are not going to let any beast like that drive us away," said the girl in as strong a voice as she could muster. "We could expect something like that any-where where men are drinking, mother. We shouldn't have come over here, that's all; this isn't a desirable part of the town."

But despite her words, Annalee again felt a tremor of doubt. Nor could she understand why some of the other men, who now were again appearing on the street, hadn't taken a hand in the affair. Her lips curled in contempt. Were they all afraid of this bully? Had he driven them to cover with half a dozen pistol shots and his roaring voice? Then she was struck with a sudden thought. Suppose all the shots had not been wild! Would this man have killed if any one had tried to interfere?

Now that it was all over, the girl felt weak. Perhaps her mother was right. In any event it appeared to be a man's job—this carving a home out of a raw country. But she bit her lip in resolution.

When they entered the hotel lobby she saw several men talking near the door and caught a glimpse of flashing stars on their vests. She asked the porter to bring her some ice water, and when he came shuffling to the room she told him of the occurrence on the west side of the tracks.

"Oh, I reckon thet was Jake Gruger," said the porter, with a grin, displaying his tobacco-stained teeth. "Yes, that was Jake, all right. The kid was hep to him. He's been to the Falls an' he allus comes back on a tear when he's been down there. They don't cross him when he's takin' on likker, an' he don't make no fuss onless it's serious, when he's sober, which is most of the time."

"But—do they let him shoot like that, and carry a pistol?" asked the girl.

"I don't reckon anybody could stop him shootin'," replied the grinning porter. "He's tolerably fast with his smoke iron, an' there ain't any hereabouts that I know of as would want to try to beat him to the draw."

"The—draw?"

"Sure. That's gettin' your gun out an' into action," the man explained. "Jake kin draw an' shoot at the hip an' hit a dime sideways further'n some folks kin see!"

46

"But there are officers in town," the girl pointed out. "I saw them downstairs."

"Oh, them?" said the porter with a deprecating gesture. "They're tryin' to locate the man that held up the stage from Choteau early this mornin'. They ain't figurin' on botherin' Jake."

"A holdup?" faltered the girl. This was another side to the country which she had come to adopt.

"Oh, yes. Some gent was short of change, so he borrered what the stage driver was carryin' down to the express office. That happens now an' then; there's still a few live ones hereabouts."

Annalee stared at him in amazement. "But—do they know who did it?"

"If they do, I don't reckon they want folks to think they do," cackled the porter. "Between you an' me, I 'spect they think Silent Scott did it; but they'd have about as much chance with Silent as they would with Jake Gruger."

"Oh!" exclaimed the girl, staring with wide eyes. "Is this—this Silent—a stage robber?"

"Nobody seems to know quite what he is, miss," said the porter cheerfully. "He's slick, anyways."

"And do both these men live here?" she asked.

"Naw—they come an' go. Silent's movements are about as easy to trace as a maverick steer in the bad lands. Jake Gruger lives out here apiece. He's foreman on the Capron Ranch along the river, the C-Bar, they call it, after the brand. That was young Myrle Capron with him."

Annalee remembered Neeland had said the ranch

below where she had selected the homesteads belonged to some people by the name of Capron.

"Oh—oh," she said in a queer voice as the porter left.

Then she sank down in a chair, her lips pressed tight, and fought with the depression which had settled upon her as the result of the news she had just learned.

A breeze, fragrant with the tang of the sweet grasses, filtered in through the window, which opened on the west, and brought with it the sounds of revelry in the old town across the tracks.

CHAPTER VI
RUMORS OF WAR

With the clear sunlight and crisp air of another perfect morning, Annalee Bronson's spirits revived. She sang as she dressed in a natty, brown suit which set off her hair and complexion, and went often to the window to look at the rolling prairie which flung its green mantle to the foothills of the purple mountains.

Mrs. Bronson, too, was more cheerful. The invigorating quality of the climate was beginning to make itself felt, and she forgot her fears in admiration of the radiant beauty and superb health of her daughter.

The two of them were laughing as they went down to breakfast.

"I'm going to see the railroad people and find out about our freight," the girl declared. "Then I'm going to order the lumber for our little, temporary house, mother—we'll have a better one in a year or two—and arrange to have it sent out to the farm." She paused as she considered how the word sounded. Then she laughed.

"We're farmers, now, mother. And I'm going to hire some men to build the house. When we're installed in the house it'll be time enough to take up the other things, one at a time. We don't have to hurry, and no one can take our land away from us—even if we should run out of money!"

A worried look appeared for an instant on Mrs. Bronson's face. "You must be careful of the expense, dear," she cautioned; "we haven't much, you know—three thousand for the house in Coltersport was hardly enough, but I had to take what I could get. We've less than five thousand altogether."

"But that will be more than enough here, mother," said the girl, cheerfully. "We get the land for nothing, and all we have to do is build a temporary house and put in enough of a crop to see us through the first year. Don't worry, I'll watch our nest egg."

Annalee was busy the remainder of the morning. She found that the car containing the household goods they had shipped from the East had arrived only the day before them. The railroad people said they would hold the car two or three days until it could be unloaded by the various homesteaders whose effects it contained.

She visited the new lumber yard where the manager helped her with her plans, advising a three-room house of two bedrooms and a living room and kitchen combined for a starter. He said he would figure out the lumber and other materials needed and would start his men hauling them out to the location next day.

"We have some carpenters working with us," he smilingly explained; "homesteaders, too, most of them, who are taking advantage of the opportunity to earn some money before going to live on their claims, and we will send three or four of them out to put up your house."

Annalee thought this a very excellent arrangement and rented a tent in which she and her mother could live for the time required to build the house.

She then approached a man who had a small, boxlike building on the main street near the railroad tracks and who advertised:

TEAMING & HAULING
Goods Hauled Anywhere

She explained that she wanted her household goods transported to her homestead and her mother's.

"Sure—I'll get 'em there," boomed the transfer man who had long, tobacco-stained mustaches. "Where is your place?"

"It's east about twenty miles," the girl explained. "Near the river. I'll have to go out with you—but, no I won't. I'll go out with the men hauling the lumber tomorrow and you can follow them. It's right north of the—the Capron place, I believe."

The man's eyes widened, and he fingered the ends of his mustaches.

"Out there, eh?" he said vaguely. "Just north of the Caprons? How fur north, ma'am?"

"Oh, I should say a mile or a mile and a half north of the river, and I understand their ranch is at the river."

"Yes, yes," he admitted, without looking directly at her; "yes, that's where it is. The C-Bar's 'bout twenty miles east of here. Well, now, miss, come to think of it, I don't think I'll be able to haul that stuff of yours after all. That's quite a ways, although that wouldn't count if I didn't have so much to do, but—why don't you get the lumber people to take it out?"

"Why did you change your mind so quickly?" demanded Annalee impatiently. "I didn't think twenty miles was considered such a great distance in this country."

"It ain't, it ain't," said the man, agitating his mustaches some more. "It ain't so fur, but it's too fur for me right now. Anyway, I ain't haulin' anything out in that perticular locality just yet. I've got all I can tend to closer to town. That's all there is to it, lady; I wouldn't turn you down if I didn't have my good reasons fur it."

The girl walked away from him in disgust. Turning back toward the hotel she came face to face with the big man who had driven the homesteaders from the old town resort the night before.

Jake Gruger gave her a flashing glance out of his dark eyes and passed her without further recognition.

Although their gaze had met but for an instant, Annalee had detected a new quality in the man's eyes—a menacing quality, quickly appraising, aggressive, and forbidding. It was plain he was not drunk this morning, and he was a different individual, she felt sure. For good or evil he was a force to be reckoned with, and he was to be a neighbor!

Annalee shuddered involuntarily as she hurried on

toward the hotel. She recognized two of the officers she had seen the night before. They were standing by a little car outside the hotel entrance. Remembering what the porter had said, she felt the impulse to go up to them and ask them if they were indeed looking for Silent Scott. Then the red suffused her cheeks. Afraid of one desperado and interested in another! It was ridiculous.

The hotel porter had as much as said that Scott was a doubtful character; probably he hadn't told the half of what he knew. And Silent Scott's horse *had* been covered with dust from a long ride when she had seen his master dismount the morning before. Had he just come from the scene of the holdup? But, in any event, it was none of her business.

"It's an even bet, Miss Bronson."

"What's—what's that?" said the girl, looking about her in astonishment.

Andy Sawtelle was bowing at her left. "I was saying, it's an even bet, ma'am, that you're more beautiful than the morning."

"Oh, Mr. Sawtelle, where have you been?" she asked severely.

"I've been wooing the Goddess of Chance, ma'am," he replied with a sigh. "But, alas:

"An ace in the hole, ma'am, means nothing to
    me,
Though I push in my checks most high, wide
    and free.
Some guy with three deuces, or maybe a pair,
Is certain to leave me all busted for fair."

"So, you're a poet," teased the girl; "and a gambler," she added, with a frown.

"An abandoned poet and an abominable gambler," smilingly replied Sawtelle.

"I wonder," said the girl thoughtfully, "if you could give me some advice. You are—acquainted here—and about the only person I seem to know—that is—"

"Advice?" said the poet, brightening. "My long suit, ma'am. No reference to cards," he added, holding up an open palm. "Let us go into the hostelry and the wisdom of the plains is at your disposal through one of Nature's playthings."

Annalee didn't quite know why she laughed, nor why her seeming mirth appeared out of place.

In the lobby, where they seated themselves in two of the several vacant arm-chairs, she told Sawtelle of her adventures of the morning.

"You've made one mistake already," he said. "You must have two shacks—houses, I should say, Miss Bronson. We call 'em shacks out here, and most of 'em are just that. You must have one for your mother on *her* homestead, where *she* has to live, and one for yourself on *your* homestead, where *you* have to live. You see, it's the law that you each have to live on your own places. Funny that lumber fellow wouldn't know that much, but he's just come—well, everybody's raw at this new game, ma'am."

The girl readily saw the wisdom in what he had said. She told him of the sudden change of heart on the part of the transfer man.

"You should have told me what you wanted to do in

advance," he complained. "Didn't I tell you I'd be happy to be of service? Now I'll see that lumber fellow and tell him what you want in the way of two small, practical, two-room shacks—houses—and I'll get somebody to haul out your things. All you got to do is pay the bills, miss; and this homesteading isn't as cheap a proposition as some think," he pointed out with a side glance at her. "By time a homestead is made into a farm it'll cost as much as it would to buy an improved place first off."

The girl missed the significance of his last sentence. She was finding his assistance welcome, and she was reflecting on that fact. Also, she wanted to ask him about Silent Scott and the stage robbery, and tell him of Jake Gruger's performance of the night before. But, somehow, she couldn't bring herself to speak of these things.

"I'll gladly pay the bills, Mr. Sawtelle," she assured him; "and I'll be ever so much indebted to you for your—your help and courtesy."

He waved a hand and looked at her quizzically with lifted brows.

> " 'Tis not for thanks I do this, ma'am;
> But for the busy fraud I am!"

She laughed delightedly. "You are a most ambiguous poet, Mr. Sawtelle. I never know quite what you mean. But I'm going to thank you whether you want me to or not. Now I must run up to mother and tell her everything will be all right."

"Tell her you have reason to *think* so, anyhow," said the poet gravely.

She looked at him quickly. "Mr. Sawtelle, tell me," she said impetuously, "will the Caprons like it because we have taken up land down there near them?"

Sawtelle shrugged. "They're old-timers. They forgot this land belonged to the government and thought it was theirs, they had run cattle over it so long. All the stock people were that way. But they'll get over it—and they can't very well fight a woman."

Annalee again felt a tinge of misgiving as he moved away.

So that was it. They couldn't fight a woman! She found herself wondering what Jake Gruger could be expected to do in the case of a man.

Late that afternoon Sawtelle came to them with the information that all arrangements for their settling on their homesteads had been made.

"I took the liberty of cutting down a bit on that lumber gent's plans," the poet explained. "He had some high notions about fancy doors and such that I chased out of his head. I assumed that you want two practical, moderately expensive houses; and they'll be located close to the dividing line between the homesteads, so you will each be on your land but close together. They start out with the lumber in the morning, and I've found a homesteader who'll haul out the furniture and baggage. About day after to-morrow you might plan to slip out there—"

"No," said Annalee in quick decision; "we go right out to-morrow. We want to be there from the start."

Sawtelle shrugged. He had a habit of agreeing, protesting, or washing his hands of a matter by his shrug.

"Then I'll have to see about your conveyance," he said.

"Maybe Mr. Neeland would run us out in his car," suggested the girl.

Sawtelle's eyes widened, and he laughed. "You couldn't drag Mr. Neeland out there at the end of a rawhide lariat!" he said cryptically.

"And why not?" Annalee demanded.

"Because Mr. Neeland has decided his hide isn't puncture proof," replied the poet with a puzzling smile. "I'll have to see him to make sure of your locations."

Annalee and her mother were too busy getting their personal belongings ready that evening to do much thinking about the veiled insinuations which had come to their ears regarding impending trouble because of their homestead locations. Nor did the girl give these subtle hints much credence. To both of them the matter now became an exciting adventure; they were anxious to begin the struggle to make their dreams come true. To Annalee the adventure appeared haloed by the glamour of a strange romance; to her mother it was a hoped-for practical means of making her daughter independent.

Early next morning Sawtelle came for them and took them down to a spring wagon in which their personal belongings had been placed. He said he had hired the wagon and horses and would drive them out himself.

They left the town behind and were soon in a sea of

green prairie. Two miles out, at the crest of a rise of ground, they looked back and saw three wagons loaded with lumber and other supplies following them.

It was the only sign of movement in that vast plain which soon was to be dotted with the shacks of home-steaders and scarred by the barbed wire of the vanguard of agriculture.

"Mother!" exclaimed the girl in an excited voice. "We're pioneers!"

Mrs. Bronson smiled bravely and pressed her daughter's hand.

Sawelle tickled the backs of the horses with the whip and looked steadily ahead. Once he turned and spoke.

"It's a funny thing that green and gold so often go together. These prairies will be as yellow as a canary's wing in three weeks."

His gaze roved the line of cottonwoods along the river in the south.

CHAPTER VII
DEVELOPMENTS

Nightfall saw a strange scene on the virgin prairie north of the river. The last glow of the sunset tinted the white of a tent a faint pink and touched with gold a pile of lumber. A streamer of smoke trailed above a small camp stove about which two women hovered, preparing a meal. Trunks were ranged on one side outside the tent, a cloudless sky promising immunity from rain, and two horses were eating grain from the rear of a spring wagon, tended by a lanky individual who hummed a queer tune to himself.

They ate in the open—Annalee, Mrs. Bronson, and Andy Sawtelle. A lantern, hung high in the tent's opening, shed its yellow rays over the repast, which was simple, and mostly garnered from cans, but appetizing, nevertheless.

Sawtelle was moody and non-communicative. The girl and her mother showed the excitement of adolescents at a picnic.

"I'll go down first thing in the morning and get a load of furniture," Sawtelle said when the supper was finished. "The carpenters will be up with the lumber wagons by noon. They'll bring their outfits with them, but I expect they'll look to you to cook for them."

He looked questioningly at the women. Annalee nodded cheerfully. Then she thought of something and gazed at him in dismay.

"Where—where will you sleep?" she stammered.

The poet waved an arm in a gesture of depreciation. "Under the stars, where I belong," he said simply. "I've had the ground for a pillow and the sky for a cover ever since I can remember—almost. And I took the precaution to bring along a pair of blankets," he added with a smile as he built a brown-paper cigarette.

"You women seem to think this is untamed country," he went on, the light of his cigarette burning a hole in the misty twilight. "Is isn't. It's warm and friendly, when you get to know it. It can't be bad when the meadow larks prefer it."

He rose and went out to look after the horses and make his bed on the prairie.

Annalee went to the spring for a cool drink while her mother retired into the tent.

The girl stood for a long time looking out over the brooding land under the first stars. From somewhere, far off, a coyote began its nocturnal serenade—a last survivor of the wild life that had teemed on the plains. In the whisper of the scented wind, the moving shadows and the coyote's plaintive cry, Annalee sensed something of the romance of the new country she had dreamed about; caught something of the significance of that seemingly boundless expanse which had lured strong men and wrought strange miracles with their minds.

It was nearly midnight when she fell asleep, with the weird droning of the prairie wind drumming its unintelligible message into her ears.

Sawtelle was off early for town next day. The women were busy making their temporary canvas home as comfortable as possible. They soon found the heat of noonday unbearable and walked down to the shade of the tall cottonwoods along the river.

They found many well-worn trails and pushed on through the timber until they came to a fence and a gate. They could see a big field in the river bottom, with growing grain thrusting its green shoots up through the soil.

"Look, mother, it's proof!" cried Annalee. "They are raising wheat or something, right here close to us!"

Beyond the field they could catch glimpses of the slow-moving surface of the river.

Suddenly, before the women could withdraw, a man

on a horse burst into view and came galloping across the field toward the gate. The girl's lips tightened as she recognized the young man who had interceded the night Jake Gruger had accosted her.

"Hello," he called as he rode up to the gate. "What're you folks doin' out here?"

"We were wondering what is growing in that field," said the girl. She resented the vivid interest he showed in her.

He looked around with a blank expression. "Oh—that? Oats." He smiled at them complacently. "Did you come out here to see 'em? They'll grow here in the bottoms, but they won't grow anywhere else. We raise a crop every year for the stock. Want to come over to the house?"

"I—don't believe so," Annalee answered, while her mother surveyed the horseman critically.

"Might as well," the youth urged. "This is the C-Bar—Capron place—I'm Myrle Capron. Guess the womenfolks would be glad to see you; they don't have any too many visitors." He smiled at her.

"We couldn't come to-day," said the girl, relenting in the face of his frankness and invitation. "We are expecting some carpenters up to our place and more lumber and other things from town, and—well, I guess we're too busy to pay any calls to-day, but—"

"*Your* place!" Myrle exclaimed, showing intense astonishment. "Where's *your* place?"

"We have located on a homestead, or two home-steads, rather, about a mile north of here," explained Annalee.

"Oh, now, you're handin' me one," said the youth derisively. "You don't figure on tryin' to farm in *here!*"

"We've taken up land with that object in view," said the girl severely.

Myrle Capron looked at the two of them in wonder; then a shade of displeasure, mingled with disbelief, flitted across his gaze.

"You're haulin' in lumber, an' bringin' out carpenters—" He stopped speaking, looking dumfounded.

"Is there anything so strange in that, young man?" asked Mrs. Bronson sharply. "It is customary, is it not, when one settles in this new country, to first build a home?"

"This ain't a new country, ma'am," the youth retorted wryly; "it's older'n you think. Maybe it's too old to learn new tricks!"

"Let's not be arguing about it, mother," said the girl impatiently. "The viewpoint of these people, who are stock raisers, is different from that of the home seekers, as I've been given to understand."

"Anyway, I'll agree with anybody that we've got a good-looking neighbor," said Myrle with a grin.

Annalee turned her back to him and drew her mother away. When she looked back from among the trees she saw him sitting his horse, looking after them.

"I'm afraid the young men in this lonely place are going to prove irritating, dear," Mrs. Bronson observed; but Annalee merely laughed.

When they emerged from the trees they saw that the lumber wagons had arrived. They hurried back to the home site and found the three men, who were to build the houses, eating their lunches which they had brought with them.

"We'll have your shacks up in no time a-tall," promised the spokesman of the carpenters. "We ain't minded to make this any long job with the hot weather right on top of us."

And they proved true to the man's word; for they set about laying the foundations of six-by-six timbers as soon as they finished eating.

It seemed to the girl and her mother that they could see the small houses take form under their very eyes during the afternoon. Sawtelle had run a line, marking the division of the two quarter sections, according to the information he had received from Neeland, and the carpenters began building the houses facing each other—one on the south side of the division line, and the other on the north side. In this way it would be possible for Annalee and Mrs. Bronson to be near each other, and yet each would be living on her own land, thus complying with the law.

Sawtelle arrived in mid-afternoon with a large wagon load of furniture and other belongings from the car on the railroad siding.

"Borrowed a tarp from the lumber people to put over this stuff till your roofs are ready," he said cheerfully, displaying a big canvas.

The lumber wagons, unloaded, started back to town, one of the drivers telling Annalee that he would be back with the last of the material, and the shingles, in the morning.

Sawtelle called upon the carpenters to help him in

unloading the furniture and packing boxes, and when that had been finished he turned to, in the late afternoon, and lent his aid to the carpenters while Annalee and Mrs. Bronson set about the task of getting supper for all.

They were thus busily engaged when the rapid pound of hoofs came to their ears, causing them to look up from their tasks. Three horsemen were galloping up the gentle slope from the line of trees to the south.

The carpenters stared with interest at the sight of the men in chaps and broad-brimmed hats; Mrs. Bronson looked worried, while the girl bit her lip and glanced apprehensively at Sawtelle, who was frowning and muttering something to himself.

The leader of the three riders pulled up his horse a scant three yards from the workmen. It was Jake Gruger, and his black eyes were darting menace.

"What's going on here?" he demanded.

The spokesman of the carpenters stepped forward hesitatingly, a puzzled look on his face. "We're— building a couple of shacks," he announced.

Gruger's thick lips curled in a sneer. Myrle Capron, sitting his horse behind the C-Bar foreman, looked on with amusement. The third rider, a lean, dark-faced man, toyed with the ends of his black, drooping mustaches, and stared tolerantly at the group. Gruger did not look at Annalee or her mother. He glared at the carpenters and Andy Sawtelle. It was Sawtelle whom he now addressed.

"You taking a hand in this?" he asked curtly.

"I'm working here at present," replied the poet.

"These ladies have filed on two homesteads here. I've looked at the corners and think they are on the right land."

Gruger's brow gathered into a black frown. "It's the first time you ever saw much in work," he snapped out. "Maybe the skirt's got you locoed. You ought to know it can't be done here. This is C-Bar range. Now, you fellows"—and he turned his blazing eyes on the startled carpenters—"get going. You hear me? Get going an' get going fast!" he roared, jerking his gun out of the holster on his right thigh.

Mrs. Bronson shrank back at sight of the weapon, horrified. The girl was stunned by the force in Gruger's voice. The man meant what he was saying.

Sawtelle stepped forward as the carpenters drew back, cowed by the C-Bar foreman's attitude.

"You ain't figuring on making war on women, are you, Gruger?" he asked, a nervous inflection in his voice.

"You rhyming prairie tramp, keep your mouth shut!" shouted Gruger. "Stick to putting words together an' don't get to meddling with men! You'll get your fool head blowed off if you mix up in this!"

The carpenters were hastily gathering their belongings together. They had heard something of the animosity displayed by certain of the stockmen against homesteaders. They realized they could work in more peaceful surroundings.

Annalee had meant to interfere, but Gruger's rage, Myrle Capron's warning look, and the satisfied, evil gleam in the eyes of the dark-faced man beside Gruger, deterred her.

In the lull which followed Gruger's outburst, galloping hoofs were heard again, and a man came riding down the slope from the rise of ground to northward.

The girl felt a thrill of hope as she recognized Silent Scott. He rode down to the group with a mildly questioning look in his serene blue eyes.

Gruger was frowning heavily. Myrle Capron appeared surprised. The third man from the C-Bar stared at the newcomer narrowly.

"Evening," Scott greeted.

Annalee was amazed at the softness of his voice; puzzled by the quality of his smile.

"What do you want?" growlingly inquired Gruger.

"Answering that would be a big order," drawled Silent Scott. He looked askance at Andy Sawtelle.

"This girl and her mother have filed on homesteads, here," the poet explained quickly. "These three men are carpenters, and I was helping them start the houses when Gruger busted in and ordered 'em out."

"Shut up!" roared Gruger. "I'll do what explaining is needed, an' there's none coming so far's he's concerned." He nodded angrily toward Silent.

"The man has the right of speech, Gruger," Scott said softly. "Why bother the women?"

Gruger shoved his gun into its holster and edged his horse toward Scott's. "You aimin' to horn into this?" His voice was sharp.

"I'll help to see that women who are strangers here get a fair deal, I reckon," Scott replied evenly.

The carpenters, genuinely frightened, were on the point of taking to their heels.

"Stay here, you men!" Scott ordered crisply.

"You forgettin' I told 'em to go?" cried Gruger.

"But they've just heard different," said Scott coldly, meeting Gruger's blazing glare. "I reckon you're forgettin' it's women that's filed here, Gruger." Scott's words came like the crack of a whiplash.

"An' I reckon you're playin' to bring things to a show-down," Gruger gritted through his teeth.

"If it's gun play you're threatening, Gruger, we'll leave the women out of it," said Scott sternly.

The girl gasped as she saw the look in the two men's eyes and their tense postures with hands poised above their guns.

"Don't!" she managed to get out in a loud whisper. "Oh—don't!"

For what seemed minutes, but which was only a few seconds, the two men looked into each other's eyes, each ready on the instant to answer the slightest indication of a move on the part of the other.

Then Gruger's eyes widened and his lips curled. "You, too," he said sneeringly; "but you're callin' the turn, Silent."

He whirled his horse and, with a flashing look of rage at Sawtelle and the carpenters, drove in his spurs. Myrle Capron and the man with him galloped after their leader.

Scott looked smilingly dawn at the girl.

She drew a long breath of relief. Then she noted that Scott's left hand was roughly bandaged with a handkerchief.

"Oh—you're hurt!" she exclaimed.

"Lucky it was in the left hand," he muttered in a low tone that carried only to Sawtelle's understanding ears.

CHAPTER VIII
AN ENIGMA

Silent dismounted with a whimsical look at the girl and her mother, who were regarding him curiously, and approached Andy Sawtelle. He was smiling, tipping his head a bit to the left, almost swaggering in graceful awkwardness in his black chaps.

"You helping build the shacks?" he drawled out.

Sawtelle nodded with a grimace. "Neeland picked the spot for them," he said, indicating Annalee and Mrs. Bronson. "Gruger was down in the Falls a few days and Neeland got busy. Nice land," the poet added in a vague voice.

"Good as any north of the Teton," Silent agreed, drawing papers and tobacco from his shirt pocket.

He scowled at the bandage on his left hand as he gingerly fashioned a cigarette with his right. He snapped a match into flame with a thumb nail, lit his smoke, and frowned at the three carpenters.

"You boys better hop to it an' get your work done," he advised. "I'll hang around close till you've finished, but I'm not aiming to wait here long. Come on—quit staring an' get busy."

The carpenters hesitated, looking from the speaker to the line of trees in the south and back to Sawtelle. The poet grinned and went back to work. After a few moments of indecision the carpenters followed his example. Then Scott turned back to the two women.

"You've had some hard-boiled neighbors wished on you," he said with another smile.

Under the spell of his smile and his eyes, Annalee forgot the hints she had heard about this man. He was looking at her queerly now—questioningly, she thought, with just a trace of amusement—and he had, somehow, the bearing of one who belonged there. Certainly he had befriended them. The carpenters had been about to go—thoroughly bluffed or frightened—and Sawtelle very evidently was not a match for the aggressive Gruger. Now that she thought of it, she didn't believe for an instant that Gruger had been bluffing. Nor had the man before her been bluffing. There was something underneath it all which she didn't understand; some hint of deadly menace. Yet Silent Scott looked anything but a desperado or a bandit.

These thoughts finally brought a smile to her lips which he applauded with his eyes.

"You can be sure we wouldn't have selected any one like that—that Gruger, for a neighbor," she told him.

Scott laughed. It was a good laugh, boyish and genuinely mirthful. Then he sobered and stared quizzically.

"Well, it's too late to change," he announced. "You've made your locations an' you've got to stick to 'em now. You've as much right here as anybody else, I suppose, now that the country's all shot to pieces."

"Why—don't you believe in homesteading?" faltered the girl.

"I do an' I don't," drawled Scott. "But stopping this land rush the way Gruger would try to stop it would be

68

like stopping a bunch of stampeding steers by wavin' a pink handkerchief in front of 'em."

He was smiling again, nodding confidently to Mrs. Bronson, who hung on his words with much interest.

"But I don't reckon Gruger will try anything as raw as he pulled to-day for a while," he went on. "Gruger ain't got as much sense in some ways as he might have. He's run the C-Bar outfit with a high hand so long he's let it get a hold on his brains. They'll try to get you out an' they'll likely keep others from coming in here—till next year, anyway. The locators have steered clear of this spot. I see you've got some of the springs," he concluded, lifting his brows as though in surprise.

Sawtelle came over to them, leaving the carpenters again working feverishly at their task.

"Pardon," said the poet with excessive politeness, a twinkle in his eyes. "Mr. Scott this is Miss Annalee Bronson and her mother, from Pennsylvania. Ladies, this is Mr. Silent Scott, one of our permanent residents who's growing up—I guess—with the country."

Scott lifted his hat in brief acknowledgment of the formal introduction, glanced suspiciously at Sawtelle, and smiled at the girl and her mother. The latter nodded at him.

"It's right thoughtful of Andy to spare this short time from his work," he said pointedly.

Sawtelle went back to his labors as Annalee laughed.

Then the girl suddenly became practical.

"Mr. Silent, you will have to attend to your injury," she said severely. "That hurt hand will have to be washed and sterilized—I guess that's what they call it.

Anyway, we have some iodine and you'd better put some on."

Scott frowned at the bandaged hand.

" 'Spect you're right," he agreed. "I'll go over below the spring an' tend to it."

He walked toward the willows and a few moments later the girl followed him. She carried some clean bandage rolls and a small bottle. She found him bathing his hand in the cool water trickling down below the spring.

"Let me see it," she insisted, stepping to his side.

He held his hand out for her inspection, looking at her closely.

There was a small puncture in the flesh of the palm.

"Oh!" she exclaimed. "That looks like a bullet wound."

"You said it, ma'am," he said, composedly. "But it don't amount to anything."

"It might—if it wasn't looked after," she pointed out. "Now, stoop down here."

She took the hand, annoyed at the subtle thrill she experienced. After washing the wound carefully she applied the iodine. She looked up at him slyly to see if he would wince, but he was staring moodily across the weaving willows.

She wanted to ask how he had received the wound, but could not bring herself to do so. There was a reserve about him that restrained her. Her heart beat faster as she thought of the intimation of the hotel porter that the officers might be looking for this man. Had he, then, had a skirmish with the sheriff and his deputies? Had he been wounded in a fight with them,

70

and—she shuddered at the thought—had he, perhaps, shot one of the officers? Was he a fugitive from the law?

It *was* a strange country!

When she had bandaged the injured hand he thanked her softly.

"Whatever brought you out here to try to farm?" he asked in a strange, far-away voice. "Two women—you just a girl—*alone!*"

"It will restore my mother's health," answered Annalee. "And we can hire men to work for us. That is we can hire them if—if that Gruger—"

She left the sentence unfinished and saw Scott scowl darkly.

"Jake Gruger will leave you alone," he said bluntly.

"But, Mr. Scott," she said quickly, "you must not get into any—any trouble on *our* account. I—I didn't quite understand what was beneath the surface in what happened this afternoon, but I'm sure there was big trouble in the balance. We—we wouldn't want any trouble to come about just because we came out here to live. We—oh, I didn't dream it would be anything like this!"

The dying sun turned her hair a rich bronze—almost red.

Silent Scott raised a hand as if he would touch her hair and suddenly desisted.

"Trouble an' this country go hand in hand," he told her seriously. "Seems like it wouldn't be what it is if there wasn't any trouble. You've got to expect it. But you ain't got the kind of trouble comin' to you that

Gruger's tryin' to hand you, and you won't get it—if *I'm* around."

Annalee knew what the man had said was not intended in a boasting vein. She looked at him hopefully; then lowered her gaze as he met her eyes.

Why was he so anxious to help them? Why did he look at her that way?

Suddenly she blushed. An instant later she stamped her foot with irritation.

"Well, trouble or no trouble, we're here to stay," she said defiantly; "whether you're around or not."

She regretted it a moment after she had said it. But he did not resent it.

"That's the spirit, Miss Bronson," he said quietly. "An' I don't reckon that C-Bar outfit would pull anything rough on you or your mother. They'll try to take it out of your men—the men you hire to help you work your land. An' they'll probably give it up as a bad job when they see they can't drive you out."

"Oh, I hope so," said the girl impetuously. "Now I'll have to help mother get supper for the men. You'll stay, won't you, Mr. Scott?"

"There wouldn't be a chance to rope me an' drag me away from a meal a woman had cooked to-night," he answered laughingly, following her toward the tent where her mother already had a fire in the stove and supper under way.

She watched him with surreptitious glances as he looked after his horse.

"What's his name?" she asked as Scott came back from tying the big, black gelding where the feed was particularly good below the spring.

"Nightmare," replied Scott with a grin.

Annalee saw the horse raise his splendid head and look at his master as he heard the name spoken.

"Nightmare!" the girl said, astonished and amused.

"Yes," returned Scott. "I named him that because he's given more than one party a nightmare tryin' to catch up with me."

"Oh," said Annalee. "Oh—I see."

It didn't sound particularly encouraging. Why should persons be trying to catch up with him? It was the most puzzling thing that had ever come to the girl's attention. And what a situation! Here was a man of mystery who might be an outlaw protecting her and her mother! If it became generally known—if what she could not help but surmise were true—would it be considered ethical on her part?

In the end, Annalee gave it up and accepted the situation for what it was. They sat down to supper with the sunset flinging its crimson banners athwart the western sky. They ate silently, the girl's attempts to start conversation proving futile. Mrs. Bronson was content to study the features of Silent Scott. She did not know just why he inspired in her a feeling of security.

The men returned to work after supper and kept at their tasks until it was dark. Scott had taken the slicker roll which had been tied behind his saddle and had retired to the other side of the willows about the spring.

Next morning when the little company rose they found that Scott had gone.

Annalee was surprised. He had virtually promised to

remain to see that Gruger did not again interfere with the men who were building the two small houses. They showed nervousness as the result of his absence, but evidently did not wish to further show the white feather before the two women, so went to work after breakfast.

The girl asked Sawtelle what he thought of it all.

The poet's answer was not satisfactory. He merely shrugged and said, "I dunno. Maybe he thinks Gruger's scared away."

"But why—how did he scare Gruger away?" Annalee persisted.

Sawtelle gazed at her speculatively before he replied.

"Silent Scott," he said slowly, "is one of the fastest, most accomplished experts that ever fanned the hammer of a six-gun."

CHAPTER IX
A NEW MOVE

It was not hard for Annalee to associate Sawtelle's statement, that Silent Scott was a formidable gunman, with the remarks the hotel porter had made about Jake Gruger's draw. It was apparent that both these men were skilled with their weapons; that they did not regard the use of them in the same light in which men in the East held such matters. She thought she now understood what the attitude of the two men sitting their horses, looking steadily into each other's eyes, hands above their pistols, had portended. Instinctively she shuddered at the recollection.

She walked over to where Sawtelle was working.

74

"Mr. Sawtelle," she said coolly, "I believe you said you were going into town again late to-day to bring out the balance of our shipment to-night."

The poet nodded in affirmation. "I'd rather make the trip when it's cool," he said. "Won't be so hard on the horses—or me."

"Very well, Mr. Sawtelle—"

"Why not make it 'Andy'?" he broke in complainingly.

"All right, Andy, then," the girl acquiesced. "I'll give you some money, Andy, and I wish you would buy me a good revolver and a supply of ammunition."

The poet's eyes started. "A gun—ma'am?" he questioned. "You want a gun?"

"Certainly," said Annalee crisply. "If men are to come around my place brandishing such weapons, I think it would be well for me to take steps to protect myself. Only I will not threaten—I'll shoot!"

She left him gasping; but the incident seemed to imbue the carpenters with renewed courage, and much of their joviality returned.

The work of putting up the framework of the houses progressed rapidly, and by afternoon the carpenters were nailing on the sheeting. There was no sign of movement in the direction of the Capron Ranch in the south, and no indication that Silent Scott was in the vicinity.

"I wouldn't be surprised if it was a put-up job between that Gruger and Silent Scott," Annalee told her mother, tossing her head. "They can't scare me with their wild antics. I believe the people who live here are having a lot of fun with the newcomers. Well, here's one they won't have much more fun with."

Mrs. Bronson shook her head in indecision. "I don't know, deary. But I *do* know that I've had so many shocks in the last few days that I don't seem to have any nerves left."

"Fine, mumsy!" cried the girl with a cheering laugh. "Now you're talking like a real pioneer. Anyway, there's no use worrying."

She remembered afterward that she had forgotten the matter of Silent Scott's wound. Well, perhaps he had received that in a fight with the authorities. On the other hand, it might have been the result of an accident. Men fooling with pistols had been known to shoot themselves in the hand—and the head, for that matter. In any event, there remained the fact that Scott had disappeared and Gruger was keeping out of sight.

Sawtelle left for town in midafternoon, and the carpenters kept hard at work, rushing the houses to completion.

"You'll have at least one roof to sleep under tomorrow night," the boss carpenter promised.

The poet returned around midnight when the others were asleep. In the morning his load was taken off and work resumed on the building. That night one of the houses was indeed virtually completed, and Annalee and her mother moved in.

Two more peaceful days passed and the houses were finished.

Incidentally, the hammering of the artisans was punctuated at certain intervals by the report of a gun.

Annalee was beginning to practice with the big weapon Sawtelle had brought her from town. She hadn't succeeded in hitting anything she aimed at, but, as she told her mother, the mere firing of the gun was a great moral victory. All this was done against Mrs. Bronson's wishes; for the girl's mother urged her not to touch "that horrible thing."

"I've at least got to know how to make it go off," had been the girl's spirited defense.

On the sixth day after their arrival the carpenters gathered up their tools and Sawtelle started with them to town, taking with him a long list of supplies to bring back. Annalee had paid the men and the lumber concern and had sent a draft to be deposited in the State Bank of Brant.

When the spring wagon had rolled away, the girl and her mother were alone for the first time in their houses. Carpets had been laid and furniture moved in, and now they enthusiastically set about the task of putting on the finishing touches which make an abode for women.

They were interrupted late in the afternoon by the thundering approach of a horseman.

They were in Annalee's house at the time, and the girl hurried to the door to see a large, florid-faced man carefully lowering himself from the saddle.

When he was on solid ground he removed his big hat and wiped his forehead with a faded red bandanna. He looked at her shrewdly from small, gray eyes set above a large nose. A gold chain of large, heavy links sprawled across his vest, accentuating his bulk.

"You Miss Bronson?" he asked in a gruff voice.

"I am," smilingly replied the girl. "And this is my mother." Mrs. Bronson had stepped behind her daughter.

"Glad to meet you," said the stranger, with a jerky bow.

"I'm Capron," he announced, walking toward them.

"Won't you come in?" the girl invited sweetly.

"Well—yes," said the rancher.

He looked about with a frown before he entered the little house. He settled his ponderous weight in the one rocking chair in the small combination kitchen and living room, and stared keenly under bushy brows at Mrs. Bronson and Annalee.

"No place for you women," he said presently. "I don't know what the government is thinking of!"

"We thought it was rather pleasant, Mr. Capron," said Annalee cheerfully. "Don't those white curtains look nice? We brought all these things all the way from Pennsylvania."

"They should have stayed there!" he grumbled. "I was down in Great Falls and didn't know what was going on up here, or I could have saved you women a lot of trouble."

The girl looked surprised; then she smiled. "If you mean you would have forbidden your man Gruger coming up here, you needn't apologize," she said. "He did act rather foolish; but he merely amused us. I suspect he thought he was going to scare us with his bad-man bluff, but he didn't."

Capron's eyes were popping by the time she finished. "Did you think he was bluffing?" he asked incredulously.

"It would seem so, Mr. Capron, in view of the fact that he had no legal right to do what he tried to do," replied Annalee coolly. "Three hundred and twenty acres of this land in here, Mr. Capron, is now our property, and we will not welcome such boisterous trespassers!"

The rancher's look indicated that he had received another shock. He gulped and shook a thick forefinger at the girl.

"Young lady, don't you ever get it into your head that Jake Gruger is bluffing," he said sternly. "Jake Gruger don't know what a bluff is. And don't forget that I'm not always around to see what Jake does. He's been my foreman for years, and he's been a good one. He worked cows for me in this country before the government ever thought of surveying it, let alone bringing folks in by telling 'em they could farm here. Farm!" Capron indulged in a sneer.

"Why, you couldn't farm this in a million years! It's all we can do to get an oat crop in the bottoms. This is cattle country, young lady, and it'll always be cattle country. In five years every fence the homesteaders put up will be buried in tumbleweeds!"

He wiped his brow and face after the exertion of his speech. The girl's face was pale, and Mrs. Bronson again looked worried.

"But it ain't your fault," Capron hastened to say. "I don't blame you none. You took the literature and the pictures for granted and came out here thinking that all you had to do was file on the free land and let a farm grow. Free land! Do you know what you've got to do?

You've got to fence, and dig a well—that spring dries up in the summer, or I'd have located it long ago. You've got to plow and harrow and summer fallow and all that. And you won't get a crop unless you have rain, and we don't get rain here. Why, it's the first of June now, and the rain should be starting. Do you see it? Not a drop. *Not a drop!* And the hot winds will be here in a fortnight!"

"Mr. Capron, I can't help thinking that you are trying to discourage us for reasons of your own," said the girl coldly.

"Discourage you? Limping coyotes, girl, if I *can* discourage you, I'll be doing you a favor. Wait till you've seen the hot winds. This green grass will be yellow in less'n a week! If that'll happen to hardy grass—native grass—what'll happen to grain? If you got one crop every five years you'd be doing well. We have about one wet year in five. I know. I've had to figure on feed for my stock for more years than you've lived. No, the best thing you can do is give it up for a bad job and let it go at that."

"We can't do that, Mr. Capron," said Annalee decisively.

"I understand," he said. "You're in for this lumber and carpenter work, and your fare and one thing and another, but maybe we can smooth that out."

"I don't believe I understand you, Mr. Capron."

"Well, how much do you want to get out of here?" asked the rancher bluntly.

The girl's face flamed, and she rose from her chair.

"You either misunderstood me, or you are purposely

insulting, Mr. Capron. We are not asking you for any-thing."

"Don't be foolish," growlingly replied Capron. "Of course you expect something back for what you've spent. And I'm willing to pay you because I don't want you in here setting an example for other poor, deluded Easterners. If we can keep the homesteaders out of here till they've given this thing a try-out and found out what they're up against, I can keep this range."

It was Mrs. Bronson who now spoke in a cool, culti-vated voice. "We had expected, when we came West, Mr. Capron, to find some neighbors who would reflect the spirit of hospitality which visitors to the East from this part of the country have flaunted. If we can't have neighbors who are ladies and gentlemen, we can, at least, have the privilege of declining their acquain-tance. I do not believe the tenor of your remarks is such as to indicate that you belong in the first classification," she concluded acidly.

Both Capron and the girl stared at her. It was evident that Mrs. Bronson was genuinely annoyed.

Capron started to speak, then rose with a red face. "You can hint that I'm not a gentleman, ma'am, but before you're through with this business you'll find out that what I've told you is straight goods, and that I was doing the square thing in offering to buy you out. I've made you a legitimate proposition. I'll give you a month to think it over."

"We will hardly require that length of time, Mr. Capron," said Mrs. Bronson with great dignity. "I believe my daughter has given you your answer."

"Great Scott!" exclaimed Capron. "Do you two women think you can make a farm out of this pin-head parcel of land by yourselves? I own forty thousand acres, and I wouldn't think of trying to farm it even with all the help I've got!"

"I can think of no reason why we should discuss our affairs with you," replied Mrs. Bronson in a precise voice.

Capron stared about the room with a frown. Suddenly he started. His gaze had fallen on the gun which Annalee had left upon the table with a box of cartridges beside it.

"Well, I'll be—"

He slammed his hat on his head and started for the door. He paused on the threshold and regarded them belligerently.

"Whether you want to or not, think over what I've said. Think it over till the first of July, anyway. By that time you'll know something of what the hot winds are and what chance you've got of raising crops in here."

"By that time we'll have our fence up and some land plowed," Annalee asserted.

"*Fences!*" Capron's face purpled. "You don't need fences in here," he stormed. "There isn't going to be any stock up here this season—at least, it wasn't my intention to run any up here. It'd look bad for a fence to go up."

"But it would keep the stock out if you should decide to run some up this way," said the girl with a knowing smile. "We don't intend to take any chances, Mr. Capron."

The rancher stamped out upon the little porch and down the two steps. "Remember," he said loudly, reaching for the reins dangling from his horse's bridle; "remember I'm not entirely responsible for Jake Gruger."

"If that's a threat, Mr. Capron, you can tell Jake Gruger he will be dealt with according to law if he comes here again," called the girl as the rancher swung heavily into the saddle.

Capron glared at them angrily. "That'll scare Jake, I reckon," he said sarcastically as he rode away.

Annalee's laugh carried to his ears.

"Oh, mother!" she cried, throwing her arms about the older woman's neck. "You told him. Good for you, mumsy; you're getting to be your old self again. It's all a bluff to frighten us away. What is it they say when a bluff is stopped—oh! We called their bluff, mumsy; and now I'll bet they'll be good and leave us alone."

But if the girl and her mother could have seen the grim look on the rancher's face, and the hard quality of his scowling gaze as he rode southward toward his own domain, they might not have felt so confident.

CHAPTER X
PRAIRIE LOGIC

Andy returned that night after the women had gone to bed. He did not disturb them, and in the morning when they told him of Capron's visit, he shook his head dubiously. He quickly changed the subject and talked of the stirring scenes in town. Brant was crowded with homesteaders and was enjoying a run of prosperity such as it never before had experienced. A big Fourth-of-July celebration was planned.

But Annalee and Mrs. Bronson were more interested in affairs nearer home. When the girl told him they were convinced that Capron and Gruger were trying to bluff them out, he pursed his lips and recited:

> " 'Tis when it's pleasant, calm, and warm
> That one should look for signs of storm."

"Now what does *that* mean?" asked Annalee with a trace of irritation.

"That's prairie logic," Sawtelle replied succinctly; "and it hasn't anything to do with the weather. Did you think Silent Scott was bluffing, too?"

"I have an idea that the heroics we've been treated to in the past few days were engineered for a purpose," said the girl in a vexed voice.

"I don't think any of the parties concerned know the meaning of that word 'heroics'—and things are not so often engineered in this country," said the poet slowly. "Things just naturally happen here. I wouldn't say that, Miss Bronson. Silent is close-mouthed and doesn't try to set right a lot of things he's blamed for. He isn't like that fellow Lummox, who was with Gruger and Myrle Capron up here that day. 'Member the fellow with the snapping, black eyes and the long, black mustaches? He's a boaster. Gruger likes to have tough hombres in his outfit," said Sawtelle in matter-of-fact tones. "Lummox is not only a gunman—he's a killer."

84

"A—killer?" gasped out the girl.

"With half a dozen notches on his gun butt," Sawtelle affirmed.

Annalee rose from the table. "Now I *am* convinced that a lot of this talk about your men out here is for our benefit," she said severely. "Please do not speak again of gunmen, Andy Sawtelle."

The poet shrugged and silently turned his whole attention to his breakfast.

After the meal he unloaded the supplies. Then he came to the door of Annalee's house and bowed.

"I'll take the horses back this morning, if you don't need anything else hauled, and if you should need me again, send word and I'll be glad to come out."

"Why, Andy!" exclaimed the girl aghast. "You're not going to leave us. I had counted on you staying with us right along. We—we've got to have help—some one we can depend upon. Why, there's the fence—and the plowing!"

Andy Sawtelle looked startled. "You—ah—expected me to work here all summer?" he faltered.

"Of course—didn't we, mother? Of course we did, Andy; and we will pay you good wages."

For a moment the poet appeared crestfallen. Finally, he smiled wryly, "Gruger was right," he observed. "I'm a rhyming prairie tramp. I never saw much in work, and you've got me locoed. I have to tell you, miss, that I don't know any more about farming than I know about flying an airplane, which is much—not enough to speak of."

Annalee laughed. "But you can learn," she said

enthusiastically. "You will have to have a man to help you, and you can hire a man who does know. I make you our foreman, Andy. We'll call this the—the—Twin B Ranch! There's two of us, mother and I; we have two homesteads, and our last name begins with B. Won't you take the position as foreman of the Twin B, Andy?"

Sawtelle frowned darkly and compressed his lips to suppress the smile which hovered on them. Then he sighed as if in resignation.

"I can try it," he said dubiously. "But I'm not promising anything. And there's something you maybe haven't thought of, Miss Bronson. This fencing and plowing and one thing and another—how you going to do it without horses?"

"That's right," said the girl thoughtfully. "Well, Andy, I guess you will have to buy us a team and—and what we need."

Sawtelle threw up his hands. "Responsibility!" he exclaimed with an exaggerated gesture. "Something I have avoided all my life! And now I've got to swim in it!" He looked at Annalee and Mrs. Bronson reproachfully. "I'm going to town and hire a good Irishman!" he announced decisively.

Sawtelle was as good as his word. At the end of a week, during which time there were no further visits from Capron or any one south of the line of trees, the poet came back from town driving the team he had purchased for the Bronsons, with a man sitting in the front seat of the new Bronson wagon.

"New hand," he announced laconically.

"Oh!" exclaimed Annalee, looking at the short, red-faced man with the upturned nose and the twinkling blue eyes.

"What—what is your name?"

"Pat," replied the grinning employee. "Pat McCarthy."

"Well, Mr. McCarthy, we're glad to have you with us. This is my mother, Mrs. Bronson. We're—we're part Irish ourselves. Did you bring your things with you?"

Pat jerked a thumb toward a bundle which Sawtelle had dropped from the wagon.

"Well, your quarters will be in the tent with Andy," said the girl, concealing her surprise at the small amount of the new hand's belongings. "Later, when the barn is finished, and the fencing and plowing done, we will build a house for our men; but just now—"

"Tent suits me," said Pat shortly. "Cool an' airy— good place in hot weather. I'll be puttin' me things away, if it's all the same with you."

Mrs. Bronson sniffed in disapproval at the odor of the man's pipe.

"A bad smelling pipe means a good working man, mother," the girl said laughingly. "Something tells me Pat is competent."

In the three weeks that followed, the small barn was finished, Sawtelle, hauling the lumber from town; a plow, harrow, and seeder were purchased and brought to the Twin B; wire for the fence was obtained, but work on the fence could not be started as posts were not available. The lumber company expected posts any day, the manager had explained.

Pat began plowing, something which Andy Sawtelle

said he could not and would not do.

The homesteads began to take on the look of a regular farm. But Capron's prediction that it would be a dry season proved true. Little rain fell—only an occasional shower. The hot winds came and the green of the plains turned to gold, and dust clouds swirled upon the horizons. No other homesteaders located in the fertile district north of the river. This was a significant fact and caused Annalee to ponder.

There was no further molestation from the Capron outfit.

"Didn't I tell you it was all a bluff, mother?" the girl pointed out.

But even as she said this, she marveled that none had come to file on the land near them. In the end she assumed that Gruger had succeeded in bluffing out others who had contemplated locating there.

The thing, however, that bothered Annalee and her mother the most, as time went on, was the lack of women neighbors, or even casual acquaintances.

"Do you realize, mother, that in the five weeks or so that we've been here we haven't seen another woman?" said the girl one night after supper.

Mrs. Bronson nodded with a sigh. "It is indeed a lonesome country," she complained.

"It wouldn't be if that Capron crowd were shown a few things and others would come in here and locate," said the girl with spirit. "I'll tell you, mumsy, we'll go in to Brant for the Fourth-of-July celebration. It's only about a week away. Maybe we can induce somebody to come out here and locate. It ought to reassure them to know that we're here and doing things."

Sawtelle appeared both pleased and dubious when he heard of the plan to go into town on the Fourth.

"We'll leave Pat here to watch the place," he decided.

"We will not!" protested Pat. "There's two days I aim to be in town; one's Christmas an' the other's the Fourth of July. An' I'll be takin' me wages to date along with me in case of emergency, if you don't mind, ma'am."

"You can have them," said the girl. "We will have the horses with us, Andy, and I don't believe it will be necessary for anybody to stay and watch the place. We're all entitled to a holiday."

"We ought to go in on the night of the third to get the benefit of everything," Pat suggested.

Andy Sawtelle was the only one who didn't laugh.

CHAPTER XI
THE COWARD

G ruger and his man Lummox rode at a jog toward town. The hot, noonday sun beat down upon them, and the dust rose in an enveloping fog.

"Goin' to be a hot Fourth," Lummox commented, biting at the ends of his drooping mustaches. His small, beady eyes appeared to be fixed on the road ahead, but he was watching the foreman furtively.

"*Should* be hot," Gruger replied savagely. "Allers *was* hot. Suppose these hairbrained, would-be farmers will be looking for showers. Fat chance!" He laughed harshly.

"How do you suppose them two came to locate back there north of the river?" said Lummox with a jerk of a thumb over his shoulder.

"Some fool locator's doings," returned Gruger. "I aim to find out who sent 'em out there."

Lummox seemed smiling to himself. He cleared his throat several times. "I been thinking, Jake, that this country is did for," he said finally, drawing a plug of tobacco from his pocket. "I been wonderin' if it wouldn't be a good thing for me to slope out of here— go somewheres, Jake—somewheres where they's still something doin', you might say. I hear there's such a place left, Jake?"

"Where you mean?" asked Jake curiously.

"Mexico," replied Lummox reverently.

Gruger started. He had often heard the rumor—never voiced in its subject's presence—that Lummox had originally come out of Mexico and had drifted north when the trail herds were being driven from Texas to Montana.

"I didn't think any man would figure on goin' that far unless he had a good reason for making the trip," the foreman observed with a keen glance at the man riding beside him.

Lummox did not turn to look at him, nor reply.

A sudden alertness seemed to have seized upon Gruger, however.

"How soon had you thought of goin'?" he asked, almost eagerly.

"I hadn't figured on quittin' you till we'd shipped this fall," said Lummox. "I reckon you savvy I'm not

90

plumb cheerful at leavin' your outfit, Jake. I've done the best I could; but, with these homesteaders flockin' in an' moralizing, the crust's goin' to begin to get thin."

Gruger nodded and pulled his hat closer down over his eyes. Lummox had done his best. Gruger remembered gratefully several deals the law might not have looked upon with favor which Lummox had helped him put over. He remembered, too, the man's quick temper and his quicker gun hand.

During the remainder of the distance into town there was silence between the pair.

Through habit they galloped wildly into town, down the short, new extension of Main Street—called Central Avenue after the principal thoroughfare in Great Falls—over the railroad tracks into what was the old cow town.

They put up their horses at a livery, and Gruger took leave of Lummox, promising to meet him in the Green Front resort in the old town at supper time.

A breeze had sprung up in the late afternoon, fanning the town with its cooling breath, as Jake Gruger walked swiftly across the tracks into the modern section of Brant.

The street was crowded, aflame with the national colors, aflutter with bunting and flags. Gruger gazed out of scowling eyes beneath the brim of his hat and jostled rudely out of his path those who got in his way. When he reached a small, white building near the eastern end of the street, he paused and looked through the window past the gilt sign. He grunted with satisfaction. Then he threw open the door and entered a small office.

The man at the desk swung around and stared at the intruder with popping eyes. It was fully a minute before he recovered sufficiently to execute a weak motion toward a chair.

Gruger ignored the invitation and stepped quickly to the side of the desk. "Neeland, who located the Bronsons out our way?" he demanded in a vicious voice.

"Why—why—sit down, Mr. Gruger," stammered the locator with an attempt to smile.

"I didn't come in here to sit down an' have any sociable chat," shot out Gruger. "I asked you a question, an' I expect you to answer it."

"But—I—the Bronsons?" Neeland wiped his forehead.

"Don't stall," snapped the foreman. "An' if you know me an' know what's good for you, Neeland, don't lie!"

The locator looked hopefully toward the closed door and again gazed apprehensively at his formidable visitor.

"Why do you think *I* know who locates everybody that comes here for a homestead?" he evaded. "There's half a dozen locators in this town—"

"An' you do more business than all of 'em put together," thundered Gruger, smashing his fist down upon the desk with tremendous force. "What's more, you keep track of things. You know, Neeland, an' if you don't want me to stampede in your direction, you'll start talkin' an' talkin' straight pronto—here an' now."

Neeland wet his lips with a dry tongue. "Well, you can sit down and be less—less antagonistic—while you're getting your information, can't you?" he asked plaintively. "There's more to this than you suspect, Gruger—"

"An' more than *you* suspect, Neeland. Now bust out with it. Who located the Bronsons?"

"I—I located them—now wait a minute, Gruger! Wait a minute!" Neeland's voice had risen to a scream. "I didn't think you folks would object to women—"

"They're land grabbers, ain't they?" roared the infuriated foreman. "They're settin' an example for others out there, ain't they? They've built two shacks, an' a barn, an' they're plowin', ain't they?"

In his rage his huge hands seemed about to close on the locator's throat.

"But there's a mistake!" exclaimed Neeland, pushing his chair back against the wall in the corner where the desk was situated. "I tell you, there's a mistake. I didn't know they were going out there to live right away!"

Gruger sneered in contempt. "Oh, you didn't know that?" he ridiculed. "You thought you'd get their money while Capron an' me were away, an' get some more from somebody else the next time we went away, an' then light out by time they came to live on the places. I believe I'll wring your neck, Neeland!"

The locator was trembling. Cold perspiration stood out on his forehead in glistening beads. His breath was labored.

"There's another mistake, Gruger," he wheezed, almost eagerly. "I located Miss Bronson on the wrong quarter section accordin' to the way they've built their houses. I didn't exactly do it intentional, you understand, but the girl is on the wrong quarter. They've got changed around, from what I hear from Andy Sawtelle, and I—I haven't said anything about it to 'em yet."

Gruger stepped back, his eyes widening. Then he leaped at Neeland and grasped him by the throat.

"Are you lying?" he asked through his teeth. "If you're lying, Neeland, I'll shake your neck till you die like a rat!"

"True, s'help me," Neeland managed to gasp out. "They're changed around." He could hardly speak.

Gruger shut off the locator's wind for a moment, then released him and stepped back, grinning at the blue marks left by his fingers on the man's throat.

"Then they're each livin' on the wrong land?" he demanded with a fierce glare.

Neeland nodded weakly, feeling his throat, terror showing in his eyes.

Gruger dropped into a chair and pulled it close to the locator.

"You keep what you know to yourself, see?" he said. "Don't tell that fool poet, don't tell the Bronsons, don't tell *anybody*—you hear me? Do you think you can keep your mouth shut to save your neck?"

Neeland was not capable of resistance even if he had had any such remote idea. He wanted to be rid of the menace Gruger so potentially represented. Inwardly he was thanking his stars that an error *had* been made on the Bronson place!

"I'll keep mum," he promised with a ghost of a smile.

Gruger rose and strode to the door. As he opened it he turned. His eyes burned with contempt and subdued rage.

"You better!" he cautioned grimly. Then he went out.

Neeland shivered in his chair as he saw the big man pass before the window on his way down the street.

Gruger walked fast, shoving people right and left in the failing light of the sunset. His face was a queer mixture of grim determination and elation. He was evidently pleased with the information he had forced out of Neeland, and it was apparent that he was working out a plan. So busy was he with his thoughts that he did not acknowledge the occasional greetings which were spoken to him, mostly by men garbed similarly to himself.

He glanced casually across the street as he passed opposite the hotel and—stopped dead in his tracks. He saw Silent Scott pushing his way through the throng in front of the Thompson House.

As Scott disappeared and the crowd closed in, Gruger walked on. The only change in his expression had been the narrowing of the lids over his eyes. He crossed the railroad track into the old town and hurried toward the Green Front.

CHAPTER XII
THREE MEETINGS

On the day before the Fourth, Annalee accepted Pat's repeated suggestion that they go to town on the eve of the celebration and announced that they would start for Brant late in the afternoon.

Pat accepted the news and his wages with undenied cheerfulness; but Sawtelle's face was grave as he took the check Annalee handed him in payment for his services.

"Of course you know, Andy, that what you have done for us, and your courtesy and kindness from the time of our arrival out here, cannot be paid for in mere money," said the girl gratefully; "and we know you were not thinking of wages when you offered to come out here with us after that drayman, whoever he was, showed he was afraid to come."

"I wasn't thinking of work, either," said Sawtelle whimsically.

"Andy, don't you like to work?" asked Annalee. "Tell me honestly now."

For reply Andy attempted to glare at her. "This ain't been so much work as it has been a novel experience."

Which was all she could get out of him on that subject.

They drove to town during the sunset and the long twilight. The drive was a revelation to the two women. They had never seen the land so lovely. The plain was like cloth-of-gold under the crimson skies. A vagrant breeze whispered in the waving grasses. Then, as the crimson banners of the sunset faded to amethyst and blue, streaked with silver, the purple haze of the soft twilight draped itself over the prairies, leaving only the painted peaks uplifted above its curtain in the west.

Night was gathering as they drove slowly into town. The scene which greeted their eyes caused them to thrill with excited wonder. The street was thronged with holiday crowds. Cow-punchers were there decked out in their festive regalia—gay colored shirts and scarfs of purple, pink, and yellow; great, high, broad brimmed hats, some black with red binding and bands, some gray, some saffron colored, some brown; trousers tucked into shining riding boots; belts and holsters embellished with gleaming silver ornaments; many ivory-handled guns as further adornment, and some gauntlets trimmed with silver.

Homesteaders from the East, the Middle West, the Palouse country of Washington, wore their blue-serge Sunday best and flaunted neckties in flaming colors.

Gay youths sported mail-order suits of natty trim, belted and buckled in the most extravagant styles of the day.

There were even a few straw hats—a decided rarity in a country which had always favored dependable felt in its headgear.

Girls in white, with flowing sashes of pink and blue; portly dames, red-faced from wind and sun, in the proverbial black silk; stockmen showing great expanse of vest front adorned with heavy, gold watch chains; children trying to pattern after their elders—more quiet and subdued, too, it seemed to the Bronsons, than children of the cities.

Scores of horses were tied to the hitching rails, dozens of dusty, rust-streaked automobiles of small caliber were parked in the vacant lots; dogs were everywhere.

Bunting was stretched between the buildings across the street, above the heads of the merry-makers; it streamed in the breeze from the posts, porch roofs, and store fronts; small fir trees were tied to posts and nailed to the corners of buildings here and there, adding a touch of vivid green to the more brilliant hues of the decorations; flags fluttered and waved from every vantage point.

A band, imported from the Falls, was playing a stirring march. Shouts, laughter, voices raised in song were heard at intervals above the music of the brass instruments and the booming of the big drum, and in the occasional lulls came the tinkling of music boxes, and the screeching of phonographs. Now and then all this medley of sound was punctuated by the sharp staccato of a six-shooter emptying its load of blank cartridges or hurling its leaden messengers harmlessly toward the star-splashed sky.

Annalee and her mother were assisted from the spring wagon at the Thompson House by Sawtelle, while Pat carried their baggage inside. Then the two men went to put up the team and the women approached the desk.

"We're full to the brim, plumb full," said the clerk; "but I'll find a room for you, Miss Bronson."

And he did. But Annalee and Mrs. Bronson found it impossible to stay in their room or on the balcony outside the little front parlor on the second floor. The spirit of the holiday seized them and they went downstairs.

Almost the first persons they saw in the lobby were Myrle Capron and his father. The rancher saw them moving away from the foot of the stairs and made his way to them immediately.

"Figured you folks would be in," he said in a more

gracious tone than he had used on the occasion of his visit to the homesteads. "I was coming up to your place long 'bout the first of the month, but I've been pretty busy."

Mrs. Bronson nodded to him coldly.

"We've been busy, too," said the girl, with a dancing light of devilment in her eyes. "We've started our plowing, Mr. Capron."

The rancher's amiable look fled. "What do you think you'll plant up there?" he asked, his curiosity getting the better of him momentarily.

"Winter wheat," replied Annalee sweetly. "We're plowing deep, so the moisture can be held in the ground."

"Wheat!" Capron exclaimed. "You couldn't grow wheat on that dry land if you plowed clear through to China!"

"Pat—a man who is working for us—says there will be more rain here when the country is farmed," was the girl's rejoinder.

"All theory!" Capron exclaimed. "They've got more theories about farming this land than the stargazers have got about Mars or the moon! Don't you think, if wheat would grow here, us old-timers would have been planting it long ago?"

"No, you were not farmers and didn't wish to be," said the girl with conviction. "You could farm now, if you wanted to; there's nothing to stop you."

Myrle Capron was grinning at the girl from behind his father's back. She felt a vague resentment at this.

"Look here," said Capron gruffly, "you've got sense,

and you've got red-headed spunk. I'll give you five thousand dollars to relinquish those homesteads out there and go somewhere else and file. Now don't get mad and flare up—this is a straight, business offer. We've got some of our homestead rights left out on the C-Bar, and we want to locate those homesteads and some more around 'em. I've leased the school sections up there and I want enough land to join 'em up so I'll have some range left north of the river. That's how the play lays."

Annalee felt that Capron was speaking the truth, and there *did* appear to be something in what he said, and a reason for his wanting the land in question. But she shook her head.

"You forget, Mr. Capron, that if we relinquish our homesteads, especially for a consideration, we cannot locate again. We couldn't very well swear that we didn't receive anything for relinquishing, and we cannot afford to lose what we have invested out there. There are plenty of other homesteads out there, are there not? Why don't you people take up some of those?"

Capron shook his head impatiently and scowled. "You could buy a small, improved farm down toward Great Falls for five thousand," he pointed out. "And you'd have your horses, wagon, and implements left."

But the girl's decision had long since been made. "It is more romantic and thrilling to make a place yourself, Mr. Capron," she answered him. "We feel like pioneers, you might say; and some day it may be worth something to say, 'I was a first settler.' And there's the increase in the value of the land to be taken into consideration."

The rancher looked at Mrs. Bronson. "Is that the way you feel about it, ma'am?" he asked with a grim smile.

"I believe I made my position clear when you visited us," replied Mrs. Bronson.

"In that case I won't bother you with any more offers," snapped out Capron as he turned abruptly on his heel.

Myrle Capron approached them as they went out on the hotel porch. "Glad to meet you again, Miss Bronson," he greeted, ignoring the girl's mother save for a flashing glance.

Annalee was vexed and showed it in her manner toward him. She merely bowed.

"I was wondering if I could have a dance with you at the big ball to-morrow," he went on, oblivious of his cold reception.

"It's not probable that we will go," said the girl.

"Oh, you don't want to miss that, Miss Bronson. They've built a big pavilion just for this celebration, and brought an orchestra from the Falls. You'll be there all right, an' I hope you save me a dance. You know," he went on, lowering his voice to a confidential tone; "you know I don't always agree with dad an' Jake Gruger. I'm more broadminded, *I* am. I don't mind homesteadin' neighbors, if they're the right kind—" He broke off as the girl turned away in disgust, taking her mother's arm. He looked surprised.

They did not wait to listen to what else he had to say, but mingled with the throngs in the street. Soon their holiday spirit returned, and they found themselves laughing gayly with the crowds of merrymakers.

"We don't get a chance to celebrate often, but when we do, we *celebrate!*" This from a matron with whom they collided in the crush.

The woman passed on; but they had caught something of the attitude of the celebrants from her and understood why these people entered so enthusiastically into the fun making.

They were returning to their hotel late in the evening when they suddenly came fac to face with Silent Scott. He doffed his hat and smiled at them.

Annalee glanced instinctively at his left hand and saw that it was no longer bandaged. "Your injury is well again?" said the girl, her voice sounding foolish even to herself.

"Thanks to your help," he said, again favoring them with that baffling smile.

To the girl's irritation she could think of nothing to say, and they were jostled apart by the crowd.

"Let's go to our room, mother," said Annalee, almost angrily.

CHAPTER XIII
TWO CONTESTS

Annalee lay in bed trying to analyze her thoughts long after her mother had fallen asleep. The shouts and laughter of the holiday crowd continued in the street after midnight; but the girl did not hear them as she lay staring at the fluttering muslin curtains in the open window.

She resented the offers of Capron to buy them out, and the bold advances of the son, Myrle. She was interested and yet annoyed in so far as Silent Scott was concerned. But more than anything else, she was irritated because Silent Scott puzzled her. She could not fathom his looks or his actions. He was either wonderfully capable and deep, or he was merely shallow and spectacular. She could not decide which was the correct deduction. But she was annoyed with him simply because he puzzled her.

She finally fell asleep, amused at her concern with the artifices of the men who claimed the country for their own.

Morning saw scores of horsemen, wagons, and automobiles pouring into Brant. The crowd was augmented to three times its size of the day before. Early in the day it became apparent that although but one celebration had been advertised, there really were two distinct celebrations—one in the old town, and the other in the newer section of Brant proper. Rivalry between the two factions soon developed.

In the new part of town the big, open-air dancing pavilion had been erected, and dancing began at eleven o'clock in the morning. Here, too, were held races and other contests before noon. But the old town had reserved the big riding events for itself, and the bucking-broncho contests, roping, bulldogging, and horse races were scheduled for the afternoon on the open prairie beyond the old buildings on the west side of the railroad tracks.

Annalee and her mother followed the band and

parade to the old town rodeo in the early afternoon. Bleachers had been erected about the field where the contests were to be held, and the two were fortunate in getting seats. A Mrs. Clarendon, on Mrs. Bronson's right, proved a hospitable soul as well as a literal fund of information. She had lived on the north fork of the Teton for thirty years, the wife of a cattleman and the mother of a family of five.

"We've sold out an' are goin' to Californy to live," she informed them. "Most of the cattle people are drifting down there. We've had enough blizzards to last us the rest of our life an' worked hard enough to deserve a rest. Besides, we want the children to have a good schoolin'—something they can't get aroun' here."

She did not seem to resent the fact that Mrs. Bronson and her daughter were homesteaders. Instead, she sympathized with them.

"You'll sure earn your farms, all right," she averred. "Believe me, I know what you've got coming. It won't be play, Mrs. Bronson."

She chuckled to herself. "But it's better'n the East," she declared hastily. "This air will put you on your pins in no time, Mrs. Bronson. Even the winter will tone you up."

Mrs. Bronson warmed toward her. She confessed her loneliness, at times, for women neighbors.

"That's what I call tough—havin' to live near them Caprons," said Mrs. Clarendon. "He just worked his wife to death, and now he's got a housekeeper who's just as overbearin' as himself. An' the Capron girl is so snobbish—without any reason—that she can't get along with anybody! There's that big bully foreman of theirs, now."

She pointed to where Gruger was standing near some horses at one side of the field. Mrs. Bronson and the girl made out the man Lummox also.

"Last pre-lim-i-naries to the buck-ing broncho contest!" sang a gayly dressed horseman through a megaphone.

Mrs. Clarendon had explained the nature of the various contests as they had taken place so the girl and her mother could understand.

"Winners of the pre-lim-i-naries to try to ride Cyclone, Hope-less, an' Te-ton Steam-boat," sang out the announcer.

"Them's outlaw horses," Mrs. Clarendon explained. "Cyclone's the worst; he's a man-killer, I'll say. It'll take a good one to stick on him."

Several riders who essayed to stick on the bucking horses in the preliminary were thrown.

"Ain't got the riders left in the country," Mrs. Clarendon apologized.

But the girl and her mother were greatly interested and excited, and when one man, announced as "Little" Joe Wheeler, qualified, they cheered and clapped their hands in approval.

"Well, if that little runt ain't got himself in the public eye at last!" exclaimed Mrs. Clarendon. "He works for us, or did, till we sold our stock. Gettin' let out must have put some sense in him! He ain't drinkin', or he'd never stuck on that hoss!"

Even Mrs. Bronson laughed delightedly at this.

Lummox, the dark-faced assistant to Jake Gruger, was the next to qualify.

Annalee became aware of an excited group at the edge of the field almost directly below them. She saw Andy Sawtelle waving his arms and slapping some one on the back. The poet had affected an artist's tie and this, under his long face, combined with his flapping, worn hat and slender figure, gave him something of a mawkish appearance.

Then Annalee saw that it was Silent Scott he was pounding on the back. Pat McCarthy was in the little group also. He was standing on the edge, his short legs braced well apart, hat jammed back on his head, pipestem in one corner of his mouth and the bowl of the pipe upside down.

"Looks as if he had been drinking!" exclaimed the girl.

"What's that?" called Mrs. Clarendon. "Lor' me, deary, it's most of them that have been takin' on some likker this day."

Silent Scott went out to ride. Annalee watched him curiously, and saw him qualify for the finals with more ease than any rider had exhibited.

"Another chance to show off," she murmured, although she had not been able to help admiring his superb riding.

With the finals on, Little Joe drew the Teton Steamboat, a rangy bay with a wicked look in his eyes. In less than a minute Steamboat had thrown his rider, to the derisive hoots of the spectators and Mrs.

Clarendon's cries of encouragement.

"There goes that half-Mexican of Capron's," scoffed Mrs. Clarendon as Lummox went out to ride the horse, Hopeless. "They say he carries a knife in his boot, an' I wouldn't put it past him. Supposed to be a killer, too."

Hopeless had to be blindfolded before he could be saddled, and he showed more viciousness than the horse which had thrown Little Joe. He was a big, black horse, so tall that the hazers had to come to the assistance of the wranglers in putting the leather on him.

Gruger was on the field, whispering in Lummox's ear. When he retired from the field he joined a group some distance from where Sawtelle, Pat, and Silent Scott were standing with some others. Annalee felt a sense of misgiving as she realized that her employees had ostensibly allied themselves with Scott.

Hopeless was off to a series of crow hops the instant the bandage was pulled from his eyes and he felt Lummox's weight in the saddle. Then, without warning, he began to sunfish. Up he went and came down low to one side and then to the other until Lummox's stirrups nearly touched the ground. Failing thus to dislodge his rider he whirled in mid-air, changing ends, and Lummox lost his right stirrup.

A howl of excitement went up from the crowd. Gruger and the others with him were shouting madly. Lummox kept his hand from the horn, scorning to pull leather and lose the contest in that way. But he couldn't regain his stirrup. His right spur slipped into the cinch band and the judges shouted to him. This hold, however, availed him nothing, for a second later he went spinning over Hopeless' head and landed ignominiously in the dust. There was a shout of delight.

Annalee could see Sawtelle and Pat cheering wildly and swinging their hats. Gruger's face was nearly purple as he witnessed this demonstration, and Lummox's eyes were darting fire as he scrambled to his feet and took himself off the field.

This left Silent Scott as the one remaining contender for the prize, and he walked slowly out to where Cyclone, a sorrel, blindfolded, and with a "twist on his ears," was struggling with the wranglers. Three times the saddle blanket was dislodged before it was put there to stay, followed by Scott's saddle.

Shouts of derision were coming from the Capron group while Andy and Pat were yelling encouragement.

The girl became so interested that she forgot her mother and Mrs. Clarendon, who were keeping up a running fire of conversation.

Annalee noticed that Scott hadn't effected the gay attire favored by many of the other men who had lived long in that country. But neither had Gruger or Lummox, for that matter. She wondered if there was any significance attached to this coincidence.

She stared breathlessly as the blindfold was pulled from Cyclone's eyes and Silent Scott swung quickly into the saddle. The wild animal seemed to tremble; then it lunged forward in short leaps, whirled, and spun in the air, as the rider raked it from shoulder to hip with his spurs.

Cyclone then resorted to sunfishing, but Scott stuck

easily in the saddle, frustrating the infuriated horse's frenzied attempts to cast him off. Then Cyclone again whirled as if on an axis, all four feet in the air, and began swapping ends with a rapidity which brought a wild roar of applause from the excited spectators. The outlaw corkscrewed and sunfished and swapped ends in a final furious burst of energy, providing an exhibition of wicked bucking that caused the encircling hazers to gasp.

As Silent Scott fought the outlaw horse, Annalee Bronson fought another contest in her own mind in which her inspired admiration of the man's undoubted physical skill was matched against a naïve skepticism of his mental merits.

Suddenly she screamed. Cyclone had reared back. For an instant he hung straight in the air, balanced on his hind legs; then slowly he tipped backward!

The girl's breath stopped as Silent slipped from the saddle and from under just as the horse fell upon its back. As the animal scrambled to its feet, Scott again threw himself into the saddle, and drove in his spurs.

Cyclone stood an instant, shaking in every muscle; then he dashed away on a run with the hazers closing in on him.

He had bucked less than three minutes, but he had tried every trick he had at his command, and Silent had ridden him as the judges and crowd now acclaimed.

Annalee looked down upon him, pale, a peculiar look in which aloftness and congratulation were commingled in her eyes, as he came off the field with the judges.

She frowned with displeasure as she noticed the antics of Andy Sawtelle and Pat McCarthy. The two were singing and dancing, raising a cloud of dust, their arms about each other and their heads bare. They made a grotesque picture, she thought.

The crowd was leaving the field, and Annalee and her mother began the descent of the board seats to the ground. When they were still several tiers of seats from the edge of the field, the girl saw Gruger and Lummox pass below. Lummox was looking at Scott's back.

The girl smothered a startled exclamation—suppressed a desire to cry out—as she saw the black venom in Lummox's eyes.

Gruger, on the other hand, seemed strangely satisfied. He grinned evilly as he accidentally caught her eye.

She shivered as she turned her gaze quickly away.

"Don't forget to come to the big dance," Mrs. Clarendon was calling to them from above.

Annalee waved her handkerchief in a gesture of consent.

CHAPTER XIV
IN THE OLD TOWN

T he celebration reached its height with the coming of night. The games and contests were over and nothing remained but the dance and the gathering of men in the streets and the various resorts to talk, greet old acquaintances, renew friendships, or indulge in the games of chance which were running full blast.

Annalee gave herself up to the wild spirit of pleasure which prevailed in the big dancing pavilion, and while her mother sat with Mrs. Clarendon, talking, watching, meeting other women and their menfolks, she danced with whoever asked her.

Men fought for her favor, and at the conclusion of each number she was beset with requests for the next.

Myrle Capron was feverishly eager to be her partner, and though she maneuvered to outwit him several times, she finally relented and gave him a dance. After all, it was best to be on as good terms as possible with her neighbors, she decided.

But they were no sooner on the floor than she regretted her decision. Myrle's face was flushed, his step at times none too sure. He kept holding her off and looking down at her with an intent, burning gaze out of eyes unnaturally bright. She did not need the scent of his breath to inform her that he had been drinking.

"You look won—wonderful to-night," he said, pressing her hand.

"If you start talking and acting this way, we won't finish the dance," she reproved him. Then, to change the subject, she asked: "What have you been doing all day? I don't believe I've seen you."

"Gambling," he said in a confidential tone. "But I didn't have any luck. I tried every—everything; stud poker, blackjack, craps, an' the wheel. No good. I dropped a wad. I wouldn't want dad to know how much." He winked at her openly.

"You should know better," she said severely.

"Oh, we all gamble out here," said the youth lightly.

"You ain't got hep to us yet. We're different than they are in the East. You'll catch on. Lots of things go out here that wouldn't go back where you come from."

"I'm not so sure of that," replied the girl gravely. "But I'm not going to preach—especially when I know it won't do any good." She laughed lightly. "Did you see Mr. Scott ride?" she asked purposely in retaliation for his belittling speech.

Myrle scowled. "He was lucky, that's all," he said thickly. "Lummox would have beat him out if he hadn't got a poor break."

"Why, it looked all fair to me," said Annalee, surprised.

"You couldn't be expected to understand," he said almost patronizingly. "Takes an ex—expert eye to see the little twists of the game. Anyways, Scott better be careful."

Annalee pricked up her ears. "What do you mean by that?" she asked.

"Oh, he's got an idea he's the whole rodeo aroun' here, an' somebody's liable to take him down a few pegs," said Myrle mysteriously.

"I guess Mr. Scott can take care of himself," said the girl airily, then waiting breathlessly on his answer.

"He hadn't better monkey with Lummox," said Myrle sourly. "Lummox'll just naturally leave him for the coyotes to pick, an' that Mex ain't feeling any too good to-night after being beat outa the bucking prize."

"I don't believe Mr. Scott deliberately goes looking for trouble, does he?" asked the girl.

"Maybe not; but he's got a chip on his shoulder just

the same," was the reply. "An' you ain't always got to look for trouble to run plumb up against it. The other man might be lookin' for it, an' you wouldn't know a thing about it?"

The orchestra ceased playing, and they walked to the bench where Mrs. Bronson was sitting.

Annalee dismissed Myrle, against his will, with a smile. She was worried over what he had said. He had seemed to imply that there might be trouble between Silent Scott and Lummox. Annalee felt that if such should prove to be the course of events, it would partly be the fault of Gruger. Did Gruger hate Scott because the latter had come to the rescue of the Bronsons the day the foreman had attempted to stop the work on the houses? Had that affair, then, been just what it had looked to be? She remembered Lummox's look at Silent after the bucking contest; but it seemed to her that Gruger's leer of satisfaction had carried more significance. Was Gruger pleased because Lummox hated Silent Scott, whatever the reason?

During the next intermission the girl walked to the open end of the pavilion. There her worried glance spied Andy Sawtelle peering at the lights and movement within. She stepped down and pushed her way through the crowd about the entrance.

"Oh—Miss Annalee!" He removed his hat and indulged in an exaggerated bow a bit uncertainly.

The girl looked at him suspiciously.

"I have to report that the celebration is a unanimous success," he announced without replacing his hat. "Are you enjoying yourself, Miss Bronson?"

"Andy, you've been drinking!" she accused.

A look of supreme dejection spread over the poet's face. "It is all too true," he murmured. "I have been caught in the treacherous whirlpools of conviviality even as poor Pat"—there were actual tears in his eyes—"has sunk."

"You mean Pat is—is—"

"Completely out, Miss Bronson," sighed the poet. "He made the unfortunate mistake of trying to—ah—accompany me while I was visiting the various points of interest in search of old friends to whom I owed my regards, and indulging in the resulting formalities.

"And now he sleeps in the scented hay
Above our horses across the way.
He'll doubtless wake from a pleasant dream
Sufficiently sober to drive the team."

"Oh, Andy!" exclaimed the girl, stamping her foot. Then her face cleared and her frown was succeeded by a look of resignation. "I suppose you have the right to observe your holiday as you choose," she observed, shrugging her shoulders.

"Thank you, Miss Anna. It's my temperament. Sometimes I have no control over it at all, and my imagination runs away with my judgment. But if you want me to promise I will not take another—"

"No," said the girl, shaking her head. "I'm not going to exact any promises. But—how long can you keep this up?" she asked curiously.

"That, ma'am, is a natural question from you. You

are amazed, possibly, that I am making such an excellent showing. You will notice that even my articulation is unaffected. Very well, I shall tell you."

He put his hat back on his head and fondled the artist's tie, fixing her with his bright gaze.

"Early this morning I felt myself about to succumb to the entreaties of my numerous friends that I join them in a round of regards. I had the foresight to take a wine glass of pure olive oil. That's the secret, Miss Anna. If they don't slip something across on me, I'm good for all night, all morning, and if necessary, all day tomorrow and the rest of the week!"

"It won't be necessary," said the girl coldly, uncertain whether to be angry or amused.

"If there is something you wish me to do, I assure you I am anxious to execute your commands," said Andy eagerly.

Annalee could not resist a smile. In any event, Andy was loyal.

"Nothing? Sure?" he asked wistfully.

"Andy, have you seen Mr. Scott to-night?" the girl asked suddenly.

"Why, yes," he replied, lifting his thin brows. "He's down in the Green Front in a stud game."

"Gambling?" The girl seemed to ask herself the question. "Who else is there, Andy?"

"Every cow-puncher in town," said the poet.

"Is—are Gruger and that Lummox there?" she asked hesitatingly.

"Why, I 'spect so," said Andy slowly, looking at her questioningly. "You heard something?"

"I danced with Myrle Capron," confessed the girl, "and he gave me the impression that there might be trouble between Scott and Lummox. I was wondering if—that day he had that run-in with Gruger—might have anything to do with it."

Andy's eyes had become alert. He smote a palm with his fist. "By the snakes!" he ejaculated. "I'll bet Gruger's putting that Mex up to go out after Silent! You thought they were bluffing, ma'am, didn't you? That would be just like him. Lummox could beat it and the C-Bar'd be clear. I wonder—I wonder—"

"That's just it, Andy," said Annalee in a worried voice. "I'm wondering, too. And I'm wondering if Mr. Scott knows anything about it."

"He's a suspicious cuss," observed Andy. "He'd be likely to catch on."

"But he should know—in advance," said the girl in an excited tone. "I feel that he would rather avoid trouble than—than meet it halfway. And, if there is trouble—should be trouble—I'd feel that I—we—were partly responsible. Oh, I don't know my own mind, but—we must warn him, Andy." She looked up and down the crowded street.

"I'll saunter down there and put a bug in his ear, Miss Bronson," said Andy with a nod of affirmation.

"And I'll go with you," the girl decided, "to make sure."

Andy bowed and took her arm as they made their way to the street.

"I don't blame you in the least, ma'am, for wanting to go with me," he said as they walked toward the railroad tracks. "Those who are not acquainted with my—er—accomplishments on an occasion like this are often misled as to my ability to keep my head and retain my equilibrium. Here, I will demonstrate."

They had reached the tracks which were momentarily free of other pedestrians.

"Look, ma'am!" cried the poet, removing his hat and holding it high above his head.

An instant later his right foot shot up and the toe of his right boot knocked the hat from his head.

"You'll notice I didn't lose a particle of my balance after the kick," he pointed out as he retrieved his hat.

The girl laughed softly as they resumed their walk to the old town.

"You must be part French to kick like that," she intimated.

"Native American," said Andy morosely. "A prairie tramp, just like Gruger said. But I've read the books, and that's more than most of 'em have done."

They walked on in silence, threading their way through the crowd which jammed the street until they reached the Green Front resort.

The swinging doors had been taken off; removed, doubtless, to facilitate the movement of the scores passing in and out of the place.

Annalee started as she looked inside. The floor was packed, and the bar lined with patrons three and four deep. She could not see the gaming tables, but she could hear the checks clicking in a lull in the sounds within the resort. It was the clear tones of a voice which had caused her to start.

"You know you were dealt a fair hand, Lummox." She recognized the voice of Silent Scott coming from somewhere near the door.

Andy left her side and slipped quickly within.

"An' I say you went to the bottom for that queen!" came harshly from Lummox.

There was a sudden movement on the part of a number of the spectators who edged away to either side. In the gap thus created Annalee saw Lummox's back at a table and the calm face of Silent Scott across from him.

She saw the other players as if in a daze, and Gruger standing to the right of Lummox while Andy Sawtelle was pushing to his left.

Even as she stared, she saw Silent Scott's face grow a shade paler. A queer smile played upon his lips.

"Lummox, you're not so interested in that paltry pot, an' you know I don't cheat at cards," he said evenly. "You've busted in here huntin' trouble—that's the size of it. I ain't sidestepping any responsibility, but I'd like to know what's eatin' you before the hostilities get under way."

His coolness appeared to madden Lummox, who partly rose.

"Sit down!" Scott's command came like a pistol shot. "You can't have the advantage of the grudge an' the draw, too, Lummox!"

"You're two-faced!" exclaimed Lummox. "You're playing to the land grabbers! You're worse than a card sharp, Scott, you're a double crosser!"

"Too late!" the girl whispered to herself. She wanted

to cry out, but her tongue clung to the roof of her mouth.

The spectators had broken away from behind Scott. Now those who were near Annalee shifted their positions to the side, for she was just without the door, directly behind Lummox. She could not move.

Scott's eyes had narrowed. Now his words came cold and clear, penetrating to every corner of the room and carrying to the farther side of the street.

"That's a lie, Lummox!"

For ages it seemed to the girl the two men locked gazes; then Lummox leaned to the left, and his right hand darted like lightning. But, fast as he moved, Andy Sawtelle's right foot moved swifter, and his booted toe caught Lummox's right elbow as it crooked back.

The man screamed with pain and rage as his gun clattered on the floor. He kicked his chair back, half falling in the act.

Gruger had leaped toward Sawtelle with a curse.

Then Lummox's right hand came up from his boot, and Annalee screamed as she saw the flash of cold steel in the light of the hanging lamps.

The close air of the room split to the crashing report of a gun, and Lummox bent suddenly forward and leaned on the table. The knife, slipping from his grasp, jangled on the chair and hit the floor at his feet.

There was a moment of intense silence. The girl saw a little curl of blue smoke rising from Silent Scott's right hip. Lummox slumped forward on the table. The crowd closed in, and there arose the murmur of hushed voices. Then confusion, and the girl relaxed. The scene swam before her eyes, and she dropped limply into the arms of Andy Sawtelle, who came running to her.

She heard him speaking, heard shouts, and the stamping of feet. Then darkness settled over her.

CHAPTER XV
SONGS IN THE NIGHT

Annalee recovered swiftly as Andy Sawtelle bore her through the gathering throng toward the railroad tracks which marked the division of the town. There he put her down and steadied her as she regained her strength.

"Oh—Andy!" she sobbed. "Did you hear what he—said?"

She fought for composure as he drew her gently across the tracks toward the hotel.

"It wasn't the horse contest, Andy; it was us! Lummox accused him of being a friend of the—the land grabbers. The contest just got him mad, that's all, and Gruger took advantage of his feeling toward—toward Silent."

It did not seem untoward to her that she should use the name by which Scott was generally known among the men.

"You're right," agreed Andy. "It was Gruger's doings. He figured Lummox could put Silent out of the way, and then he'd have plain sailing out there. He's been a raging volcano ever since Silent butted in that day."

"And I thought it was stage play!" groaned the girl.

"Andy, I want to go to my room."

The crowds were surging toward the old town and the Green Front resort. Everywhere there was excitement. Home seekers and other newcomers to the town were calling to each other almost in triumph.

"There's been a killing!"

"Caught a guy cheating at cards!"

"All happened in a minute, they say."

Annalee shuddered as she heard the remarks passed back and forth. The injustice of it all struck her with sinister force. The shooting *had* been forced on Silent Scott. But a question kept intruding. Had Silent hoped to avoid the meeting? Had he tried to avoid it? It all had taken place so quickly that the girl had not been able to get a true perspective on the progressive steps of the tragedy.

When they reached the hotel, Andy entered with her and escorted her up the stairs. At the door of her room he removed his hat and spoke earnestly.

"Now, Miss Anna, you mustn't think too much about this. You seem to be trying to blame yourself, and that is wrong—very wrong. There's been bad blood between Silent and Gruger for a long time, just because Gruger's been jealous of Silent. Gruger is worse than a coyote. He's had Lummox pull more than one dirty stunt for him. Lummox was sore because Silent beat him in the bucking contest, but he didn't have to pick a ruckus with him on that account. The Twin B didn't have anything to do with this. It was just Gruger and Lummox trying to put it over on Silent, and I've got a hunch that they thought Silent would back down.

That's all. Now you lie down for a spell, and I'll be back with any news—"

"Yes!" the girl interrupted eagerly. "I want to know if—if Lummox—do you think he was killed, Andy?"

Andy shrugged. "Silent had to stop that knife," he said noncommittally. "He hadn't started to draw, hardly, when I kicked Lummox. But when he came out with that knife, well, Silent didn't have much time to pick a spot for his target."

The girl opened her door and entered her room. She lit the lamp with trembling fingers. The room had two windows on the east side of the building, and she could hear the excited exclamations of men in the hotel bar which was situated under her room on the first floor; its several windows opened below hers.

She dropped upon the bed, striving to readjust her mental processes. Yet, at that time, it seemed she could remember nothing but the grim face and keen eyes of Silent Scott under the hanging lamp, and the swift moves of the man Lummox. She shivered with memory of the gleam of the knife.

In all her life she never had seen men so aroused, and here there was a deadly, quiet confidence about certain men. She felt herself shrink from the thought of Silent Scott. In some intangible way he had seemed different—perhaps he had merely been conspicuous. Anyway, this thing had come between her thoughts of him—had made him seem another and totally different man to her. He was no longer a bluff, as she had foolishly chided herself; but, in being the other kind of man, he seemed automatically removed from her ken.

122

The door opened, and her mother came in, accompanied by Mrs. Clarendon.

"The poor dear," Mrs. Clarendon was saying.

Annalee's mother put her arms about the girl and kissed her. The older woman seemed to have recruited strength from her daughter's ordeal.

"Don't worry, and try to forget as much of it as you can," said the practical Mrs. Clarendon. "Lor' me, those are things any woman is li'ble to see in this country. Look at me—I've seen three perfectly good killings an' a man cut his own throat!"

"Mrs. Clarendon!" exclaimed Mrs. Bronson in an awed voice.

" 'Sfact," affirmed the good woman with a vigorous nod of her head. "But I'm sure glad that C-Bar Mex got his!"

"Oh, how can you say that?" Annalee reproved her.

"How? Why, because that's the way I feel about it," replied Mrs. Clarendon heartily, sitting in the rocking-chair and rocking violently. "Him drawing a knife! From what that shiftless poet told us—excuse me for callin' him that since he's workin' for you two an' I reckon he's a good sort—Silent let him go the first time. He would have been justified in lettin' daylight through him the second he went for his gun. Then the hound tries to throw a knife into him! I ain't got any use for any knife throwers!"

Mrs. Clarendon's manner was a source of amusement to the girl, despite her concern over what had happened.

"Let me tell you something, Mrs. Bronson, since

you've come out here to live, and you, too, deary," Mrs. Clarendon went on. "You've got to change your ideas out here an' broaden out—I guess that's what they'd call it. You got to take things as they come an' get used to these men of ours. They're more or less boys—grown-up boys. They've had a lot of room to play aroun' in an' they get peevish when their range is cut down. The law ain't been much—usually every man for himself, you might say. They ain't got over that, either. An' there's no stopping them when they get it in for one another. You might just as well let 'em fight it out any way they want an' be done with it. My man lost half his hair an' three front teeth tryin' to shove our ranch bound'ry two feet west. He couldn't make it stick, but he was satisfied after the fight. That's the way they are. You can't reason with 'em. All you can do is feed 'em good an' trust to luck. They tame down in time—when they get old. An' there ain't no better male stock in America or Californy than right here!"

Both the other women smiled at this outburst, even as they gleaned the current of common sense in it.

"So don't be blaming this Silent Scott," Mrs. Clarendon admonished. "That Mex put the play up to him an' he had to go through. An' don't be blaming yourselves, either. It wasn't any of your fault. Most of these grudges are too deep for us women to see through because they start in some silly way an' the men that's on the inside are usually close-mouthed. That's one thing you got to hand it to the men for—they don't tell on each other like us women."

As she finished speaking a knock was heard on the door.

"Come in," called Mrs. Clarendon.

Andy Sawtelle opened the door. But he made no move to enter.

"Lummox ain't dead—yet," he announced, looking at Annalee. "The doctor's working on him, and he may pull out of it."

"Oh, that's good news!" cried the girl. "Thank you, Andy."

Mrs. Clarendon smiled wryly as the poet withdrew. "That fellow acts like he was feeling some responsibility," she observed. "Well, you folks have done more'n anybody in these parts ever was able to do before. You've got him working!"

"He practically volunteered," said Annalee with a laugh. She felt better after having heard the poet's news. "Maybe he didn't receive the proper encouragement before."

"He rode the line an' dodged jobs for twenty years that I know of," said Mrs. Clarendon dryly. "You must have him hypnotized, young lady."

Annalee blushed under the critical gaze. She began quietly to prepare for bed while her mother and Mrs. Clarendon gossiped on a wide variety of topics. The conversation seemed to do Mrs. Bronson good, the girl reflected.

An hour later Mrs. Clarendon left, after she had invited them to visit her at her place west of town before she and her family left for California in the fall.

Mrs. Bronson chattered on as she prepared to retire.

She blew out the light in the lamp and soon fell asleep.

But Annalee couldn't sleep. She kept going over the events of the day in her mind. The noise from the barroom below kept her awake also.

Suddenly she sat up in bed and listened intently. Some one was singing in the barroom, and the words drifted distinctly to her ears.

> "They buried him out on the lone pra-air-ee,
> With a cac-tus at his head;
> 'It's powerful sad, but his aim was bad,'
> Was what the mourners said."

Annalee recognized the thin, tenor voice as Andy's. There seemed to be some vague significance to the words of the song. The vocalist was applauded vociferously. Annalee wondered if the song could have any connection with the tragedy of that night. This singing of burying—

She worried the matter in her mind. Would Silent Scott be tried for murder if Lummox died? Was Lummox dead? Was Silent even then on his way to jail?

In the end she got up silently, wrapped herself in her dressing robe, put on her slippers, opened the door, and stealthily stole out into the hall to the head of the stairs. As luck would have it she saw the porter moving below and called to him.

"Will you please tell Andy Sawtelle to come to the stairs for a minute?" she asked in a low tone. "He's in—the bar, I think."

The man obeyed, and a half minute later Andy came

hurrying up the stairs. His face was the picture of grave concern.

"I heard you singing—about burying somebody," she explained. "Did it have anything to do with what happened to-night? Is Lummox—dead?"

"No such luck," said Andy. "He's too tough to die when he ought, that bird. I was just entertaining the boys a little. Are you awake yet, Miss Bronson?" he concluded stupidly.

"Andy, you've been celebrating again," said the girl with an exasperated frown.

Andy bowed. "Bacchus hangs on the fuses of the firecrackers," he said solemnly. "You didn't ask me to promise, and so—" He waved an arm in a gesture of abandon.

"Have they—done anything to Silent Scott?" asked Annalee.

"Not that I've heard of," replied Andy, surprised. "I reckon Gruger will call it a day and lay off a while."

"No, I mean have they—arrested him?"

"What for?" Andy demanded. "He acted in self-defense. And, besides, Lummox isn't dead yet!"

"We will go home in the morning—early," said the girl severely as she turned back to her room.

Before she fell asleep she again heard the poet's voice raised in song.

> "I'm lost on the lone pra-air-ee,
> I cannot find my way-y-y;
> I'll stay here all night in the stars' soft light,
> Till the dawn of the break-ing day-y-y."

There seemed a sad note in Andy's voice. It quavered. Evidently his celebration was working havoc with his normal cheerfulness.

But Annalee detected a subtle meaning in this verse, also.

"Till the dawn of the breaking day."

Why should that line linger in her memory? What was it she could not understand? Why did she have a feeling as if she were lost?

"The foreman asked, 'Where was you going?'
'To get more hosses,' the hoss thief said.
'Hang him to that cottonwood!' the foreman
    yelled;
'Hang him high till he's good an' dead!'"

Andy's mood apparently had changed in the brief interval when glasses had tinkled.

Annalee turned over and drew the covers over her ear. In a short time she slept.

CHAPTER XVI
THE SILENCE IS BROKEN

On the way to the ranch the morning following the celebration in Brant, it was Mrs. Bronson who was most talkative, Annalee being preoccupied and Andy and Pat observing a decorum which was not their natural bent.

Pat drove, an unlighted pipe between his teeth, and Andy nodded in the seat beside him.

From the rear seat Mrs. Bronson directed a lecture at the pair, which they gave no sign of bearing, while Annalee occasionally smiled in quiet amusement.

As the sun mounted toward the zenith, Mrs. Bronson desisted in her friendly, almost motherly tirade and opened a parasol which she held over herself and her daughter. They drove on silently through the heat of the day, Pat refusing to push the sweating horses, and Andy dozing in fits and starts.

It was midafternoon when they reached the homesteads and found, to their intense relief that nothing had been disturbed.

"I didn't think that old Capron would have the nerve to bother anything here," said Annalee with false conviction.

"It wouldn't be policy," said Andy dryly.

"He's done enough as it is," the girl retorted.

Andy shook his head gravely. "I don't believe Capron is responsible for Gruger's schemes and actions," he said slowly. "He's sore, and he wants to buy you out; but I think that's about as far as he'd go himself. He's pretty sure to respect the code that men can't make war on women hereabouts and get public opinion to back them up."

"Well, he can't say as much for his foreman," said Annalee, tossing her head.

Andy looked at her thoughtfully. "Gruger isn't directing his attack directly at you," he pointed out.

"Oh!" The girl stepped back as if she had been struck.

"I—I know what you mean, Andy."

Pain and remorse were reflected in the poet's face.

"Miss Anna," he said contritely, "please don't misunderstand why I said that. I just wanted to show you—honestly, I did—what a skunk Gruger is. You—you misunderstood him. I don't blame you. You thought he was blustering—bluffing. But that isn't his way. He's dangerous. He's doubly dangerous now that he's got his back to the wall trying to keep this range. And it isn't that he's as loyal as all that to Capron and the C-Bar. It's because he wants to have his own way. His word has been law in this section in here by the river for years, and it drives him mad to think that any one would go against his will."

"I understand you, Andy," answered the girl gravely. "And—these are things I would like to keep from mother, if I can."

"I'll never mention a thing to her!" exclaimed Andy loyally.

"Thank you, Andy," she murmured as she turned into her house.

Andy looked after her wistfully; then he pulled his hat over his eyes and went to the barn where Pat was putting up the horses.

"There's your tapering-off medicine," said Pat, grinning, and pointing to a pint flask on the top of the feed box.

Andy took up the bottle, hesitated, with thumb and finger on the cork, glared at Pat, then flung it among the bags of feed in a vacant stall.

The Irishman stared after him as he went out.

They had supper early, before sunset, and after the meal Andy went out to inspect the plowed acreage. They were preparing a patch of forty acres for seeding, twenty acres to be on Annalee's homestead and twenty acres on her mother's land.

Sawtelle, however, did not pay any great attention to the plowed field. He sat on a pile of stone which had been picked from the surface of the prairie in the path of the plow, and stared into the south and west. He marveled, as he had all his life, at the stupendous, inspiring spectacle of the prairie sunset. He listened to the wind, which rose steadily, and held his face up to it, looking at the silvering skies in the northwest. Thus a horseman came within his line of vision and Andy stared, curiously at first, then with eyes and senses keenly alert.

He rose and waved his hat as the rider approached. The horseman saw him and came on.

In Andy's eyes rebellion, envy, admiration, and wonder clashed as Silent Scott reined in his mount and smiled down upon him.

"What's new?" he asked.

"Still kicking," said Scott. "I hope he don't pass out," he added with a frown.

Sawtelle indulged in a shrug. "You're too liberal," he said. "He had it coming. Going for a knife, that way."

"I know," Scott admitted. "But there are folks that wouldn't understand—" He glanced toward the houses in the distance. "An' I ain't hankerin' to nick up my gun butt."

"A man like you can't help having notches in his

131

gun," said Andy. "Been riding long?"

"Since morning. I started for up on the Marias."

Andy's eyes clouded. But they cleared presently, and his brows lifted. He squinted at Silent Scott quizzically.

"Going back to the Brakes?" he asked.

Scott's gaze flashed toward the river. "Maybe. For a time. Did you tell 'em, up at the house, that I was in there for a week after Gruger was up here?"

Andy shook his head. "They think you beat it out and left them cold," he replied with a short laugh. "You don't take much credit to yourself for what you do, Silent."

"What did it amount to?" asked Scott scornfully. "An' they probably wouldn't understand. How can they when I don't understand myself, you might say!"

Andy laughed. But it was a mirthless laugh.

Scott eyed him narrowly.

"Look here, Silent, you come on over to the house," said Andy suddenly.

It was Scott's turn to laugh. "What for?" he scoffed.

"I think that girl's got it coming to her to know something about you," said Andy, frowning. "At least she's entitled to the chance to get you right; I mean, to feel that she's better acquainted with you. It isn't nice to think you're under obligations to a total stranger."

Scott winced, but he essayed a smile. "You've got to take some things for granted in this country," he observed dryly.

"But they haven't been brought up that way, Silent," Andy pointed out earnestly. "It ain't fair to them—to the girl—to put them in such a place. Last night's business came with something of a shock. The girl saw it, you know."

"She—saw it?" gasped Scott.

"Sure. Got a hint from young Capron that Lummox was gunning for you and dragged me over to the Green Front to warn you—went with me to be sure I tipped you off."

Silent Scott stared with an expression of blank amazement. "An' you say they haven't been brought up our way!" Scott blurted out. "Where was she when it happened?"

"Out front," answered Sawtelle with a scowl. "Waiting for me. I'd just gone in. They got out from behind Lummox so's not to stop any stray bullets and gave her a good view of the proceedings."

He started toward the house, where the lights were shining, and Scott followed him, walking his horse.

"Say, that kid's sure got spunk!" declared Scott.

"Oh, you're just guessing," Andy flung sarcastically over his shoulder.

Silent Scott smiled as he rode on behind the poet.

Annalee was standing on the little porch of her house when they came up. She looked rarely beautiful in the deepening twilight, with a greeting and a question in her eyes.

Scott swept his hat low.

"I couldn't go on without stopping, after what I heard to-night," he said in a low voice as Andy took a hurried departure.

"Oh, you have bad news?" asked the girl with immediate concern.

"None whatever," Scott assured her, dismounting. "I want to thank you, Miss Bronson."

"Thank—me?"

"For thinking of me last night," he said smiling.

"I—don't believe I—quite understand," faltered the girl.

She marveled that this boyish-appearing man could, on occasion, be the cold, formidable-looking person she had seen across the gaming table from Lummox the night before. His eyes, his frank speech, his smile—everything about him belied the reputation he must have as a gunman and perhaps an outlaw.

"I believe you sent Andy Sawtelle in to wise me up about that fellow, Lummox," he said.

"Oh! Yes, that is true. I—we—felt partly responsible."

"But when you started to warn me, you didn't know then what excuse Lummox was going to make for shooting me, did you, ma'am?"

"I don't think we need to discuss how I came to—to decide as I did," said Annalee stiffly, with heightened color. "But have you had supper?"

"No," said Scott cheerfully. "An' what's more, I don't know where I'm going to get any."

Annalee looked at him suspiciously, but couldn't resist a laugh. "Come in," she invited. "Mother has gone to her house to go to bed," she explained when they were inside. "The ride in the heat gave her a headache. I'll have to give you a cold supper, I'm afraid."

"Well, I've had two or three cold meals, so I guess I can stand one more," returned Scott, grinning, as he seated himself near the table.

"There's hot water to make tea," she pattered. "Some cold meat and potato salad—do you like potato salad?"

"You've got the most wonderful head of hair I ever saw in my life!" was Scott's irrelevant answer.

She looked at him in astonishment. Then she turned away quickly, coloring. "You evidently include flattery among your accomplishments," she commented.

"I wouldn't call that flattery, Miss Bronson," he said easily. "That's a plain statement of fact. Do you know what your hair reminds me of?"

She wrinkled her brows and risked a swift glance to make sure he was in earnest. "What?" she asked, and was partly sorry for it.

"Well, there's a time in fall, ma'am, when these prairies take on a reddish-gold look along in the late afternoon. I like 'em best then. An' your hair is just that color—with the sun goin' down in it."

"I thought Andy was the only poet on the premises," she remarked, with some misgiving.

Silent Scott laughed with delight. "You're clever as well as too all fired good looking," he said, with a mock frown.

"Mr. Scott, did you call to pass compliments?" she asked with hauteur.

"Not exactly. I stopped to thank you, as I told you first. But the compliments—if you want to call 'em that—just leaked out naturally. I couldn't help myself. You see I was born an' reared in this God-forsaken country, ma'am, an' I used to think the finest thing I'd ever seen was the prairie cactus flower. Maybe that was because there ain't many flowers here. Then—I saw you."

Annalee could not bring herself to answer this flippantly. She saw the wistful, moody look in his eyes. It was not mere cajolery on his part. He was like a boy confessing some youthful transgression. She noted the clear, tanned skin of his face and throat, the tumbled shock of blond hair, the neatness of his dress—his black riding boots shone with the luster of their polish. Then her appraising glance rested on the butt of the gun on his right thigh. Instinctively she shuddered.

"Silent—" The name slipped out naturally, and she did not correct herself. "Are you a—a gunman?" she asked impulsively.

He smiled at her. It was catching—that smile.

"I expected you would ask that," he replied quietly. "There are several ways of answering it. In the way you would think of it where you come from, I'm not; in the way that we look at it out here, I am."

"I don't believe I understand you," she said, puzzled.

"Well, it's this way," he drawled, gazing at her with a half-humorous, half-quizzical expression out of his baffling, blue eyes. "I reckon you people back there have read a lot about gunmen an' that what you've read has got you to believing he's a bloodthirsty critter, lookin' every minute for a chance to pull down his smoke wagon on some gent an' just naturally fill him full of holes. How about it?"

"Oh, no," she protested. Then she wrinkled her brows. "That is—well, perhaps we *have* been given to understand something of that nature," she amended.

"I thought so," he said. "Well, I ain't that kind,

ma'am. Now, out here, any man that's pretty handy with his weapon is liable to get to be known as a gun fighter. I guess I come under that brand."

She looked at him gravely. "You can ride, you can shoot, you can—are you perfect in everything, Silent?"

His laughter filled the room, and she flushed indignantly.

"No, miss," he said sobering. "I'm a miserable gambler. No, I know you don't like that idea—gambling, I mean. Well, it's done out here. I ain't very handy with a rope, although I can snare a straight shot now an' then. I don't know a thing about women. Now let's see—"

"You had better eat your supper," Annalee interposed, severely, overlooking the fact that she hadn't finished preparing it.

"Maybe so," he said, grinning. "What should I begin on, ma'am."

She didn't speak again until the food was on the table and he was eating.

"Don't you get good food on the ranches?" she asked seriously.

He scowled. "Did you ask me that because I was goin' at this so hearty? Well, I'll tell you. We get plenty of it, but it wasn't as good as this. We didn't hardly have potato salad more'n three times a week, an' it always happened that I was out on circle or somewheres when we had it."

Annalee laughed in enjoyable understanding. For the remainder of the meal she flitted about waiting upon him. After all, it seemed good to have a man in the house, especially a man who was hungry and not ashamed of it.

When he had finished he took up his hat and rose. "That square's another thing I'll have to thank you for, Miss Bronson."

"Don't you dare," she said impulsively. "Still— maybe you'll promise me something, Silent."

"I hate to make promises, ma'am, they're so dog-goned tricky."

"But I only want you to promise not to have any trouble with that man Gruger," she pleaded.

"I'm not lookin' for trouble with Gruger," he said with a frown. "An' I wouldn't want you to think anything's goin' to happen between us. You see"—his tone became very serious—"in a way, I'm like Gruger. I sort of hated to see the homesteaders come in. But I don't like his tactics. An' I don't like *him*. But so far's I'm concerned, ma'am, there'll be no trouble started."

Annalee beamed her thanks.

He shifted awkwardly and then walked to the door. She went out with him. The prairies were bathed in the soft moonlight; the scented wind had strengthened. Both of them breathed deeply and he turned to her with a smile.

"Miss Bronson, I did something to-night I don't think I ever did before. I went in to eat without takin' care of my horse."

He said it so sorrowfully that the girl's joking rejoinder remained unspoken.

"That's one thing I guess I *will* have to blame on you," he said.

She flushed under his compliment.

Andy appeared, leading Scott's horse.

"Took the liberty of feeding him and watering him," he said to Scott, as he handed him the reins.

"You're a good scout, Andy," said Scott mounting. "I don't usually forget Nightmare."

"I know that," said Andy as he shuffled on.

"You'll come again, won't you, Silent?" said the girl.

"Thank you," he said simply. Then he was gone.

For some time Annalee stood looking after the black shadow that swept southeastward. It was amazing, this meeting—amazing in more ways than she could determine.

Then Andy appeared again. "You better go in the house, Miss Anna, and clear off the dishes."

The girl was astonished and looked at him blankly.

"There's horsemen coming from the west, ma'am," he explained.

"Oh—what—"

She ran into the house as Andy hurried on toward the barn.

CHAPTER XVII
ALARMS

Annalee found herself going automatically about the work of clearing the table of dishes and the remainder of the food. She found herself hurrying, too, and suddenly she paused to wonder that this should be the case. Why should she hurry to clear the evidences of a meal because horsemen were coming? But she didn't attempt to carry out this thread of reasoning; instead, she quickly put the room to rights and got out her sewing.

One thing she sensed instinctively: The riders were not coming from the Capron Ranch.

Soon the pound of hoofs, which Sawtelle's trained ear had heard from afar, came to her. She took up her sewing and found herself strangely calm. She felt she knew what this visit portended, and she faced it stoically. She wondered with a thrill, if she was beginning to absorb the mannerisms of this new country.

She heard men dismounting outside, heard voices, including that of Andy.

Then boots stamped up the steps.

She looked up to see a tall, dark man of official bearing and immediately recognized him as one of the officers she had seen in town the night she arrived.

She nodded coolly and lifted her brows questioningly.

"I am Sheriff Moran, ma'am," said the officer; "and I would like to ask you a few questions."

She saw Andy Sawtelle's face behind him and was puzzled by his look.

"Won't you come in?" she invited.

The sheriff took off his hat and entered somewhat gingerly. He was covered with dust—a sign she had learned meant hard riding.

He shook his head when she indicated a chair.

"Ma'am, do you know anything about this Silent Scott, they call him?"

The girl's eyes widened in surprise. "Why, Sheriff

Moran! I've only been here a short time. I—I—don't see how I could very well."

Sawtelle had entered. He was lounging against the door.

"That isn't the question, ma'am," said the sheriff with a scowl. "I have reasons for wanting straight answers."

"Seems to me, sheriff, that Miss Bronson has given you a pretty square answer." It was Sawtelle who spoke, and the official swung on him angrily.

"You haven't anything to do with this," he said harshly. "With *that* anyway."

"I'm not butting in," answered Sawtelle. "I was only reminding you that Miss Bronson is a lady and a stranger in the country."

"Maybe not so much of a stranger as you might think," Moran returned.

Sawtelle scowled. "You're not forgetting yourself, are you?"

The sheriff was silent.

Annalee found herself feeling rather sorry for him. After all, he had his duty to perform, and it was a difficult situation. "Sheriff, let me ask one question before you put any more—will you please?"

He looked at her speculatively, then nodded.

"Lummox—is he badly hurt?"

"He's dead!" answered the sheriff shortly.

She started, and her face paled.

"That's why I'm here, miss," he said in milder tones. "You can see what I'm up against. I'm not only trying to get a line on him; I'm out to find him!"

One hand went up to her throat. Silent Scott was wanted for murder! He was a fugitive—an outlaw! Had he heard them coming and fled?

"I can answer your question more direct, sheriff," she said in a calm voice. "I answered as I did because it startled me. I don't know anything about Silent Scott except that he befriended us here, when we didn't know him at all, for that matter, and—in return—I tried to warn him that he might get into trouble for it—and—"

"I reckon that's about all I need to know, ma'am," the sheriff interrupted, dryly, in a tone which she somehow resented. "Now, ma'am, I'll ask you the second question. Silent lit out early this morning. Did you see him when you was driving here?"

"No."

"He didn't come here then?"

"I don't know where he went—when he left town. I don't know where he is now. Why should you think he'd come here?"

"Why, you just said he'd befriended you and you tried to befriend him in turn," said the sheriff in mock surprise. "Maybe he'd come here to be befriended again, for all I know. He—"

The girl interrupted. "Can't you be a sheriff and a gentleman at the same time?" she cried scornfully.

The official turned his gaze away. "Well, maybe I *was* putting it in a poor sort of way, Miss Bronson," he apologized. "Honestly, girl, I don't want to be mean—but I've got to find Silent. Jobs like this one go with this."

He turned back his coat, revealing his star of authority.

"I should have asked what I'm going to ask now in the first place. Has Silent been out this way at all, to your knowledge? Your word is perfectly good with me, ma'am."

The girl stood motionless, her hands to her breast, her face white.

"Seems to me she's answered that," drawled Andy Sawtelle.

The sheriff paid no attention to him.

Then Andy hummed softly:

"He wears a star and asks the truth,
And says at lies he'll balk;
But that's no sign it would be a crime
To plumb refuse to talk!"

The sheriff turned on him, furious. "You get out o' here!" he ordered in a loud voice.

"Mr. Sawtelle is an employee of mine," said Annalee firmly.

"Which answers that, sheriff," said Andy breezily.

"Now I know what I wanted to know!" cried the sheriff. "And I warn you, Miss Bronson, you are aiding and maybe hiding a man that's wanted by the law. You're an accessory! You know what that means."

"Whatever it means, you're mistaken," said the girl, tossing her head and eying him defiantly. "I'm not going to lie to you, sheriff, because I don't believe in it in the first place, and Silent Scott would not wish me to. I believe that much in him. He was here! When he was here, why he was here, I'm not going to tell you. Where he has gone, I do not know. Now, I'll ask you to go."

The sheriff looked at her and saw that her lips were trembling, despite her flashing gaze.

"I told you your word was good with me, Miss Bronson," he said with just a trace of sarcasm. "And I believe you when you say you do not know where he has gone. But he might have tucked himself away around here close somewhere and I ain't taking any chances." He strode to the door. "Search this place—all of it!" he shouted to the men with him.

Andy went out and stood on the little porch, whistling.

Mrs. Bronson came to the door of her house and called across to her daughter.

"Annalee—Anna—what *is* the matter? What has happened?"

The girl ran across to her and put her arms about her. She drew her inside.

"It's some men, mother; they're looking for a—a fugitive. They're searching everywhere out this way for him and—came here, too. Is your headache better? Have you been asleep. There, I can see you have. That's good, mumsy."

She soothed her mother and evaded direct replies as best she could. Meanwhile, her heart was in a tumult. She had not wanted to answer the sheriff's questions. Why? Because the trouble on the Fourth had, at least so she was inclined to believe, arisen out of Silent's interest in their behalf. She remembered the hint that he might have robbed the stage. She had meant to ask him about that. And would it have made any difference with her feelings this night?

The sounds outside had ceased. She went to the door and looked out. She saw Andy Sawtelle and Pat talking before her own door, and she called softly to Andy. He came hurrying to her.

"They were thinking of going in there, too, but I convinced his nibs he was all wrong," said the poet lightly.

"And where have they gone now? Which way?"

"They split up. Some have gone east, north, and south. They might as well have gone straight up, I'm thinking."

"But, Andy! They'll keep after him, won't they? Won't he have to—to face the charge of—of murder?" the girl asked tremulously.

"If they catch him, he will," Andy conceded. "But it wasn't murder—not that. It's the Capron layout that's behind this skunk, Lummox. Politics, maybe; or maybe they've got more cards up their sleeves."

"That's all—Andy. Good night."

The girl went back into her mother's house.

"Now, deary, what *is* the matter?" asked Mrs. Bronson querulously.

"Nothing, mother, nothing," sobbed Annalee; "nothing, and—oh, everything!"

And she buried her face on her mother's pillow.

Outside, Andy Sawtelle stood with his hat in his hand, his face upturned to the wind, a strange mist in his eyes of faded blue.

145

CHAPTER XVIII
THE RETURN

Annalee slept with her mother that night. Nor would she disclose the reason for her tears, although the older woman tried to learn what had upset her.

"Is it instinctive sympathy for this man the officers are chasing?" she asked.

But the girl would vouchsafe no reply.

"You must remember, dear," Mrs. Bronson went on; "we have always been a law-abiding people. Your forbears were among the earliest settlers in the great State from which we come. They always upheld the law— fought to uphold it. Do not forget your birth and breeding, Anna mine. They may not think much of such things out here, but they count mightily, just the same. But I know the blood in your veins will tell you what to do in an emergency."

Then suddenly a great, illuminating thought came to the mother.

"Anna—is it Mr. Scott for whom they searching?"

There was no response, and Mrs. Bronson remained silent. She did not know that Scott had been a visitor there that night. Finally she put aside the thought, decided her daughter was inclined to be sentimentally generous, and fell asleep.

But her words had left the girl dry-eyed, thinking— thinking.

It was true, what her mother had said. Moreover, it

appeared that Silent had sensed the approach of the posse and had taken flight just in time. He had no thought of being captured, of facing the charge against him, even though it might not be a just one. If such was the case, why, then, should she be concerned? The matter was in his own hands. She had—well, she had helped a little, perhaps. She had not told when he was there nor which way he had gone. She went to sleep, puzzling over the little thrill which this realization gave her.

There were no untoward events next day, and the following day the lumber concern's wagon arrived with the first load of fence posts, some spools of wire, and a keg of staples.

"Hurrah!" said Andy gleefully. "Now we can show 'em we mean business! Anyway, it takes a fence to make farms look like farms, Miss Anna."

The girl was enthusiastic. It was true that the fence would prove a finishing touch in distinguishing their domain from the rest of the world. They could follow with their eyes the lines of the wires and know just what belonged to them. But they did not realize for several days what an expensive proposition a fence could be and how much hard work it could entail.

"We can put up a cheap fence, three strands, posts eighteen feet, or so, apart," Andy explained; "or we can use four strands of wire and put the posts sixteen feet apart. It'll cost a lot more, but it'll keep cattle out of the crops and pay for itself in the end, I guess. As I say, I'm no farmer—I've just heard all this—"

"We'll put up a good fence," said the girl, while her

mother nodded. "You go right ahead, Andy."

Andy hauled the balance of the wire and posts from town while Pat quit plowing and began digging post holes.

"'Tis as much to me likin' as tryin' to keep that blamed plow pointed in the ground, anyway," he averred, to the amusement of the others.

But Andy, on his last trip, brought home a heavy sledge and announced they would drive the posts in.

"I saw 'em doing it down near town, and it worked fine," he explained.

They hitched up the team to the wagon next morning and drove out with a load of posts. Andy complained that he was not sure they had run the proper lines, as this had been accomplished by "sizing up" stakes between the corners.

"I haven't hardly got the heart to tell Miss Anna she should hire a surveyor to run her lines," he told Pat. "It means so much more money. Mother me, this place'll cost 'em a fortune before they're through with it. If there were more settlers in here we could run a party fence on one side anyway. Free land!" He snorted with indignation. He looked around disgusted.

"Anyway, it'll be easier to move a fence later, if we have to, than hire a surveyor now," he capitulated.

They tried driving the posts. One standing in the wagon box, swinging the sledge, and the other holding the post until it was started down straight. The method proved successful, except that the tops of the posts were mashed in somewhat; but it was very hard work. Andy took turns with Pat at this work and did very well, for he developed a knack the Irishman lacked. It hardened his muscles until he was himself surprised.

When they had driven posts about two sides of the plowed space, it was decided that it would be a good plan to build a fence completely about the field first, thus assuring protection for the crop which would soon have to be put in. It would take considerable time for two men to build a fence clear around the half section. This they did, and on the day the fence was completed, they had a visitor from the south.

They had just secured the last strand when they saw the rider approaching. It proved to be Myrle Capron.

He reined in his horse with a look of amused tolerance on his face and inspected the completed fence. The field was west of the houses, and he had ridden out of his way to look over the work, as both Andy and Pat knew. They spoke no word of greeting, waiting for the youth to show his hand.

"Nice job," he said finally; "but it might not hold steers if they were big enough an' mad enough."

"It wouldn't hold sheep, either," replied Andy dryly.

Myrle flushed with anger. "If you're hittin' at us, you've missed the mark," he said hotly. "We've sold our sheep."

"Yes," drawled Andy. "What you going to range on the school sections?"

"Cattle, if we range anything. You know we ain't never gone in for anything but cattle, Sawtelle. The sheep was just an experiment of dad's on that bad land below the river. We ain't never been sheepmen, Sawtelle, an' you know it!" Myrle's eyes were narrowed with passion, and his voice was shrill.

"Well, we're not trying any experiments up here," was Andy's retort.

"But you're trying some in town," flashed back Myrle, "an' you're liable to get into trouble as well as that killer, Silent Scott, if you don't watch yourself!"

With this fling, he whirled his horse, drove in his spurs, and galloped to the house at a furious pace.

Andy stared after him in amused surprise, not heeding Pat's blasphemous remarks. Then, with concern showing in his face, he started on a run for the house.

Myrle drew up before Annalee's house and swung his hat low as the girl and her mother appeared. He laughed heartily at the look of astonishment on their faces.

"Howdy," he chuckled; "don't you ever expect visits from neighbors?"

"Under the circumstances you can hardly blame us for being startled," said the girl.

He dismounted leisurely, threw the reins over his horse's head with a gesture of bravado, and walked up the steps to the porch.

"I just thought I'd run over to show you that we can let bygones be bygones," he said in his tone of exaggerated confidence. "How *are* you, to-day, Miss Bronson? You're looking well, Mrs. Bronson. It's hot, ain't it? See you've got some fence up—"

"Are you here representing your father, Mr. Capron?" asked Annalee.

"Gracious me, no," answered Myrle, looking at her

intently. "I'm representing myself, Annalee, an' I reckon I'm having a hard time doing that."

The girl stiffened at his look and mention of her first name. "You are hardly an acquaintance of sufficient standing to address me as you have, Mr. Capron."

"What've I got to be, a banker or something?" he asked, grinning.

"You misunderstood me," she replied coldly. "You've known me but a very short time and hardly at all."

"Well, that's what I come over for—to get better acquainted."

"Considering everything that's taken place, I'm afraid that will not be possible, Mr. Capron."

"Oh, you're thinking about that Lummox affair an' the carpenters," said Myrle easily; "I didn't have anything to do with that."

"But you people were not friendly in the first place, and have been anything but friendly since," Annalee pointed out. "I don't know what part you might have played, but—and I don't like to say it—you are not welcome here, Mr. Capron."

"I know what's the matter," he flared up; "you're stuck on that killer, Silent Scott!"

The girl's face went white. "You are grossly insulting, Mr. Capron, and you might as well go."

"And you might as well find out it'll pay to be neighbors with me—an' us. An' you'll never see that Silent again. He's put another notch in his gun an' beat it. If he ever shows up aroun' here again, he'll get his good an' proper!"

"Did you hear me ask you to go?" cried the girl, clenching her fists.

"You started all this trouble yourself, an' now you want to crawl out of it!" Myrle accused. "What's more, we know your man Sawtelle helped Silent, an' we ain't said nothing about that—yet."

Annalee fell back, a wild look in her eyes. "You come here to say things like *that*," she said in a strange voice.

"Did I hear you mention my name?" came from below Myrle.

The youth whirled and looked down at Sawtelle. "Oh, you?" he jeered. "You got a name?"

Sawtelle's sad face was stern. "What's he been saying, Miss Anna?"

The girl shook her head. She could not speak.

"You come here to the house to make trouble with the women when there aren't any men around, Capron?" demanded the poet.

"Well, there ain't none aroun' yet, are there?" queried the youth sneeringly, his hand dropping casually to the butt of his gun. "I don't call a clown a man!"

Sawtelle appeared to ponder this while Myrle started to laugh. Then the poet leaped up the steps. The youth drew too late, for Andy's fist, with the accumulated strength of an arm hardened by work, crashed full upon his jaw, knocking him back against the wall of the house. The gun thumped on the porch.

Myrle came back with a bound, caught Andy on the cheek with a left hook and dived for the weapon, his face black with rage. He secured it, but as he rose he came in contact with Andy's right fist again. This time he was knocked the length of the porch, and Andy tore after him, kicking the weapon aside. He grabbed his antagonist by the shoulders and threw him off the porch, leaping after him. As Myrle half rose, he hit him again, and the youth lay flat.

Andy looked about him with bloodshot eyes. Then he gradually came to his senses. Mrs. Bronson had withdrawn into the house. Annalee came running out, her eyes blazing wildly, holding in her hands the gun Andy had bought for her in town.

Myrle was scrambling to his feet, dazed. Andy secured the youth's gun, broke it, and spilled out the cartridges. He shoved it in Myrle's holster, then handed him his reins.

"Get out!" he cried hoarsely.

Myrle gathered strength rapidly and climbed into the saddle. With a look of intense hatred at the girl and Andy, he spurred his horse cruelly and dashed away.

"Now—I expect I *have* done it," said Andy sorrowfully.

"You did just right, Andy," said Annalee, breathing hard and placing a hand on the poet's arm. "He's as big a beast as Gruger."

Then she went into the house, leaving Andy standing on the ground just below the porch, with one hand on the spot on his arm which she had touched.

The balance of the day passed quietly. After supper Annalee went to the spring for water, and on her way back to the house she stopped and stared apprehensively southward, where she saw Andy Sawtelle talking with a horseman.

More trouble? She knew it was Andy's habit to walk over the prairies in the twilight. Sometimes he would walk until long after the stars had come out. Had he met some one from the Capron ranch? She could not make out the rider, for the distance was too great and the mist of the twilight too dense. She breathed with relief when she saw the rider strike off eastward and Andy start toward the house.

She waited for Andy to speak when he came up to her.

"That was Silent," he said simply.

"Silent Scott!" exclaimed the girl astonished. "Silent? Are you sure?" And then, realizing the absurd nature of the question, she asked: "Where is he going? Why didn't he come up to the house?"

"I guess he didn't want to come up here for fear they'd find out he'd been here again. He doesn't want to cause you any trouble, Miss Anna. Silent just heard a week ago that he was wanted. He's been down in the Musselshell country. He's going in to give himself up!"

"Oh!" breathed the girl. "Oh, Andy! Isn't that fine?"

The poet looked at her wistfully, with a fleeting expression of pain in his eyes. Then: "It *is* fine, Miss Anna; and it will set him free."

"Free? Oh—will they—"

Andy nodded. "Until his hearing, anyway."

"But is it necessary for him to go to jail when he is sure of being acquitted?"

"They'd probably admit him to bail—if he had it,"

said Andy. "But don't worry, Miss Anna; it'll all turn out all right."

The girl went into the house. "Myrle Capron was right," she thought to herself. "We are responsible for all this. It wouldn't have happened if we had not come here in the first place. And Silent is giving himself up."

A great thrill of joy swept over her. He hadn't known Lummox was dead and that the sheriff and his men were after him. He had ridden far—why he had ridden far didn't matter. As soon as he had learned the state of affairs he had started back. He had been stealing past the place in the shadows of evening, avoiding her house intentionally for her protection. And now he was riding to Brant to give himself up—to face any intrigue of his enemies, of her enemies!

"The sheriff was right!" she exclaimed aloud. "I'm an accessory!"

Her heart was beating wildly as she ran out to where Andy Sawtelle was walking in the cool of the early night, across from the spring.

"Andy," she said, in an excited voice, "hitch the team for me in the morning. Pat can drive. I want you to stay here for mother's protection. She must not be made to stand the trip, and it isn't necessary—"

"Why, Miss Anna, what are you talking about?"

"The team—I want the team, the spring wagon, and Pat in the morning early—"

"But where are you going?"

"I am going to town," the girl announced calmly.

Andy was silent for a time. "Very well, Miss Anna, everything will be ready. And—I just noticed something. Look down there—down south. See those moving shadows?"

"What are they?" asked the girl.

"Capron's cattle!" said Andy. "They've brought a big herd north!"

CHAPTER XIX
BRANDS OF LAW

As Annalee and Pat drove away from the farm in the morning they saw several hundred head of steers grazing in the south. The girl realized that the result of Myrle's visit was the breaking of the Capron promise not to range cattle north of the river that season. However, with the field fenced in, and the posts for the fence about the houses in and ready for the wire which could be strung in a short time, she did not much care about the presence of the cattle.

They drove rapidly, the girl's aim being to get to town as soon as possible.

"And, listen, Pat," she admonished the Irishman; "you get no money to-day. I have my reasons, so do not ask for any."

"It ain't money I'm lookin' for," Pat declared; "it's a chance to paste that young hound Capron in the eye."

"Never mind," said the girl nervously. "And don't get into any fights to-day, Pat; we've trouble enough as it is, remember that."

They reached town a little after nine o'clock. Annalee instructed Pat to put up the team in the hotel barn; then she hurried to Neeland's office.

The locator shook hands energetically, but there was a worried look in his eyes. "What's the matter, Miss Bronson? Is anything wrong? Ain't your homesteads all right?" he concluded apprehensively.

"It's nothing about our homesteads," said the girl tersely. She did not notice the look of relief which came into Neeland's eyes.

"Fine," he breathed, offering her a chair. "Sit down, Miss Bronson—"

"I don't believe we have much time to lose, Mr. Neeland," said Annalee crisply; "I have come here for a specific purpose, and as you have transacted some business for us, I naturally come to you for assistance—and I'll pay you for your time and trouble, of course."

Neeland again showed symptoms of nervousness. "Yes, yes, Miss Bronson—what is it?"

"You know Silent Scott shot that man Lummox—Capron's man—and the sheriff went after him when Lummox died—" The girl was having trouble saying what she wanted to say.

"Yes, yes, Miss Bronson," said Neeland in worried tones. "He got away. They haven't found him. Why should it bother you?"

"He came in late last night or early this morning to give himself up," said the girl quickly. "Now, Mr. Neeland, *we* were responsible for that trouble. It all arose out of our filing out there and incurring the enmity of that man Gruger, who tried to frighten our carpenters away. Silent Scott called his bluff—if it was a bluff. That's what led up to this shooting. Silent didn't know they were after him. As soon as he found out, he came back. They'll put him in jail until his hearing, anyway, unless some bail is put up, I understand. *I'm here to put up that bail, Mr. Neeland!*"

The locator wiped his forehead. He had seen a shadow pass outside his window.

"But, Miss Bronson, what can I do about it?" he asked in a querulous voice. "What can *I* do—I can't do anything, Miss Bronson—don't you see?"

"You can find out where he is and what the procedure is," said the girl scornfully. "That's all I would like to have you do, Mr. Neeland. And I'll pay you for it."

"I can't, Miss Bronson," said the perspiring Neeland. The shadow had passed outside his window again. "My dear young lady, you must see our lawyer. We have a lawyer here. It takes a lawyer for such things, Miss Bronson. Why, they'd laugh at me. I wouldn't have any standing in court."

"Where is the lawyer?" demanded the girl with a look of contempt. "You seem terribly worked up over this thing and—"

"Two doors above here, Miss Bronson. You'll find him up there. Lawyer Fredericks—that's his name—"

But the girl was gone. She hurried two doors up the street to the little office of the lawyer.

Fredericks beamed upon her and ushered her into his private office.

"You are the lawyer, of course," she began.

"Fredericks is my name," he said, nodding.

"Has Silent Scott given himself up?" she asked abruptly.

The lawyer raised his brows. "I believe he is in town intending to give himself up at justice court at ten o'clock. Why, Miss—ah—oh, yes, Bronson—are you interested in the case?"

"I want to put up bail to keep him out of jail." She was breathing fast, and her face was white. It *was* an ordeal, after all.

Fredericks whistled softly. A faint smile played on his lips. "Why have you come to me?"

"Why? Aren't you a lawyer? Don't you look after such things? What are you for?" She nearly shouted the question.

Fredericks' smile became chilly. "You are perhaps not aware that I am retained by the year by the Capron interests. They'd hardly wish me to assist in getting bail for the slayer of one of their men."

"Oh—oh!" cried the girl. Then suddenly she became calm. "Very well; I'll go to the justice himself."

She walked out of the office with her head held high. She asked the location of the office of the justice, learned his name was Nichols, and went at once to his sanctum, which consisted of one room, used as a court-room and office.

Judge Nichols was old. His hair was white but wiry, and his eyebrows, by a queer coincidence, very nearly black. He had a fierce frown.

"Sit down, young lady, and don't act so excited. Now then, what is it?"

"I've come—you see—I want—oh, no one will understand!" The girl nearly broke down.

"There, there, now, miss, don't take on that way. Just

calm down. I'm an old man, and I understand all these things. I've been a judge around here for so many years I've forgotten when I started. Just you gather yourself together and tell me all about it."

"Oh, judge," sobbed Annalee, overcome by his kindliness, but still fearful that her mission would prove unsuccessful. "It's—it's that they won't understand—I'm afraid they won't. Judge, Silent Scott got into that shooting trouble on our account, and I want to put up the bail—so he won't have to go to jail and stay there till his hearing. He's going to turn himself over to you to-day. He came as soon as he heard he was wanted. He's coming into court this morning. We haven't much left in the bank, judge, but if two thousand would be enough, I'll give you a check, and—oh, I know he would not run away—"

She broke out in tears afresh.

The old justice took a small buckskin bag from a hip pocket. While the girl sobbed he opened the bag, took out a plug of tobacco, and cut himself off a generous chew. He thrust this into his left cheek, stowed the plug in its container, and put it away. Then he glared about the office and carefully wiped his glasses on a red bandanna handkerchief.

"I've heard quite a bit about this case, young lady. Now I want you to tell me all you know about it. Just calm down and tell me everything you know. Take it easy, we've got a quarter of an hour yet till court. Now then—"

Annalee told him everything, right up to the incident of Myrle Capron's visit to her house the afternoon before.

160

"And when I asked Neeland and the lawyer to try and arrange this for me they refused. I do not seem to have any friends—and I don't care. I'm not just sure why I'm here, but it seems I should be, and—"

"By the heavens! They don't own *me!*" exclaimed the old justice. "I've been the law around here too danged long. And I'm through with their treatin' me like a maverick—"

He ceased speaking as the office door opened. Annalee turned to see Fredericks, the lawyer, entering. Outside she saw Gruger's leering features as he passed the window.

Fredericks smiled at the girl perfunctorily, and then addressed the justice.

"Judge, Silent Scott is in town and is going to deliver himself up to you in about five minutes. In the absence of the county attorney or his assistant, I am assuming the prosecution. We will ask that Scott be charged with murder and held without bail."

"The charge'll be all right, I guess," grumbled the judge, "but I'm not so sure about the other. Two thousand has been offered for security that he'll show up for his hearing—"

"You can't take it!" said the lawyer sharply. "There are the books that will prove it!"

The girl looked tearfully where he pointed, and saw a pile of law books.

The old justice rose and pointed a shaking forefinger at the lawyer. "There's two brands of law, Fredericks," he said shrilly; "one of 'em's in them law books an' the other's in here." He struck himself over the heart with his left fist. "You've assumed the prosecution, eh? Maybe that's all right accordin' to the books, an' maybe it ain't. But I know one thing—I'm going to admit Silent Scott to bail!"

"You can't do it!" cried Fredericks. "You dare not do it without the consent of the county attorney."

"But I'm *going* to do it!" roared the justice. "And now you get out of here!"

Annalee half rose, words of thankfulness on her lips; then she sank back into her chair in a faint.

CHAPTER XX
DOUBTS

When Annalee revived, she was alone in the office with Justice Nichols. The old man was bending over her with a glass of water.

"There, now, drink some of this," he said soothingly. "Maybe you better go over to the hotel an' not be here when Silent comes in, eh? Don't you think that would be better?"

"Judge—is there—anything unlawful—about what I am doing?" asked the girl in a faint voice.

"None whatever," the justice assured her heartily. "An' none about what I'm doing, either, I reckon. I never had any use for that sneaking half Mexican anyway, an' I ain't got much more for Fredericks. Now drink the rest of this water—that's it. Do you want to stay?"

"No—no!" cried Annalee. "Here—I made that out at home. The money's in the bank here, judge. I am going." She rose, swayed for a moment, and then walked unaided to the door, where she turned and looked back at the old justice who stood holding the empty glass in one hand and her check in the other, staring at her with a whimsical smile.

"You're—you are a good man, judge," she said.

"Well, I dunno," the old man answered, scowling; looking about uncertainly for a place to put the glass. "Some say so an' some don't. I reckon most of 'em don't. But I'm still judge here, an' that's about all that's needed in this case this mornin', I 'spect."

The girl found the bright sunshine of the street almost painful. Her mind again was in a turmoil. What had she done? She didn't quite realize all that had happened in such a short space of time since her arrival in town. What should she do now? She felt faint at thought of the long ride home. She must rest. Yes, she was weak and should rest.

She crossed to the hotel where the obliging clerk saw to it that she had a room at her disposal without delay. The porter brought up a large pitcher of ice water. Annalee bathed her throbbing temples and hot brow in the cold water, and it made her feel better. Then she lay back upon the pillows and closed her eyes. The reaction from the strenuous events of the morning made her drowsy. She ceased to think of her troubles and lay resting quietly.

Meanwhile there was excitement on the streets of Brant. It was known that Silent Scott was in town, had arrived early that morning, and that he was there to give himself up for the shooting of Lummox. Although most of the sympathy was with Scott, a majority of the citizens did not wish to offend Capron or incur the enmity of Gruger.

Several of the C-Bar outfit, including Myrle Capron and Gruger, had come into town shortly after daybreak, but it was known that they did not learn of Scott's latest move until after their arrival. They had been rounding up beef cattle along the river to the westward, and had merely ridden into town for breakfast, they explained.

In the old town there was little or no talk of the queer turn of circumstances. The old-timers knew Scott was justified in killing Lummox. It was a clear case of self-defense, as Lummox would have killed Scott if the latter had not prevented him. But they also knew of the feud which had developed to bitter proportions between Scott and Gruger, and they wisely refrained from taking sides. It was the rule of the country that such affairs should take such course as was directed by the principals.

It was just ten o'clock when Silent Scott walked across the tracks from the old town to the office of Justice of the Peace Nichols. Many people stared at him, some nodded respectfully—all got out of his way. But none of the C-Bar outfit was among the spectators.

He found Justice Nichols alone.

"Judge, it's a right pleasant mornin'," he saluted as the old justice regarded him with a scowl. "In fact, judge, it seems 'most too good a mornin' for a man to be coming in an' giving himself up to the law." Scott laughed bitterly.

"You thinking of changing your mind, Silent?" the

justice inquired. "Because if you are, there's nothing to stop you from walkin' out that there door an' hitting for the open country."

Scott's face clouded. "No, I ain't changin' my mind," he said, unbuckling his gun belt. "Couldn't change it if I wanted to, I reckon." He put the belt, with its holstered gun, on the justice's desk.

"I'm givin' myself up for shootin' that Lummox, an' all I've got to say is that I can't see how he dodged the right bullet so long."

"A-hem." The justice cleared his throat. "What made you come in here an' give yourself up, Silent?"

"I reckon I wanted to save 'em the bother of keeping up the hunt for me," Scott drawled. "I was down in the Musselshell an' just heard a week ago that Lummox had kicked in. Soon's I heard I started back."

"You didn't have to come back," the justice pointed out.

Scott started. "Eh—no—yes. I reckon I'd have had to come back some time, judge."

"Why?" demanded the justice, gathering his bushy, black eyebrows into a frown.

Scott looked at him in surprise. "Say, look here, judge, have I got to start right out with a cross-examination?" he asked complainingly.

But now the justice's eyes were twinkling. "Well, Silent," he said in a tone of resignation, "you're more or less of a mystery to me. You ain't no hand to talk about yourself or defend yourself when you're blamed for—things. I don't believe you're bad, but I ain't sure of it—understand! I have my doubts—both ways. But

I figure there's got to be something to a man when a good woman will come to the front for him."

He attempted to glare at the tall, bronze-skinned young man before him.

"When you're through talkin', judge, maybe you'll start explaining," said Silent Scott, smiling.

The judge ignored this. "Silent, they're goin' to put a charge of murder against you, I understand," he said impressively. "There ain't any charge here as yet, that being up to the county attorney, I guess. But, anyway, I'm goin' to let you go on bail with the understanding that you'll hang aroun' here close an' go to Choteau for the hearing when they want you up there. This may be a peculiar law angle, so far's I'm concerned; but I've unraveled it so far's you're concerned."

"Bail?" Scott laughed heartily. "How much, judge?"

"Oh, about two thousand dollars."

Scott laughed again. "I quit the last game with six hundred cash to my name, judge, an' that's the bank roll," he said frankly. "I expect I'll have to leave half of that here, or all of it, to make sure my horse is taken care of while I'm in the county hotel."

"A-hem." The justice wiped his spectacles. "The bail has been furnished, Silent."

Scott stared at him open-mouthed. "What's that, judge?" he asked sharply.

Justice Nichols scowled. "You're hearin' ain't so bad, Silent. You've lived in this country since you was born an' you've heard harder things to hear than my voice. Your bail's up!"

"Who put it up?"

166

"That's different again, Silent. I don't know as the party or parties who put it up would want me to tell."

"Judge, isn't a man out on bail entitled to know who bailed him out?" Scott demanded. "How's he goin' to know whether to jump it or not!"

The justice pondered this. "A-hem. Maybe there's something in that. Yes, I guess you're right. You should know whether to jump it or not, that's a fact." He rubbed his nose vigorously. "Miss Annalee Bronson put up the bail, Silent," he confessed cheerfully.

Scott sat down in a convenient chair and remained motionless, as if stunned.

"Lawyer Fredericks tried to stop it," the justice explained. "She asked him to arrange it for her, but being tied up by the Capron crowd, he couldn't very well do it. That bunch acts as if they wanted to put you over for this, Silent."

Scott remained speechless and inactive, save for a single move to take off his hat.

"Miss Bronson seems a nice sort of girl," the old man went on. "She drove in here this mornin' after she found out from Andy Sawtelle that you was comin' in to give yourself up. The poor, deluded female doesn't seem to want you to go to jail. Think's she and her mother are responsible for this business because they filed out there. Wants to help you—"

"Judge, I can't take it!" Scott blurted out.

"Oh, you ain't goin' to get it. Don't worry. I've got it, an' it's security that you'll show up when the county attorney wants you."

"But I can't let her put it up," Scott protested. "You'll

167

have to give her back her money, judge, an' take me."

"Can't do it," said the justice decisively. "She wants you out of jail, an' she's put up the money to keep you out. That's her business. Now clear out of this office, Silent. By golly, what d'ye think of havin' to chase a man accused of a shootin' out of the office. Get out of here, Silent, but don't forget not to go far, an' say"—the justice looked at him speculatively—"what was you doing down in the Musselshells?"

Scott rose with a shrug. "Robbing stages, probably," he replied sarcastically. "Has Miss—Miss Bronson gone home?"

"How should I know?" cried the justice irritably. "It's all I can do to keep track of cases that's goin' on in this office. Get out!"

Scott slammed on his hat and walked grimly to the door.

"You can take your gun along," the justice called to him dryly.

He turned back to the desk and buckled on his gun belt. Then he sought the street, the justice following his deliberate movements with a curious gaze.

Annalee awakened from a doze to the realization that the light in the room had changed. She glanced quickly out of the window and saw a film of cloud over the sun. In the northwest the clouds were banked in the high skies. She looked at her watch and stared at its face incredulously as she saw that it was after one o'clock. She had slept three hours!

She quickly arranged her hair and applied a little

powder from the small vanity case she carried in her bag. The sleep had done her good. The events of the morning seemed far away. Her excitement was gone. Now that she reviewed what had happened, a flush mounted into her cheeks. She shrugged, and her thoughts flew homeward. Then she heard a low knocking at her door.

She started to call "Come in," but didn't. She hesitated to go to the door, although she didn't know why. Then she walked quickly to the door and opened it.

Silent Scott stood outside, hat in hand.

"I knocked kind of softlike several times in the last couple of hours, ma'am," he explained awkwardly; "I thought you was resting—asleep, maybe."

"I *was* asleep," Annalee confessed. Strange that she felt no embarrassment. "Did you want to see me, Silent?"

"Just a minute—if you'd come into the front parlor when you're ready."

"I'm ready now," she said, leading the way to the little room which served as a parlor. "What did you want, Silent?"

"I wanted to ask you to go down an' see Judge Nichols an' get that bail money back," he said slowly, twisting his hat in his hand.

"Oh, isn't it necessary to put up any bail?" the girl asked.

"Why—" Silent Scott swallowed hard. "Yes, I reckon it is, miss, but I was thinking you'd need the money yourself. It's a tolerable fair-sized chunk to have tied up that way."

"We can spare it. And it won't be tied up for long."

"Can't tell about that," said Scott doubtfully. "They might drag this thing along—on purpose."

"In that case we can get back the bail money later just as easily as now," said the girl with a laugh. "Anyway, it's just as safe in court as in the bank, isn't it?"

"Well, yes," Scott conceded. "But there's another side to it." He didn't appear sure of himself. "It might—people talk—you know."

Annalee's face suddenly went crimson.

Scott stepped to her quickly, dropping his hat to the floor, and took her hands in his.

"We understand," he said simply. "But there's folks that like to make talk."

"Let them talk—darn them!" cried the girl, withdrawing her hands. "We—my mother and I—are only trying to do what we think is right, Mr. Scott."

With that she hurried out of the room. She wanted to run—to get away!

In the lobby downstairs she proffered money to the clerk for the use of the room, which he refused to take. She didn't stop to argue with him, but made for the door. Thus she came face to face with Myrle Capron, who was entering.

"Well, I see you kept your man on the street," he said insolently.

The girl started back, her cheeks aflame. Her man! That would be what they would say? Her man?

She saw Myrle's face suddenly blanch, heard a step behind her. Then a figure loomed beside her, an arm shot out, and the youth's neck was seized in a grip of steel.

"You know what to say, now *say* it!" came Silent Scott's voice.

"I—I—didn't mean it, Miss Bronson—honestly I didn't—"

She fled out of the door and ran around to the barn.

"My team!" she cried breathlessly to the barn man. "And—where is Pat?"

"Sorry, ma'am, but some of the boys have been showin' him the sights," said the barn man; "he ain't in no shape to drive."

"Oh—he's—he's—"

"Couldn't wake him up with a pitchfork, ma'am. Too bad. Don't believe it was his fault, for he told me he didn't have a cent of change."

"They got him in that condition to hurt me!" Annalee exclaimed. "Hitch up my team. I'll drive myself. You can tell him to come out to-morrow. The walk will be good for him. I'm going home."

"But there's a storm comin' up, ma'am; an' these electrical storms out here are a holy terror—"

"Storm or no storm, you hitch up my team!" the girl commanded. "I won't stay here a minute longer than I have to. Do as I say or I'll try to hitch them up myself—they know me, at least."

"All right, ma'am; you're the boss. But I'm advisin' against it. No, take it easy; I'll hitch 'em up."

Fifteen minutes later Annalee drove out of town, her face white and set, her eyes flashing, taking no heed of the wind and the black clouds which were steadily mounting into the skies behind her.

CHAPTER XXI
THE STORM

As she drove eastward along the six-mile lane to where the fences had their end and the open prairie began, Annalee gave scant attention to the horses. The road was before them; they knew they were going home to a good barn, good feed, and good care, and they trotted along willingly without need of guidance or urging. Annalee was busy with her thoughts.

She realized now that hers had been a peculiar procedure in the eyes of the citizens of Brant. She knew from Myrle's mean, insinuating remark that he would cause a wrong impression whenever the opportunity offered. His experience at the hands of Andy Sawtelle and Silent Scott would make him more bitter toward her. So far as she, personally, was concerned, she did not care; but he had at his disposal certain tools of hand and tongue which could damage her interests and her mother's, and place them in an unfair light before the townspeople.

Tears of mortification came into her eyes. She had meant well, had thought she was doing the right thing. It had, at least, all seemed proper and fair that morning. Silent Scott had indirectly got into trouble on their account. Was it any more than right, then, that they—she—should attempt to help him? And wasn't keeping him out of jail the least they could do under the circumstances?

Yet Silent had foreseen just how the thing would be

regarded. He had been smart enough for that and had urged her to withdraw the bail money. Could he—was it possible he could suspect she had any other reason for acting in his behalf?

Her face reddened. She felt that she never wanted to see him again. In some way, Myrle's remark had come between them. Why did she look at it that way— between them? There was nothing, had been nothing, could be nothing. Her mother was right. She had to remember her birth and breeding. She told herself this dubiously. Birth and breeding seemed to be so widely variant with this new country. It was as if they didn't count. Yet, in her heart, Annalee did not actually believe this to be true.

Of one thing, however, she felt sure. The impulse which had prompted her to come to Silent Scott's aid would be misinterpreted by the townsfolk; it would be misconstrued by the Caprons, perhaps by Scott himself! She tried to forget the pressure of his hands, the look in his eyes. Yet she dwelt upon this memory. She hated Myrle Capron for having cast the shadow; and she was even more sorry that Silent Scott had heard him and had compelled him to apologize.

She had reached the end of the lane and had swung out upon the winding prairie road when she became cognizant of the fact that it was growing dark. She looked about her with alarm and spoke sharply to the horses which were beginning to show uneasiness. She was in rather a hard situation.

The wind was blowing gently from the east, but a great, black cloud was spreading over the sky like an inky curtain from the west. She considered this phenomenon with worried interest. The wind was coming from the east, where the horizon still was bright, while the storm evidently was approaching from the west. It was extremely hot, and the land was in a queer, saffron-tinted shadow. The whole landscape looked weird—fantastic.

As if to increase her concern she saw a rider coming some distance behind her. She suspected it was one of the C-Bar men returning home, or it might be Myrle Capron, or—Gruger! She shuddered and shook out the lines on the backs of the horses. They were running now—running in the face of the hot wind. The atmosphere seemed insufferably oppressive. Annalee remembered the barn man's warning about the electrical storms of the prairie country. She had heard about these storms, but they had not had a bad one that summer. Doubtless it would come as the culmination of the period of extreme heat which had begun in July.

The black curtain was now directly overhead and rapidly flinging its skirts eastward. The girl looked back fearfully and saw forked tongues of lightning licking at the tops of the mountains. The rider seemed to be maintaining the same distance between them. Alone on the prairie, driving a team which was becoming fractious, the girl felt a sense of relief in the sight of this solitary horseman, whoever he might be.

The bright strip on the eastern horizon had been engulfed in the gray cloud film which was the vanguard of the storm. In the south she saw the cottonwood branches thrashing about in the wind, displaying the undersides of their leaves like so many silvery spangles against the gathering darkness. What was that old saying in the East? "When you see the silver of the leaves, look out for storm?" Everything about and above her seemed formidable with foreboding. Then, suddenly, the wind ceased.

She looked up in surprise. The air was perfectly still, and the heat seemed to settle down upon her like a pall. It was as if she were in a vacuum, and it was hard to breathe. She could see the road, winding like a long, brown snake ahead, with its dust whirls dying away; every blade of grass appeared to stand out distinctly; the low-lying buttes, far beyond the homesteads, appeared a scant few miles away; a bird flew across her vision like a darting arrow, without sound, and, save for this, there was a singular dearth of movement—only the bobbing of the heads of the horses.

The next instant there was a blinding flare of flashing lightning and a deafening crash of thunder as the storm unleashed its fury. The rain came down with the impact of a cataract, and the wind, coming from the west now, hurled it in sheets across the prairie.

The horses lunged forward wildly, straining at the traces, while the girl pulled in vain at the lines. She screamed as the forked tongues of lightning streaked the black canopy above and the artillery of the storm crashed and roared in her ears. She was wet through in less than a minute. The road became a running rivulet of water with the horses' hoofs splashing it into her face. She could not hold the team; she would only struggle to guide the horses, to keep them in the road.

Directly ahead was the long ridge above the homesteads. The girl sobbed in thankfulness for this. Once over the ridge, it would be but two miles or so to the houses.

The rain was falling with the ferocity of a cloudburst. The lightning was almost a continual glare, so short were the intervals between flashes. Thunder rolled and crashed and reverberated without a let-up. The girl felt a peculiar, prickly sensation of her skin; the very air she breathed seemed surcharged with electricity. It had become cold.

She was powerless to control the horses, and they left the road, plunging up the slope with the wagon careening on the unlevel surface of the prairie, studded with cactus clumps and rocks. Pieces of thick, gumbo mud flew from the wheels, striking the horses on their backs and adding to their terror, spotting her dress, hands, arms, face, and hair. The wind tore her hat away and lashed the stinging rain in her eyes. The wagon nearly overturned as they topped the rise of ground and started in a mad dash toward the homesteads.

In her struggle to keep her seat, Annalee lost the lines. She screamed with the realization that the team was running away. She could not see the houses through the blinding rain. She thought of jumping from the wagon, but she could not rise to steady herself to jump. She had to cling with all her strength to the seat to avoid being thrown over the dashboard under the horses or between the wheels.

There was a momentary cessation of the lightning, then a ball of fire seemed to burst before her eyes and the earth shook to the crash of sound. The lightning had struck somewhere ahead. The horses reared back, swerved to one side, and dashed on. She saw a shadow ahead, heard a rumble above the thunder. The shadow merged into lines, took form, and her heart stood still as she saw the herd of steers which had been put on the north range bear down upon her.

Another shadow flashed near her and hurtled through the mist of rain and wind, landing upon the back of one of the horses. The animals veered sharply to the left, rearing and plunging, then ran out of the path of the stampeding cattle, guided by the man who had leaped from his own horse.

Gradually their pace slackened. Finally they stopped. Annalee sat dumb, numbed in the wagon seat as Silent Scott climbed off the horse and gathered the lines. His own mount came up, and he quickly untied a yellow slicker from behind his saddle. He threw this on the seat and tied his horse to the rear of the wagon, keeping hold of the lines while he did so. Then he climbed up on the seat beside the girl and wrapped the slicker about her.

With a sob, Annalee laid her head upon his shoulder.

He held her tightly within his left arm as he turned the horses toward the homesteads and drove on through the storm.

CHAPTER XXII
A PROMISE

Annalee closed her eyes to the driving rain. Secure within the shelter of Silent's arm, protected from the downpour by the slicker and Silent's big hat, which he had pulled down on her head, she lost her fear of the storm in a welcome sense of security. The horses obeyed his voice and the steady guidance of his hand upon the lines. He was getting wet—he *was* wet, soaking wet. She tried to put part of the slicker about him and heard his boyish laugh. She opened her eyes to see him smiling down at her, his face and hair dripping.

She smiled back. There was something almost ludicrous in his appearance. She reached up to put a hand under his chin from which a veritable stream of water was running. He touched her fingers with his lips, but an instant afterward had to give all his attention to the horses, for they were not in the road, and the wagon was bumping along at a fearful rate.

Then the miracle of the prairie storm happened. The rain lessened and the wind suddenly abated. The lightning stopped with almost the same abruptness with which it had first flashed its warning message overhead. The thunder rolled and rolled, farther and farther away, its reverberations sounding like the booming of artillery in the distance; its rumbles and grumbles became fainter and fainter until they finally died away.

With startling swiftness the skies became light as the rain ceased entirely. A rift of blue appeared above, and Annalee sat up.

"Why—it's all over," she said wonderingly.

Silent was walking the horses. Two miles to the southeast she could see the plowed field which marked the location of the homesteads. She turned around and looked back. The cattle had disappeared over the long ridge. She shuddered. Never would she forget that sight of the oncoming steers, maddened by the storm and the lightning bolt, coming toward her, horns tossing, eyes white—and then the darting shadow and Silent on the off horse, and—safety.

He had been the lone horseman she had seen following her. He had risked his life for her! If he had failed in his leap he would have been beneath the hoofs of the stampeding herd in an instant; and she—the horses and wagon might have made a difference. She did not know. She looked up at him.

"Did you follow me from town, Silent?" she asked softly.

"Yes," he answered without looking at her.

"Why?"

"I saw you starting out alone with this team an' the storm coming on—it wasn't safe."

"I know now it wasn't, Silent, but I—I wanted to get away from town. I wanted to get away—after what Myrle Capron said."

"The little rat!" muttered Silent. "But I'm glad he said it—in a way."

"Glad, Silent? Why? It was an insult."

"Maybe so, Annalee, but it was true."

Still he didn't look at her, and she gazed up at him almost breathless.

"True—you mean true, Silent?"

"Yes," he said shortly, but in a low voice. "You kept your man out of jail, Annalee; that's what he meant when he said you'd kept him on the street."

"But—the way he said it—"

"That was where the rub came in." Silent looked down at her.

Annalee felt her cheeks burning. She was strangely thrilled—happy—uncertain. The long lashes dropped over her eyes. The horses stopped.

Then she felt Silent's arms about her. She felt his hand under her chin, raising her face. She felt hot—cold. One arm crept out of the slicker and about his neck as their lips met. She was still for a few moments, then she drew away as he again took up the lines.

She opened her eyes to find the sun peeping through the clouds. The whole landscape was fresh, brilliant; blades of grass were glistening with diamond rain-drops, the prairie was a sea of gold, broken only by the vivid green of the stately cottonwoods to the south-ward; the buttes in the east were glowing pinks and purples; the horizon was a band of silver.

"See that, Annalee?" said Silent, pointing.

The girl saw a thin stream of water, hardly moving, tracing its silvery course down toward the river.

"That's an old buffalo trail," Silent explained. "They traveled single file when not disturbed and going to water. That path is worn until it is as hard as flint,

180

almost. It's easy to trace the buffalo trails when the water lays in 'em after a storm. They'll all be plowed up pretty soon."

The information seemed irrelevant to the occasion, yet it appeared to fit in perfectly with his mood.

"I suppose you wonder why I told you that," he went on. "I mentioned it because it's a sort of signmark of the country. I was born in this country, Annalee. It's all I know, an' I think pretty well of it. It's changing, an' I reckon it's changing for the best. It'll never be anything but the West, that's sure. You're one of the changes that's come. You've—you've sort of changed me."

It seemed all a wonderful, puzzling adventure to the girl. She did not try to reason it out—to analyze her feelings or thoughts. It seemed good to be there by Silent, sitting on the wagon seat with him, wearing his slicker and his hat. She marveled at this. She was glad he had followed her, not alone because of his rescue of her in the storm, but—

She blushed again.

"I ain't never been around girls much, Annalee," he said soberly. "I've done about everything men do in this country, except steal cattle or horses, or lie, or throw my gun down on somebody for the fun of it. I ain't good. But the first time I saw you down there in the hotel I knew I'd missed something. Right now, I'm not so sure what it is—unless it's just you. I'm sorry for what I did back there. But I'll never forget it, even if I never see you again, an' I don't suppose you want me to—to see you again," he added hastily.

She tried to speak, but the words would not come.

The world was so gloriously beautiful, and his voice sounded so good.

They saw Andy Sawtelle standing between the two houses and her mother on the porch of her house as they approached. Silent urged the horses into a run, and they came up with mud flying from the wheels and the freshening wind blowing in their faces.

Mrs. Bronson took Annalee in her arms regardless of the fact that she was wet and her dress spotted with mud. She mutely thanked Silent with her eyes as Annalee pinched her cheek and told her that Silent had saved her life. Later, in the house, while she changed clothes, Annalee told her mother everything that had happened, everything except what had happened on the seat of the wagon after Silent had rescued her. That she kept to herself—and wondered at it.

Silent came walking from the barn, leading his horse. The slicker again was tied to the rear of his saddle. Annalee came out with his hat, followed by her mother. She handed the hat to him without a word, her face flushed, her eyes bright.

"Mr. Scott, I do not know how to thank you," began Mrs. Bronson. "I—"

"Then just forget it, ma'am," said Silent, smiling at Annalee. "I'm going back to town on my way to the county seat an' I'll see that your man Pat gets started out here all right first thing in the morning. I reckon Miss Bronson is right. They got Pat and fed him some raw stuff—some of the Capron crowd he didn't know. I wouldn't be too hard on him, ma'am."

Annalee had lifted her brows in questioning. "You're

going to the county seat, Silent? To Choteau?"

"To find out where we—where I stand, Miss Bronson."

Sawtelle had come up and was standing near him.

> "He neither fears his fate too much,
> Nor does he care at all
> For sheriffs, judges, and all such
> That in his way may fall."

Annalee looked at Andy in surprise as he recited this, and then, to her astonishment, he winked at her soberly.

She gleaned an idea from this, however, and turned quickly to Silent Scott.

"Silent, are you going into town to see any of the Capron men?" she demanded anxiously.

"What business could I have with them?" he countered, feigning surprise.

She walked down the steps. "Aren't you going to stay to supper?"

He shifted uneasily. "There's plenty of time to get into town before supper."

"Silent," she said slowly, "you must promise me something."

He twisted his hat in his hands, but did not speak.

"Don't you think you could promise me something, considering—considering—*everything,* Silent?" she asked tremulously.

"What is it?" he asked quietly, looking steadily into her eyes.

"Promise me that you will have no more trouble,"

cried Annalee impulsively. "Promise me you will not raise a hand against any of the Caprons—or Gruger—no matter what they say or do."

"That's a big order, ma'am," he said in a low voice.

"Will you promise for—for my sake, Silent?"

Andy Sawtelle started for the barn, whistling. Silent looked after him with an annoyed expression. Mrs. Bronson was looking on from the porch with a curious expression. Yet Silent had a feeling as if he and the girl were alone. He looked down into her eyes. Deep, misty wells of pleading they were. He held out a hand which she took in both of hers.

"I promise," he said softly. Then he turned to his horse.

CHAPTER XXIII
THE TEST

Silent rode into Brant early that evening. He put his horse up at the hotel livery and asked about Pat.

"He's been out of here an hour," the barn man explained. "Over in the old town, I guess. I gave him Miss Bronson's message."

Scott turned toward the old part of town and crossed the railroad tracks with a frown on his face. He looked into several places, but it was not until he reached the Green Front that he saw his man.

Pat was standing at the bar with some men, two of whom Silent recognized as belonging to the Capron outfit. He entered and sauntered to the side of the Irishman. The bartender was just serving a round of drinks, and Silent reached over and took Pat's glass.

The Irishman started back, then recognizing Scott, greeted him jovially.

Scott poured the contents of Pat's glass on the floor and pushed the empty glass to the astonished bartender. Then he addressed Pat.

"Come over to the hotel with me an' I'll get you a room so you can rest up to-night and go back out to the Bronson place in the morning," he said. "They need you out there, Pat, an' there's nothing in this sort of thing."

Pat wrinkled his brows and looked sheepish.

"She went off an' left me," he flared up, "an' I'm having some fun."

"She wanted to get home before the storm," Scott told him. "The horses run away, the cattle out there stampeded for her, an' I happened along just in time to help her out a bit. You ought to be ashamed of yourself, Pat."

"I only took two or three," Pat grumbled. "Guess I must have got hold of some bad stuff. I could have driven her home at that, if that danged barn man had woke me up like he oughter."

"Come on along, I'll get you a horse to ride out in the morning."

Pat started with Scott toward the door.

"That your guardian?" sneeringly inquired one of the men at the bar.

"He's a friend of mine," Pat said in reply.

"You got some queer friends," was the jeering answer. There was a laugh at this.

"You want to make trouble?" demanded Pat in a belligerent tone.

"There isn't going to be any trouble," Silent Scott broke in sternly.

"No? How do you know?" It was one of the Capron men who spoke.

Silent turned to Pat. "Did you know this fellow was working for Gruger?"

"Thunderation, no!" exclaimed Pat. "Say, is that why you was so danged hospitable?" he asked the Capron man.

The other sneered and laughed openly. "You didn't figure I was buying you drinks because of your good looks, did you?"

Pat strode up to him. "I'd throw the drinks back in your face if I could," he said. "You ain't done more'n what I've done many a time. It never made any difference with me whether a man had money or not, when I was buying, an' I didn't have any slick reason for buyin', either. If I'd known who you was I wouldn't have stood up here with you."

The other's face darkened. "You'll talk yourself into a corral full of trouble," he threatened.

It looked as if Pat would strike, and Scott stepped quickly between them.

"The trouble's come an' gone," he said sharply; "there'll be no more of it."

The man's eyes had suddenly widened. He was looking over Scott's shoulder, and Scott felt Pat touch him on the arm. He turned and saw Gruger approaching them.

"Trying to stir up something with my men, Silent?" demanded Gruger, his eyes narrowing.

The little group at the bar dissolved, most of the men sauntering to the other side of the room.

Both Scott and Gruger were armed, while the others wore no weapons.

"Your men, with you helping 'em, can stir up enough trouble on their own account, Gruger," said Scott, confronting the C-Bar foreman.

"Maybe so, but there has to be something or somebody to start it, an' you're the somebody," replied Gruger darkly.

Scott's face went white under its tan, but he spoke coolly. "That's puttin' it square up to me, Gruger, but I've got to pass."

The others in the room appeared surprised. Pat stared at Scott with a look of wonder. Scott was deliberately backing down before the Capron foreman.

"Good reason," answered Gruger. "Any man that'll take sides with the land grabbers an' then let a woman put up bail for him to keep him out of jail is just plain yellow!"

There was an ominous silence. The men in the room held their breath.

Silent Scott's eyes had narrowed to slits, and he was visibly struggling with himself, trying, at tremendous mental cost, to keep himself in check.

"I reckon you know I'm not yellow, Gruger," he said through his teeth.

"How about Lummox?" Gruger jeered. "It took two of you to turn that job, an' Lummox's gun was on the floor when you drew."

"Lummox never did depend on his gun," said Scott slowly. "He was a knife thrower, an' he'd have got me if I hadn't known it an' kept right watchful. You know that, too."

"An' I know this," roared Gruger; "if you're takin' sides with the homesteaders, you stay in the other part of town, get me? We ain't welcoming your kind over here."

Scott appeared to smile. "I'm being warned off this range?" he asked in a low voice.

"The same," shot back Gruger.

"An' if I was to drift over here an' run across you there'd be fireworks?" Scott asked mildly.

"You've said it," snapped out Gruger.

"Fair enough," said Scott with a peculiar smile. "That's all right with me, Gruger." He stepped toward the door, then turned suddenly.

"One of these days I'm liable to come visiting you, Gruger."

Gruger's laugh floated out to him as he left the place followed by Pat.

The Irishman walked at his side silently. "There was no way out of it," he heard Scott mutter. He saw Scott was frowning darkly, and wondered. It had been a clean-cut case of one man backing down before another in a feud. Was Scott afraid of the C-Bar foreman? Pat knew, and Scott also realized, that the incident would be the talk of the town. Some would suspect that Scott had a reason for letting Gruger get away with his insults; but most would assume that

Scott was afraid of the other. His reputation as a gunman would suffer, but this fact only caused Scott to smile. It was a reputation he had never solicited, a thing he never had been proud of, and which he had not tried to preserve.

They came to the hotel.

"Pat, you go in and get yourself a room and lay low to-night," said Scott. "Here's some money—no, that's all right, you can pay it back to me later. You know by now, I guess, that the Capron bunch was on your trail. They wanted to keep you hangin' around these places an' away from the Bronsons. That ain't fair to the girl, Pat. There'll be a horse for you at the hotel barn in the morning. You can bring him in when you come to town again, or send him in with Andy. Will you stay straight to-night?"

Pat promised and took the money, although he insisted on giving Scott an order on his wages.

Scott went directly to the office of Justice of the Peace Nichols.

"I reckon we've just got to turn back that money," he told the justice. "Instead of helping things it's makin' 'em worse."

In answer the old man handed him Annalee Bronson's check. "The assistant county attorney's here," he explained. "Came in a little while after you left, before the storm. He says they ain't been looking for you lately. They're going to drop the charge."

Silent Scott whistled. "Thought Capron wanted to prosecute," he said, taking the check.

The old justice frowned. "Guess they couldn't convince the county attorney there was enough evidence. Anyway, they're not catering so much to stockmen these days at the county seat. The homesteaders are goin' to control the next election."

Scott considered this. "No," he said finally. "There's something more to it. It's some new move of Gruger's. Well, I'm not going to worry."

Scott took the check to Pat and asked him to take it out to the Bronson place with him and give it to Annalee. Next morning he was at the barn when Pat showed up. Pat rode away to the ranch shortly after daybreak.

When he arrived he told Annalee what had happened in town.

The girl did not reprove him as he confessed that he had visited several places and had got in with some of the Capron crowd without knowing who they were. She listened with glowing eyes to his account of the meeting between Scott and Gruger.

"I'm glad—oh, I'm so glad!"she said when he had finished.

"Glad, miss? It looked mighty bad to me. Silent will have to go back over there sooner or later. He can't get away with it unless he wants to be pegged as a coward the rest of his life."

"Never mind, Pat," said the girl. "Silent Scott was braver yesterday than you or any of the others thought."

She folded the check Pat had given her absently.

Andy Sawtelle came up with an anxious look on his face. "It's the spring, Miss Anna. I don't know what's happened to it, but it's nearly dry. Guess it had caught us unawares. You'll have to put down a well, and meanwhile we'll have to haul water from the river."

"We can do that, can't we?" asked the girl.

"Yes," answered Andy. "But the only road is through the Capron place."

"Then I'll go and see Capron," the girl announced with flashing eyes.

CHAPTER XXIV
PROGRESS

Andy's prediction that the spring would soon be dry proved true, for within a week the supply of water from that source was exhausted. The problem was rendered the more complicated by the fact that the horses had to be watered.

Annalee had sent Andy into town to see the well drillers, and they had promised to be out to start drilling a well within a week, but the week passed without a sign of them. Andy had done some sleuthing along the river, but had not been able to find a road to water which did not pass through Capron's land.

"Does that mean that he can shut us off from water?" asked Annalee angrily, when Andy made his final report.

"He can deny us the right to cross his land," replied Andy. "There isn't a State or county road to the river near here as yet."

"But there will be, some time," the girl insisted. "It hasn't been asked for, probably. It doesn't stand to reason that the government would permit such a thing."

Andy indulged in one of his characteristic shrugs. "As I've pointed out more than once, the government is a long ways distant, while Capron is right down there by those cottonwoods."

"All right, we'll go down by the cottonwoods and see Mr. Capron," Annalee decided. "Hitch up the horses, Andy, and we'll go this afternoon."

Andy appeared dubious, but he carried out his instructions, and they drove down to the Capron ranch. It was a distance of four miles from the gate at the edge of the timber to the ranch house which was situated in a level stretch of bottom land in the lee of a sheltering bluff, with windbrakes of stately cottonwoods on either side stretching down to the slow-moving river.

They passed through several green fields of grain in the bottoms.

"Oats," Andy explained. "Below here they raise a lot of hay."

"Yet they were trying to tell me nothing would grow around here," the girl complained. "They were trying to discourage us, Andy."

"Maybe so," Andy conceded. "But these are the bottom lands near the river, Miss Anna, and they seem to be better watered. The stockmen never have raised anything in this country except in the river bottoms and in coulees where there were springs. The government experts claim the benches will grow wheat, but it has to be proved."

"Andy," said the girl in a curious voice, "I want to ask you something and I don't want to offend you. You

192

use much better language than most of the men out here. Have you—been educated?"

The poet smiled whimsically. "My mother was an Englishwoman," he explained. "She taught me some before she died; but the most important thing she taught me was the love of good books. I've read quite a bit. I've read and I've dreamed. I guess I got most of what you might call my education by dreaming."

Annalee puzzled over this. Andy never seemed to quite explain to her satisfaction what he meant, and there was a note of finality to his speech which served to thwart further questioning.

"Have you ever yearned to possess a—a reputation for riding or shooting, or anything like that?" she asked timidly.

"Well—ah—no," replied Andy hesitatingly. "I'd be afraid to be quick on the draw. I'm not a fighter, anyway, Miss Anna."

"But you—you taught Myrle Capron a lesson, or would have taught him one if he had had enough sense to realize it."

"Those were peculiar circumstances," said Andy with a frown. "It was the first time I ever engaged in such a business in my life."

"Well," and the girl sighed in resignation, "it seems as if mother and I were destined to bring strife into the country. You heard nothing of Silent Scott in town?"

Andy shook his head. "Dropped completely out of sight, Silent has. Maybe he went back down on the Musselshell. He's a sort of a lone rider." He looked at her slyly. "Would you like to see him again?" he asked.

The girl flushed. "Yes, and—no. Oh, I don't know," she confessed. "He is a man of mystery, it seems. I believe in him, and yet—he doesn't seem to want me to. I never met a man like him. Do you remember, Andy, he had a bullet wound in his hand the first day he came to our place and confronted that Gruger?"

Andy nodded silently.

"He never attempted to explain that," the girl complained. "I've wondered ever since, but I never had the temerity to ask him about it. Are they talking about him in town?"

"Quite a bit, Miss Anna. Some think Silent was afraid of Gruger, but the old-timers know better. They figure Silent has a reason for letting Gruger get away with what he did. And they are expecting to see Silent ride or walk into the old town some day when Gruger is there."

"That would mean—trouble, wouldn't it?" faltered the girl.

"More'n likely. It would be Silent's answer to Gruger's warning, and that would call for a showdown on Gruger's part. The day Silent walks west across the railroad tracks in Brant will mean gun play—the fastest, meanest piece of gun play Brant ever saw."

The girl was breathing fast. "Silent has promised me," she said softly.

"Then, if the promise is ever broken, it probably will be because of you," said Andy with a faint note of bitterness in his voice.

"Oh, Andy, what do you mean by that?" the girl asked quickly.

"Forgive me for saying it, Miss Anna," said the poet contritely. "It slipped out. I don't know if there is any truth in it or not. But I know Silent won't let you suffer at Gruger's hands."

"But he's gone," said the girl. "He wouldn't know—"

"News travels in queer ways around these prairies, ma'am. I have a hunch Silent will be on hand when you need him most—and if you should ever need him again."

Annalee felt a thrill as the result of Andy's prediction, but she didn't reply to it, as they were now driving up to the C-Bar ranch house. Andy got down and opened the gate by the barn, led the horses through, closed the gate, and drove around to the front of the house.

"We're here," he said with a doubtful smile. "Maybe the lion isn't in his lair, and we've had our trip for nothing."

As he finished speaking, however, Capron himself came out the door to the porch. He stared at Annalee in amazement.

The girl nodded a greeting. "I came to see you on a matter of business, Mr. Capron."

His eyes brightened with a shrewd look, and he rubbed his nose with a thick forefinger. Then he held open the screen door.

"Suppose you come in my office," he invited.

After a moment's hesitation Annalee climbed out of the wagon, assisted by Andy, who was the recipient of a scowl from the stockman.

"I'm afraid you've come a little late," said Capron as

the girl preceded him into the little office room in the front of the house.

"Too late?" she asked, surprised, seating herself in the chair he indicated near the roll-top desk.

"Yes, I've changed my mind," said Capron, settling his big bulk in his desk chair. "I'm not in the market for your place—your homesteads."

"But they are not on the market," said the girl with a smile. "You thought I came here to accept your offer for our relinquishments? That isn't the case, Mr. Capron."

He frowned questioningly. "Then you're here to make some complaints?"

"No complaints, Mr. Capron, unless they might be against the well drillers."

"Well drillers? I have nothing to do with any well drillers. Oh-oh, that's it, eh?" He grinned as he comprehended.

Annalee nodded soberly. "Our spring has gone dry, Mr. Capron, and the well drillers haven't come to put down our well. We shall have to haul water from the river, and the only road goes through your land. We are prepared to pay for the privilege of using the road."

"Not by a—" Capron bit off his words suddenly and fell to tapping on the desk with his pudgy fingers.

"There isn't any county road to the river—as yet," the girl pointed out. "If you refuse to grant us the use of the road I shall have to appeal to the authorities. We have to have water, Mr. Capron."

"It's a wonder you didn't wake up to that before this," he said, scowling. "You could die of thirst before you could get a road opened up through *my* place."

"That's true, Mr. Capron. But, of course, we do not intend to die of thirst. It is only a question of time before we will have a well down. It would have been down before this, but the spring gave out without warning, it seems."

Capron smiled. "Those springs up there have a way of doing that. Here it's near August an' been a dry season. I'm surprised they held out as long as they did."

"Mr. Capron, I don't know that I'm justified in depending upon your sense of fair play, but I'm doing so in this instance. You broke what virtually amounted to a promise when you put your cattle up there—"

"My foreman has charge of the range," Capron interrupted.

"But the cattle are yours, are they not?" the girl demanded. "They stampeded in that terrible storm we had a while back and nearly ran over me." She shuddered instinctively. "Now they have been driven back, and we are kept watching them. They are on our land, too."

"Your land is not all under fence," Capron then pointed out.

"That is true, Mr. Capron, and we are not complaining. You have us there. But do you think keeping us from water would be playing the game square, Mr. Capron?"

The rancher looked at her in astonishment. "You're learning fast, girl," he said gruffly. "No, I reckon I can't keep you women from water." He considered this. "But you mustn't threaten me with county roads an' such," he added grimly.

"I am not threatening, Mr. Capron. What arrangement can we make about pay for use of your road to the river?"

"Keep the gates closed," snapped out Capron; "that's all."

"That will be done," said Annalee, rising. "We thank you, Mr. Capron."

"What are you going to plant in that patch you've plowed up there?" the stockman asked.

"Winter wheat," replied the girl. "Pat starts putting it in next week."

"Well, girl, I hope you get a crop," said Capron, very much to her surprise.

"I thank you again," she said cheerfully.

"You needn't thank me; thank my banker," announced Capron. "He says this land is going to be worth something for farming. I think he's crazy, but I'm willing to be shown."

"Then you will not resent it if others locate up there where we are?"

"I'm not answering that," he retorted, leading the way to the door.

Annalee left the Capron ranch in a very puzzled frame of mind. She told Andy of her interview with the rancher and Andy gave vent to a soft whistle.

"You had him when you put in that dig about playing the game square," he observed. "But I don't just understand his come-down that other way."

"Anyway, it looks as if he did not intend to bother us any more," said the girl in a hopeful voice.

"I don't think we'll have to reckon with Capron so

much as with young Myrle and Gruger," said Andy thoughtfully. "Gruger's made it a personal issue between himself and Silent Scott, and I take it he figures anything he can do to make trouble for you is hitting Scott in the back. He's that narrow."

With this remark of Andy's a great light dawned on Annalee. It was true that Silent Scott had brought Gruger's wrath down upon his head by interfering in her behalf and her mother's. This had served to distract the C-Bar foreman's attention from them to their champion. Now she saw that the acts directed at them were indirectly aimed at Silent. But if Silent remained away, would there be further trouble? She hoped he would stay away. But she bit her lip at the thought. Did she want him to remain away? She was silent for the rest of the ride back to the homesteads.

Andy drove in to town next day and secured several large barrels which had been soaked. The following day he and Pat drove to the river for the first load of water. They saw no one and were not molested. But this served to make Andy uneasy.

The well drillers came at the end of the week, however, and began to sink for water.

Annalee, herself, walked about holding the crotched willow stick, knuckles up and palms inward, and found that wherever she went it turned downward in spite of all her efforts to keep it rigid, point outward, indicating water.

They started the well between the two houses. At a hundred feet they had an abundance of good water, but the well, casing, and pump proved exceedingly expensive—expense which they had not originally figured on.

Andy had not the heart to tell them that their homesteads should be surveyed before the fence was all built. However, with the fences about the plowed space and the houses, it was decided not to build more until the following spring.

Early in August Pat put in the crop of winter wheat. Fall came on apace, and almost in a single day, early in September, the change in the seasons became apparent. Pat continued plowing, however, outside the fence until the middle of October. Then he quit, announcing his intention of hitting South with the blackbirds. Andy began hauling coal from town to supply their winter needs.

And there was no word of Silent Scott.

CHAPTER XXV
A NEW MENACE

Everything appeared propitious as fall wore on. The wheat came up and made a sea of living green against the far-flung gold of the rolling prairie land. It was thick and several inches high when the first flurry of snow came.

Both Annalee and her mother marveled at the wheat and expressed the fear that it would be killed during the long winter ahead.

"It would have to be a mighty hard winter to kill that stand," Andy explained. "The snows protect it, and melt and soak in to water it. Pat plowed deep, and that's a big thing in its favor—and he sowed thick. With any rain at all next June that wheat will run around forty bushels to the acre."

"And that will mean that there will be some money coming in instead of all going out," said the girl with enthusiasm.

Her mother did not altogether share Annalee's optimism. It had proved a very expensive business, this making of a farm out of raw prairie land. Their balance in the bank was now less than two thousand dollars, and a good sum went for coal and provisions, which they stocked in quantity, during the next fortnight. There was the balance of the fencing to figure on in the spring, also.

Andy tactfully explained that it would probably be necessary to call in surveyors to make sure that the homestead boundaries were correct.

This unexpected item of expense caused Mrs. Bronson to throw up her hands in despair.

"If we shouldn't get a crop, we'll be ruined!" she exclaimed. "Andy, what would the government do in such a case?"

Andy's characteristic shrug was an eloquent answer. "The government only guarantees you title to the land if you live up to the requirements," he said with a smile. "But you can prove up in fourteen months by paving a dollar and a quarter an acre, and then you could borrow some money from the bank on it, I suppose."

"Mortgage it," said Mrs. Bronson with a shudder. "That's what a great many will probably have to do;

but suppose they lack the capital to pay a dollar and a quarter an acre?"

"It takes capital to make a farm out of a homestead," replied Andy. "It seems to me that the big trouble is that the cost of the thing wasn't properly explained. There's people filed on claims out here that are working right now for day's wages and haven't got twice the filing fee in bank.

"There's clerks, Mrs. Bronson, who have never had a day's experience on a farm that have filed in this big rush. There are school teachers who depend on teaching the schools around here for enough to prove up on homesteads. Most of the folks who came out to file were thinking only of the small filing fee. They understood that they got the land for sixteen dollars and let it go at that. The expense of getting located, of building the shack, of fencing and plowing and seeding, of wells and coal, even of food was put in the background against the lure of that 'Free Land' advertisement."

"That's what caught us, Andy," Annalee put in cheerfully. "Anyway, we're going through with it. We may end up broke, but we'll have something that looks like a farm when we do end up. I believe it's going to be a good year, next year, anyway."

Andy looked at her in frank admiration. "That's the pioneer spirit," he told her. "And that's going to be the case with every homesteader in this country—hope for a good year. You see they've never had a taste of the hot winds—nor the cold winters. It gets down to fifty or more below here sometimes, and—we have blizzards."

The girl looked at him in disapproval, while Mrs. Bronson sighed.

"I hate cold weather," said Mrs. Bronson.

"Now, Andy, you've been enough of a kill-joy," the girl accused. "Suppose you tell us of the prairies in spring—that's poetical and pleasant."

The poet's face broke into a smile. "I could tell you of the prairies in spring by the hour," he said dreamily, "but right now I think you and your mother should be told something to prepare you for the winter, although spring comes in the winter frequently at that, you might say."

"Is that another of your enigmas, Andy?" scoffed the girl.

"No." Andy shook his head gravely. "A blizzard in this country is the terror of the winter. They last three days or more. You'll see me putting up wires from your house to your mother's and from both houses to the barn and my place over there. There'll be wires to the well—"

"For goodness sakes, Andy," laughingly inquired Annalee, "are you going to install telephones?"

"Not telephones, but a means of communication just the same. When a good blizzard comes swooping down from the north you won't be able to see six feet in any direction in it. The wires are to follow to the different spots so you won't get lost. Folks have died in blizzards because they got lost within a few feet of a house or barn and wandered around this way and that, and in a circle, till they froze to death."

Annalee turned to him with a sudden change of

expression. Her face was serious, and she regarded him with a measure of astonishment.

"You can't live in that half-tent house all winter. It's miserable of me, but I'd forgotten about your quarters. You'll have to put a board roof on that place out there and line it with tar paper or something, and put in a stove right away. Why didn't you say something?"

Andy evaded her eyes. "I've slept in tents in the winter," he confessed. "That place won't be so bad. I've banked up the earth around it which fixes the floor. It'll be all right. And I forgot to tell you about the spring coming in the winter. It's the Chinook wind, Miss Anna. It may be thirty below zero and with a foot or two of snow on the ground when the Chinook starts to blow from the southwest. In half a day it'll be above zero, and the snow'll be melting fast."

"Is that an Indian fairy tale?" the girl demanded dubiously. "It sounds like one."

"It is a fact," said Andy earnestly. "Snow and ice and cold disappear like magic when the Chinook wind begins to blow. When the blizzard is over the temperature will drop, but sooner or later the Chinook will begin to blow, and it'll be as balmy as spring in a few hours. The wind is cold at first, blowing across the snow, but it warms up gradually till it's April weather. The Chinooks are what made this such a good cattle country."

"Well, anyway, your house has to be fixed," the girl persisted. "You'll have to go to town and get the lumber and what you need to-morrow—those are my orders, Andy."

"It'll make that much more expense that could be avoided," Andy pointed out.

Annalee looked at him in surprise at his wistful look and voice. "Why, you're not trying to save expense for us at the cost of your meager comforts here, are you?"

His look was humiliating, but something in his pleading gaze made the girl flush. She turned away.

"You will have to fix it up," she insisted. "Mother and I would be worried, and from what you say there will be enough worry from the winter not to take on any more. You must bring back a small stove for your quarters, too."

Andy bowed meekly. It was an example of his odd courtliness which to Annalee had always seemed strangely out of place with his surroundings. A sudden impulse seized her.

"Andy, why don't you file on a homestead yourself?" she asked.

He looked at her in astonishment. "I can't afford it, in the first place, and, in the second place, I'm not a farmer."

"But you've been doing so well here; and you'd have the land tied up, at least. Maybe by the time you started living on it you would be more inclined to do so."

"There are enough of them filing now to tie up the land," he observed with a frown. "If I were to file, I'd keep my quarter section all my life no matter what I was offered for it."

He was off with this puzzling remark which Annalee construed was intended to convey some of his affection for the country in which he had always lived. Were they all like that, she wondered? She smiled as she remembered the statement of Mrs. Clarendon, wife of the cattleman, who had said they were going to California because they had earned it.

But Andy's remarks about the severity of the Northern winters caused her to think a lot, and her mother was much worried.

"We are so far from town and doctors, or any kind of help if we needed it badly," was Mrs. Bronson's complaint.

Men from the C-Bar came and drove away the cattle. They did not come near the house, however. Annalee thought this was further evidence of a more liberal attitude on the part of Capron, but Andy explained that they were driving the cattle to town for shipment to the Chicago market. He explained that Gruger would probably travel East with the stock shipment and be gone about two weeks. This would be followed by two weeks of celebration in town, so they could expect no molestation from that source for at least a month.

Andy fixed up his quarters and installed a stove. He had a table which was littered with books and papers, and Annalee, on her visits there, frequently found scraps of paper with verses written upon them. Some of the verses she was surprised to find quite good.

He brought in prairie chickens and ducks which he shot in the brush and on the river. Then came a night when they heard the honking of wild geese in the sky, and Andy announced they were flying south, ahead of a storm. His prediction proved true, for two days later a storm arrived, with snow and cold, although it was hardly a blizzard. It was the real advent of winter, however, and afterward there was continual cold weather.

These were days of loneliness when they saw no one abroad upon the plain. Both women yearned for the company of other women, for the chance to gossip, to compare experiences, and enjoy the companionship that women love. Andy, with nothing to do except take care of the horses and attend to the chores, became morose and taciturn. But as Thanksgiving approached and Annalee announced plans for a big dinner of turkey and other good things, he became more cheerful and entered enthusiastically into the plan.

Four days before Thanksgiving Annalee sent Andy into town with a long list of provisions and delicacies to bring back for the feast.

"And listen, Andy," she said, "if you want to stay in town overnight and come back to-morrow, it will be all right. Here's a check for your wages, too. And, Andy, if you should—hear any news—keep your ears open."

She looked at him wistfully, and Andy nodded knowingly and looked aside. He drove rapidly away without further speech, and Mrs. Bronson shook her head.

"Andy is in love with you, Anna, dear," she said softly.

"Mother! That is preposterous! He's never said anything or looked—"

"Oh, yes, he has looked, dear; but you haven't seen him. He's been careful to guard against that."

"I think you are jumping at conclusions," said the girl irritably. "I won't talk about any such a thing. Andy has too much sense."

"And he has a silent, peculiar nature," observed her mother. "He is deep."

The next day dawned cloudy, and both women searched the skies anxiously. Gradually the skies became gray and cold, and at noon the girl cried to her mother to come to the door. Then she pointed toward the northeast, where a gray veil was creeping across the prairie.

Her mother nodded and looked quickly toward the road to town. But there was no sign of Andy returning.

"It's a blizzard, mother," said the girl in a worried voice. "I hope Andy will get back before it reaches here."

But an hour went by without a sign of Andy, and the blizzard raced down upon them.

CHAPTER XXVI
A MAN IS PROVED

On the way into town Andy Sawtelle hummed softly to himself. At intervals he looked into his inside coat pocket where a number of folded sheets of paper reposed beside the list of Thanksgiving provisions which he was to buy. He seemed fearful of losing these sheets, and his eyes glowed and sparkled with unusual luster each time he peered into the pocket.

He drove fast and seemed in unusually good spirits, as if the approaching holiday had worked an agreeable change in him.

"There'll be no staying in town overnight for us," he said aloud.

His eyes clouded as he remembered Annalee's statement that he might do so if he wished. He knew the
purport of her words. She was agreeable that he spend
his check as he wished. But Andy had no desire for a
celebration; and he was hurt to think that the girl might
have ascribed his preoccupied air of late to a wish to
engage in a session in the resorts of Brant. He patted
his bulging inside coat pocket and smiled whimsically.
They did not know; but when they found out—

An hour before noon he arrived in town and put up
the horses at the hotel barn. Then he proceeded immediately to the general store, where he left the order to be
filled. After this he went to the hotel for dinner, and
then he began a round of the various resorts in both sections of the town. He refused to drink and took the
gibes of acquaintances good-naturedly.

In the Green Front he saw Myrle Capron at one of the
gaming tables. The boy's face was flushed, and his eyes
shone unnaturally bright. Andy surmised he had been
drinking, and as if to confirm this conjecture Myrle at
that moment called to the bartender to bring him a
"snort."

The youth hadn't seen him; in fact, he saw no one
outside the ring of grim faces at the table. Then Andy
noticed the boy bet a stack of blue chips amounting to
a hundred dollars, at least. He gasped with surprise and
dropped into a chair to watch the play. He had heard
that young Capron was a slave to the tables, but he had
never known him to play so heavily.

For some time he watched the game silently, and
twice Myrle Capron bought chips. He was buying two

hundred and fifty dollars' worth at a time. It was apparent to Andy from the number of house "boosters" in the game that the boy was being taken for his roll. Probably the game had run all night.

There was every indication by the looks of the players and their actions, that they had been sitting a long time. In that case, if Myrle had been losing steadily, the youth must be several hundred dollars loser—perhaps several thousand! His season's wages? Andy was aware that the boy played steadily, and he did not believe that he would have that amount of money coming to him at the end of the season. He was inclined to draw his wages as fast as he earned them. When Andy finally left the place the boy was buying more chips and demanding the services of the bartender.

A short distance across the railroad tracks in the new section of town, Andy met Neeland, the locator.

Neeland was all smiles and shook hands enthusiastically with the poet.

"Have you heard the news?" he demanded.

"Maybe so, maybe not," replied Andy, surprised at the locator's genial manner. "Which particular bit of news are you all heated up about?"

"You haven't heard it," said Neeland, taking his arm and leading him in the direction of his office. "Come on down to the place, and I'll spill it. It means quite a thing for me and for you people out there."

Andy pricked up his ears at this.

"Listen," said Neeland, when they were in his little office, "Capron has seen the big light!"

Andy looked at the locator with suspicion. He had never known him to be under the influence of liquor so early in the day.

"Are you starting on your Thanksgiving ceremony three days in advance, Neeland?" he asked accusingly.

Neeland laughed excitedly. "Nothing like that," he denied. "Listen, Andy, Capron has come to his senses. The bank has finally hammered into him the fact that the homesteaders coming in is going to put the price of deeded land way up above what it's worth for grazing. He's put his ranch on the market!"

Andy whistled. "So that's why he was so nice about the water!" he exclaimed. "And that's why he told Miss Anna he hoped she would get a good crop. He thinks that a good crop up there would help him to sell his ranch for farm land."

Neeland nodded and grinned broadly. "That ain't all, nor half of it," he declared. "He's already sold a third of it; closed the deal a few days ago." He waved an arm in triumph.

"Get the money for it?" Andy asked.

"I don't know that part of it," Neeland answered. "He might have got some of it, but whether he did or not, he'll get it all. A company bought it to cut up into farms and exploit. They're figuring on buying all of it later."

Andy was thinking rapidly. Did this explain why Myrle Capron was gambling so heavily? Had he received money from his father? Suddenly he thought of something else.

"How is all this going to affect the Bronsons, as you hinted?" he asked.

"That's the part of it you haven't heard," said Neeland, grinning. "Capron don't care how many people file out there now, and I'm taking in a big party to locate within a week!"

"Thanks for that," said Andy dryly. "For the sake of the women folks I'll be glad to see neighbors. What does Gruger think of all this?"

Neeland's face clouded, and he looked hurriedly out the window. His fingers tapped nervously on the desk, and he regarded Andy with a worried expression.

"Gruger's been wild about it," he confessed. "Went on a big tear as soon as he heard it. Knows it means his job and blames the Bronsons and—and me!" Neeland got the last out with an effort.

"If he blames you, it's a wonder he hasn't tore into you already," observed Andy.

"Well—he—he's sort of had something on me—that is, he thinks he has," stammered the locator, wiping his forehead.

"How's that?" demanded Andy.

"Oh—nothing. I shouldn't have mentioned that." Neeland rose and began to pace the room nervously. "It's nothing I can't fix as soon as he's calmed down and maybe out of the way."

"Look here, Neeland," said Andy sharply, "what are you getting at? Is it something in connection with the Bronsons?"

"It's nothing I'm going to talk about now," said Neeland firmly. "Later, perhaps; but Gruger's in town somewhere, and I'm not going to take a chance on stopping any bullets. He's in a shooting mood, that's all. This business has got down 'way under his skin. He was making it a matter of his own to keep the home-steaders out of that north piece, and now his schemes have gone by the board. Besides that, he's just pouring down the raw liquor, and that'll drive any man crazy. I tell you he's dangerous and—"

"And you're just naturally scared to death of him!" cried Andy in a tone of contempt as he rose to go. "Neeland, if you've pulled anything crooked out there, you're liable to the government. There's fire on all sides of you. I remember what you said last spring, and I take it you figure to locate this bunch out there and then beat it. But you may have to face the music yet, if anything's wrong, and you better be fixing to set your-self straight."

Andy left the office with a thoughtful face. He walked up and down the street for a time, and then he went to the bank and cashed his check. After a trip to the barn to leave instructions regarding the care of the horses, he went to the depot, where he took the after-noon train for Great Falls.

"Going to have to stay overnight, after all," he said grimly to himself.

In the city, late that afternoon, he hurried to the land office where he remained for half an hour. There was no train north that night, so he stayed in the city and took the first train out in the morning.

He was worried about the weather and was again guarding the inside pocket of his coat carefully, for there were other papers there besides the sheets he had brought with him from home.

By the time he had reached Brant, the blizzard was sweeping down. He hurried to the barn for the horses and drove around to the store for the supplies. He had loaded them into the wagon and covered them with a tarp, when he saw a familiar figure in the swirling snow in the street.

For some moments Andy hesitated, a variety of expressions flitting over his face. The snow swept down the street on a terrific wind while he struggled with his thoughts. Then, with a grim look in his eyes he ran after the figure which had passed.

Silent Scott stared at him in wonder as he gripped his arm.

"What're you doin' in town?" he demanded.

"Came in for the Thanksgiving supplies," yelled Andy against the blast. "Come in somewhere; I want to talk to you."

"You figuring on startin' back—now?" shouted Silent in his ears.

"Yes—soon's I've talked with you."

Silent took him by the arm and led him back to the wagon. He climbed into the seat and took up the reins himself. Against Andy's shouted protests he drove around to the barn.

"Put 'em up," he ordered the barn man crisply. Then, turning to Andy: "Are you a plumb fool? How far do you think you'd get in this after you left the lane? You couldn't see ten feet; you couldn't see past the heads of the horses in that out there. It's a shame the women are out there alone, but you'll have to wait till it slacks up a bit before you try it—an' I'll go with you!"

Something like agony was in Andy's eyes, but he managed a shrug and then faced Silent bravely.

"All right," he said in resignation. "And now, Silent, I want to talk to you."

They beat their way from the barn to the hotel, where they sat for an hour in the lobby while Andy talked feverishly.

Silent rose, then, with a scowl. "I'm goin' to talk to Neeland," he announced.

"I'll go with you," said Andy, and he followed him out of the door.

They forced their way across the street to Neeland's office and found him in.

The locator's face paled when he saw Scott, but he invited them to sit down and tried to appear composed.

Silent dropped into a chair and rolled a cigarette before he spoke.

"Neeland, we're here for a show-down," he said suddenly. "We want the whole story about your little mistake out there at the Bronsons."

The perspiration stood out on the locator's forehead, and he wiped it hastily.

"All right," he said in a strained voice. "Wait till I get my pipe."

He stepped into the little living room at the rear of his office.

Scott looked at Andy and smiled. He smoked idly while they waited. Then they felt a sudden draft of cold air.

Silent Scott leaped to his feet and strode into the living room, Andy hurrying after him. They found the rear door open. Scott slammed it shut. Neeland had gone.

For several moments the two looked at each other.

"I suppose he's hit it over into the old town," said Andy.

"That's about it," Scott agreed.

"And Gruger's there!" cried Andy.

"Sure," drawled Silent Scott; "that's why he went!"

Andy stared at him, white-faced.

Silent strode to the door.

"Where are you going?" cried Andy.

"I'm going after Neeland," Silent called back sternly.

"Wait!" shrilled Andy, as he ran to Silent and grasped him by the shoulders. "He'll be with Gruger. He's sure gone to Gruger, thinking that if you follow him there'll be trouble and then he can squeal his story to the one that comes out best. It's a trap, Silent; it's a trap!"

Silent Scott stood with his hand on the knob of the door.

"Surely you can see that," Andy pleaded.

Then the poet stepped back with a cunning look in his eyes. Suppose Silent *were* to go over there. It was bound to mean trouble. And Gruger might kill him! If not, and Annalee knew Silent had gone there—

Andy struggled with this thought as Silent Scott stood in indecision. Just a word of encouragement and he would be gone, and Annalee Bronson would think he had betrayed her trust. Andy looked about him with unseeing eyes. In his heart was a great yearning. He struggled with his secret—the secret which had changed his life. Should he let Silent go? Then his hands dropped to his sides and he leaned wearily on a chair.

"Silent," he said softly, "if you go over there it will mean trouble with Gruger. Do you remember your promise to Annalee? It's one fine thing that she cherishes. This—would destroy something in her heart, Silent. You—you just can't go!"

Scott turned slowly away from the door. He stepped to Andy and put his hands on the drooping man's shoulders.

"You're right," he said simply, as Andy slipped down into the chair.

CHAPTER XXVII
INTO THE STORM

All that long weary afternoon and evening Silent Scott and Andy Sawtelle waited in the lobby of the hotel with alternate trips to Neeland's office to see if the locator had returned. These trips were futile, and Scott struggled mightily with his desire to cross into the old town. He was aided in his resolve to keep his promise to Annalee by Andy, who frequently spoke a word in commendation of Silent's decision.

Persons in the hotel lobby and bar looked at Silent in a queer way. They knew of Gruger's threat. And Silent, conscious of the undercurrent of thought which was damaging his previous reputation for courage, avoided their eyes, and this made it appear as if he felt guilty of the weight of cowardice.

"Great guns!" he groaned to Andy. "This is awful. It's putting a man in a hard situation for sure, Andy. It ain't that I'd openly seek trouble with Gruger or that I want to smoke him up; it's just that people think I'm afraid—that's what they think."

Andy consoled him with the thought that he was showing greater bravery than if he crossed the tracks.

"Do any of 'em know that, or think it?" asked Silent scornfully.

"Some day they'll learn the truth—they're bound to," Andy pointed out.

"Some day," said Silent in deadly seriousness, "I'm goin' to have to meet Gruger. I'm goin' to have to meet him over in old town in his own way at his own game. It's in the pictures, an' we can't wipe it out."

Andy was silent in the face of this prediction, for in his own heart he felt this to be true. It was the code. Newcomers might not understand it, but they couldn't overcome it. It would just have to be.

He looked at the tall, well-knit figure of Silent Scott in admiration. Women liked this kind of man, and men respected him. Andy suddenly felt a pang because he, too, was not this type of man. He pressed the bulge in his coat pocket and looked waveringly at the bar.

"Silent," he whispered, "I'm going to take a drink."

"Why not?" asked Scott with a look of surprise.

Why not, indeed, thought Andy. That was it. Why not? He realized that the thing that kept him from the bar was the thing that kept Silent from the old town. Only it was different. Annalee did not know of it—she didn't know of this thing he had promised himself because of her. Andy suddenly felt a thrill of joy in realization of this fact. He turned to Silent with a smile.

"You know the old saying, 'It's death to drink in a

blizzard,' " he said jokingly. He turned his gaze away.

"You're queer, Andy," observed Silent. "I guess that's because you're a poet."

Andy smiled, but made no reply to this.

Outside, the blizzard swept down the street on a stinging wind straight out of the north. Signs rattled as the blast shrieked past, and most of the time it was impossible to see across the street. The temperature was dropping, and men were bundling themselves in fur coats and caps and overshoes. It was a wild, fearful storm, such as the northern prairie country often knows in November.

Twenty-five miles to the eastward the world was a swirl of white. Roads were covered with a raging sea of drifting snow. Cattle drifted blindly before the wind, but no human could live in such a storm.

In this sea of white, Annalee Bronson's little house shook in the force of the wind. The girl peered fearfully out into that raging maelstrom with terror gripping at her heart. On her bed lay her mother, hysterical at first when she realized that Andy might have been lost in the storm, sick and numb now that they were alone, cut off from the rest of the world as completely as if they were on top of the highest peak of the Rockies, invisible in the west.

The girl tried to cheer her mother, but her own torment of worry shone in her eyes, and her words proved of no avail. Then, as she looked at her mother's white face on the pillow, she fell on her knees beside the bed and broke out into sobbing. Her mother laid a trembling hand on the girl's head. This nearly maddened

219

Annalee, and she was still more terrified at the thought that she might break down herself in the crisis. This thought, however, lent her strength.

"Mother," she said in a stronger voice, "we are very foolish. We are both forgetting something. God is still with us in this storm. He hasn't forsaken us. Why, mother, it is really God's storm! He is showing us His power, and He wouldn't let Andy die in it. I just *know* He wouldn't, mother."

And then Annalee knelt by the bed, and her voice rose in prayer above the shrieking of the wind.

It gave her strength, and she prepared some tea which her mother drank.

"We are safe, mother," she said, striving to put a sincere note of confidence into her voice. "We are in a house, protected; we have a fire and food, and this storm can't last forever. Why, we were shut up in the train nearly five days coming out here and didn't think anything of it. The blizzard can't last as long as we were in the train. Let's play we're in a train going somewhere, mother; that's what we'll do."

All the balance of the afternoon the girl talked encouragingly and read aloud. It was the wild howl of the wind which made it hard; the shrieking of the icy blast and the fact that nothing could be seen out of the windows.

It became dark early, and the girl found it would be necessary to go out for coal. She put on a heavy sweater and cap, which she pulled down over her ears. Then she took the coal scuttle and shovel and opened the kitchen door. The wind swept in with a shrill whistle, extinguishing the light and nearly throwing her off her feet. She pushed herself forward against the blast and, pulling the door shut after her with a great effort, she started across the little porch. A sudden blast of greater ferocity threw her back against the side of the house. With a sinking of the heart she realized that she would not only be unable to reach the front of the porch and the wire which led to the coal pile, but that she was in danger of being thrown off the porch and carried away in the storm.

Her fingers gripped the window ledge and she held on, dropping the coal scuttle, which slid away in the inky blackness. For the space of a few seconds the force of the wind broke, and she hurled herself along the wall to the door. It seemed as if the breath of the blizzard itself threw her inside.

She heard her mother calling her hysterically. She lit the lamp with numbed, trembling fingers and went in again to try to reassure the older woman. She was calm, now, with the realization that they would have to fight to keep alive in the cold. She returned to the kitchen. In the kindling box was an ax. She coolly removed the cover from the table and overturned it on the floor. They must have heat.

She began chopping up the table, not knowing that her mother had fainted.

Morning showed Brant, snow-ridden, feeling less of the blizzard's strength. Silent Scott and Andy Sawtelle were at the windows at dawn. Their faces were pale, for all night they had been kept awake by thoughts of the women alone in the shack on the eastern prairie.

"Looks like it was lettin' up a bit," said Silent. "I've known a blizzard to do that—to slack up for three or four hours. If it would do that, we could make it."

Andy nodded. His eyes were haggard.

"Silent," he said, "I'll go over and have the team hitched up, and if it looks later as if we could start out and make a run for it, we'll do it—or—or I'm willing to go alone."

Silent swung on him, looking at him keenly. "All right—go hook 'em up," he said.

He followed Andy down to the lobby, where he was stopped by a man who had just come in.

"Hello, sheriff," he greeted in surprise.

The sheriff nooded to him coolly. "Heard the latest?" he asked with a touch of sarcasm.

Silent's brows lifted. "That the way you feel this morning, sheriff?"

"It's funny—mighty funny, Silent—that you happen along in Brant every time within a few hours after the Choteau stage is held up. Last spring you was along here a few hours afterward, and you was seen west of here a short time before. This time you drift in again just after the stage is held up at the start of the blizzard."

Silent Scott's eyes narrowed. "You making an accusation, sheriff?"

"I'm stating facts," snapped out Sheriff Moran. "You're suspected of this job and the other, Silent. I left Choteau by train to the Falls and came up this morning on a freight to catch you here."

"So?" said Scott coldly.

"Exactly. They want to talk to you over at the county seat."

"All right. Tell them I'll be over within seventy-two hours."

The sheriff laughed harshly. "It took you a lot longer than that to show up when you knew we was after you in the Lummox affair," he said grimly.

"I came as soon as I heard about it," replied Silent sharply.

"Well, that won't be soon enough in this case," Moran returned.

"You haven't anything on me in these stage holdups," replied Scott. "You haven't got enough evidence of any kind to take me to Choteau, an' you know it."

"But I can still take you on that Lummox shooting," snapped out the sheriff. "And I'm going to do it."

"Not in this blizzard," said Scott dryly.

"Oh, yes. By the way of the Falls on this morning's train."

They eyed each other narrowly. Then, without warning, Silent Scott's right hand and forearm moved with lightning swiftness and the sheriff, startled by the suddenness of the movement, was looking into the black bore of Scott's gun.

"I got business to tend to before I go to the county seat," said Silent. "I warn you, Sheriff Moran, I won't be stopped!"

He backed away while the official stood glaringly helpless. Another moment and he was through the dining-room door, running swiftly for the kitchen and the rear door. He dashed into the barn as Andy was finishing harnessing the team.

"Here, you," he called to the barn man, covering him with his gun. "Throw two heavy coats into that wagon seat!"

He followed the man to the little office and saw him get two fur coats hanging there and throw them into the wagon seat.

Andy, realizing instantly that there was need for extreme haste, was already climbing in. Silent Scott jumped into the seat beside him.

"Make for the lane!" he ordered.

In another minute they were plunging eastward.

CHAPTER XXVIII
THE BATTLE

Andy urged the horses to the fastest pace they could make along the snow-filled road which ran the length of the lane. They donned the heavy coats as a protection against the icy wind which hurled the snow in their faces. Silent kept a lookout behind, but occasionally shouted to Andy that they were not followed. He did not attempt to explain at that time what had caused the sudden departure; and Andy had no opportunity to ask questions, for the horses required all his attention.

The town was soon invisible in the white veil behind. The horses kept well in the road, with the fence on either side of the lane to guide them. Both Silent and Andy stared unceasingly ahead, for they knew the great test would come when they left the lane and struck out across the miles of open prairie.

There was certainly a lull in the ferocity of the storm. The wind was sweeping down from the north with less force, permitting a view for some distance in every direction. At times they caught sight of the buttes far ahead by means of which they could keep in a straight line for the Bronson homesteads. If the storm held off as well as it was doing, they would have no trouble making their objective. There was a chance, too, that the horses could be depended upon to keep to the road home, or, at least, to keep in the general direction.

In less than an hour, driving at a furious pace, they left the lane and were on the prairie road. Andy began saving the strength of the horses for a dash, in case the storm should close down upon them again at its worst. At first it was an easy matter to follow the road by its "feel," but this became increasingly difficult as they began to encounter drifts. They saw no more of the buttes, but now and then glimpsed the gaunt forms of the cottonwoods along the river to the south.

The thoughts of both men were on the women alone at the Bronson place. They knew the ordeal of facing a first hard blizzard alone, even though one might be secure in a shelter, they knew the sense of isolation; but what worried them was the fact that the women would have to go outside the house for coal with which to keep the stoves going. They could not know, however, to what measures the girl had had to resort during the night to keep heat in the little house.

Andy and Silent looked at each other from time to time with troubled eyes. The lives of Annalee and her mother might depend upon their reaching the homesteads in time. Meanwhile, the menace of the blizzard was upon them, threatening them not only with the frustration of their plans, but with death itself.

Only once did Silent Scott speak to Andy of anything save their mission.

"Did you see Myrle Capron in the old town?" he called.

Andy nodded vigorously.

"Gambling?"

"For all he was worth!" Andy shouted in reply.

Silent asked no more, but looked moodily ahead, his face grim.

They had lost the road and were driving on the open prairie, which was one vast field of white, with the snow blowing across it like heavy mist. The wind began to gather strength. It was growing colder, too. Andy knew the signs and urged the horses on. The going was hard in spots where the drifts were deep, but on those stretches where the plain was swept nearly clean of snow, as was the case on the crest of the ridges, they made excellent time. They climbed the long ridge west of the slope leading down to the homesteads and for a fleeting moment caught a glimpse of the little group of buildings ahead. With a shout of exultation Andy gave the horses their heads, and they lunged forward as the storm closed in upon them with a howl.

"Keep the wind to the left!" Silent shouted against the blast, while Andy signaled that he had heard.

But the attempt was in vain. The blizzard seemed to swirl in on them from all directions. It was impossible to see more than a few feet beyond the horses' heads. But the horses kept on, pulling the wagon through drifts and across nearly bare patches of ground where it bounced on the surface rock, while the men fought to keep their sense of direction. They had to fight, too, for breath in the face of the icy, snow-laden wind. With barely two miles to go they were suddenly lost, swallowed in the storm, dependent upon the horses to keep to the course.

Silent Scott looked at Andy's face, pinched and blue with cold, the eyes red and deep-sunk. The poet's lips were moving, and Silent knew the man was mumbling his verses. The lines were loose in his hands, and Silent reached for them. Andy fought to retain them and attempted to strike the other. Then Scott realized that he might have to fight a man gone temporarily insane; for the strain was telling on the other in a way which has often been the case under similar trying circumstances.

Scott felt a coiled rope under his feet. He had known the rope was there for some time. It gave him confidence, the feel of that coiled lariat, for it had been a tool of his trade on the range. If matters came to a certain point—He braced himself for the possibility.

Andy Sawtelle was screaming wildly and pointing off to the left. Silent shook his head. He had gained the lines and was keeping them tight. Something told him the horses sensed their direction, although as to this he could not be sure. Then Andy made a lunge and grasped the lines with unnatural strength. Silent, hampered by the big coat he wore, tried to fight him off, but did not succeed. Realizing the horses were turning as

227

Andy pulled, Silent raised a fist and drove it full on Andy's jaw. The poet dropped the lines and fell back. Scott quickly regained control of the horses and turned them back to what he thought had been their course. But he couldn't be sure.

Andy was huddled in the seat, and Scott had to keep him from falling forward over the dash or from the side. Then gradually Andy came to his senses, stared at Scott, and turned his face from the stinging bite of the wind while they literally bored their way into the white, seething maelstrom of the storm. It seemed unending.

"A fence!" Scott yelled in his ear. "Keep watch for a sign of a fence!"

There was no answer from Andy, though Scott believed that the man had heard. There was a good chance for them if they come upon one of the fences on the homesteads.

As they continued on in the storm, battling with wind and snow and cold, grave doubts began to present themselves in Silent's mind. He felt that they had gone far enough to have reached the houses of the Bronsons, and yet they had seen no sign of them or of the two fences, one about the field of grain and the other about the houses and barn. More than that, the wind seemed to be hurling itself into their faces with unusual severity. Had they swerved north?

Scott realized that if they were going north they were going in a direction away from the homesteads, away from the river with its protection of trees and under-brush, directly into a great, open region which was as yet unsettled and where they could wander until horses and men gave in to the storm. He was worried about Andy, also, for the poet sat huddled in the seat, apparently lifeless. In that condition he might freeze to death.

A little later Scott became aware of a new angle to the situation. For some little time he could not determine what had happened to provide this new element of uncertainty. It was impossible to keep the eyes open any length of time against the wind and the stinging snow. Thus it was some time before he sensed that they were going up hill!

To be traveling toward the homesteads they should have been going down a very gentle grade. With the knowledge that they were climbing, he realized that one of two things had occurred: Either they had turned around and were progressing up the ridge west of the slope, or they were going due north up the higher and steeper ridge in that direction. He decided the ridge was too steep for the one to the west and, watching the track left by his wheels, turned around and headed in the opposite direction from that in which they had been going.

The wind now appeared more at their backs. He shook Andy, but got no response. He turned the poet around so that he could look into his face, and he saw that his eyes were closed. He slapped Andy in the face several times until he opened his eyes. Then ensued a struggle to keep the poet awake so that he would not freeze to death and to keep the horses in a given direction southward. Pounding Andy with one hand, while he kept a tight rein on the horses with the other, Scott held the team to a southward course as well as he could.

Then, suddenly, the horses stopped. Silent felt a wild thrill of hope. He looked ahead, but could see nothing. He jumped out of the wagon and staggered around to the head of the team. There he shouted with joy, for he found the horses had stopped against a wire fence. Through the fence he could see a few shoots of green through the blinding snow and knew they had arrived at the field west of the house.

He climbed back into the seat and shook Andy until the poet was able to hold out his hands and arms.

"We've reached the fence—the fence of the field!" he shouted in his ear as Andy turned a dull eye upon him.

He turned the horses to the left and proceeded slowly along the fence. Scott, himself, was feeling the effect of the cold. While his body was well protected by the big coat, his hands and feet were in danger of freezing. He beat his hands on the coat and stamped his feet continually; then, looking for the fence to the right, he saw no sign of it.

But the horses were running fast, and in a short time Scott felt a lump in his throat as they stopped again. Dimly he could make out the wire strands of a fence ahead. Then Andy tumbled from the wagon and staggered out into the storm. Scott could see his form also, but faintly. Andy, crazed by the blizzard, was blindly giving himself up to it. Scott dropped the lines and grabbed the rope in the bottom of the wagon. In a few moments its loop was singing over Andy's head, and then it shot out into the swirl of snow. It was carried aside by the wind, and while Andy swayed, Scott prepared for another throw.

There was no time to tie the horses and run after Andy; and if he left the horses to their fate it was likely that both he and the poet would be lost in the storm. So, for the second time, Scott threw his loop, allowing for wind as best he could; and this time the loop settled over Andy's shoulders and Scott drew him back to the wagon, where he collapsed and fell down into the snow.

Scott lifted him into the wagon and drove around the fence. They turned a corner, and he saw a shadow to the right. The horses stopped of their own accord before the gate. Scott climbed down to open it. His feet and legs and hands were numbed, but he succeeded in getting it open. Climbing back into the seat, he let the horses find their own way to the barn. He opened the door and let them in out of the storm.

Then he lifted up the still form of Andy, found the wire leading to the house, gripped it with one hand while with the other he dragged the poet, and stumbled to Annalee's house. Up the steps to the porch, across the porch, he fumbled at the door. Then it was opened from the inside and the girl, muffled in her sweater, let them in with a cry of fear and relief.

At a glance Silent Scott saw what had happened. Practically all the furniture in the kitchen was gone, and the floor was littered with chips and bits of wood; but there was a good fire in the stove.

The girl smiled at him. "The storm wasn't so bad this morning, and I got in some coal," she said faintly.

Silent went to work on Andy, rubbing his face and hands with snow, taking off his shoes and treating his feet in the same manner. Finally the poet opened his eyes with a faint smile. Then Scott built up the fires and put the coffee pot on the kitchen stove. His own circulation restored, he went out and attended to the horses and brought in coal and water and the provisions from the wagon.

Thanksgiving Day dawned clear and cold, with the girl getting breakfast and Scott sleeping the sleep of utter exhaustion on a pile of blankets on the kitchen floor.

CHAPTER XXIX
A SHIFT OF SCENE

There was no Thanksgiving dinner at the Bronsons' that day, at least not such a dinner as had been planned. Mrs. Bronson lay ill in bed, and Andy stayed near the stove, imbibing hot drinks, for he had caught a deep cold. The experience in the blizzard had affected him mentally as well as physically. He had no recollection of his attempts to obtain the lines when Scott was driving, nor did he remember the blow, for which Scott felt thankful.

Silent helped the girl about the house, brought furniture from Mrs. Bronson's house, and attended to the chores. The wind had died, and it became steadily colder. Late that day Annalee decided to take her mother to town, as soon as it would be possible to move her, so that she would be near a doctor. Indeed, the idea of remaining on the homesteads for the balance of the winter was practically abandoned at her mother's oft-repeated suggestion.

That afternoon Silent hitched up the team, and to the surprise of every one, announced that he was going to pay a visit to the Capron ranch. He shook his head when he saw the concern in Annalee's eyes.

"Our old enemy is not at the ranch," he told her; "leastways, not unless he rode out this morning. He was in town when we left, an' I don't think he could make it in the blizzard, an' if I know anything about Gruger's habits, he'll be in town most of the time now till spring."

"It—it isn't anything concerning us, is it Silent?" the girl asked anxiously.

"No. I'm going over there on a little private business of my own. An' I don't reckon there'll be any trouble this time, of any kind whatsoever."

The girl was relieved, but still worried. She watched the white expanse to the southward until she saw Silent driving back.

He appeared cheerful to a marked degree when he came into the house, and all of them were in a lighter frame of mind at supper.

Silent built a fire in Andy's house, where he and Andy were to live, and where the poet insisted on going, although Annalee offered him the use of her mother's house for himself and Silent.

It seemed to be generally assumed by all of them that Silent would remain until they went into town. Annalee had taken his arrival for granted, as it were. She realized that she had expected him to come back—that she had wanted him to come back. That he should arrive in

233

a time of suffering and trouble seemed natural. She did not ask him where he had been, what he had been doing, or why he visited the Capron ranch. Her silence thus bespoke her confidence.

Andy, however, was worried. Silent told him of the encounter with the sheriff in Brant; also of his determination not to be taken back to Brant or anywhere else until he had seen the Bronsons safe in town. This would mean trouble if the sheriff and his men should show up. However, the extreme cold and the lack of a good road to the homesteads evidently kept the sheriff away. He did not put in an appearance that day, nor the next, when Annalee prepared the belated Thanksgiving dinner.

Mrs. Bronson looked out on the bleak landscape and shuddered. In every direction the white plain reached, cold and glistening under a sun, the rays of which could not offset the intense cold in the few hours in which it swung across the southern horizon. The temperature dropped to forty degrees below zero the day after Thanksgiving.

In the afternoon they were thunderstruck to see a wagon coming from the east. It proved to be a homesteader from the country near the buttes, who had been unable to find the road which wound northward, and had struck straight westward in search of a town or habitation.

"We have no coal and are freezing to death," the man explained.

Annalee gave him a good dinner while Silent Scott and Andy filled his wagon box with coal.

The man got out a worn purse and gingerly drew from it a number of small bills, but Annalee shook her head. It was all too apparent that the money was the last the man had. She remembered Andy's words about the many who were striving to build themselves a home on insufficient capital. Here was an example brought home to her.

The man insisted upon paying, but she only laughed.

"No, we are going into town for the worst of the winter," she explained; "and if we leave the coal out there it will be doing no one any good and will probably be gone by the time we come back, anyway. You must take it. You can pay us back in grain or—or something next summer."

Gratitude shone in the man's haggard, worried eyes as he put away the purse.

Andy watched him go and softly droned:

> "When the spider leaves
> The web he's spun,
> Jack Frost'll see
> That his work is done."

Silent scowled. "Andy, you're gettin' back to yourself, I guess."

"The winter never agreed with me—except in town," sighed Andy.

"Well, you don't show that you cared much about being in town the last time you was there," replied Silent. "You wouldn't even take a drink when I know you wanted one."

Andy's face flushed as Annalee looked at him quickly.

"Is that true, Andy?" she asked.

"All except that part about my wanting one," admitted Andy. "Silent gets some queer ideas in his head."

He walked away toward his quarters, but Annalee smiled after him gratefully. "It's because he thought I wouldn't like it," she said to Silent. "Andy is loyal."

"He's all of that," said Silent. "He'd have tried to make it out here alone if I'd let him. That fellow would just naturally die in a blizzard for you folks."

That night Silent and Annalee sat in the warm kitchen. Mrs. Bronson was sleeping, her condition having improved during the day. Annalee was finishing some fancy work; Silent stared moodily at the stove. Several times he seemed on the point of saying something which was on his mind, but each time he desisted with a smile at her.

Andy had told her how he had met Silent in town; but he had said nothing about his trip to the Falls or about Silent's meeting with Neeland and what followed. She wanted to ask him if he had been in town most of the time since she had seen him last, but she felt that sooner or later he would tell her everything about himself. It pleased her to note that he did not wear his gun around the place. There was nothing about him to hint of the sinister reputation which was his.

Suddenly Silent raised a finger. She listened and heard the wind moaning lightly. A look of alarm came into her eyes, but he shook his head smilingly. He went to the door and motioned her outside.

"It's from the southwest," he said.

"Oh! Andy was telling me. It's a—a—what is it called?"

"A Chinook," he said cheerfully. "By morning it will be warm again, an' the snow'll be starting to go. We can drive in to town to-morrow."

This proved to be true, for when dawn came the wind was blowing warm from the southwest and the snow was melting.

Mrs. Bronson was anxious to go and insisted that she could stand the trip. So Annalee packed what they wanted to take with them in a trunk and two bags while Andy and Silent put things in order about the houses and barns. At noon they started, Andy driving, with Silent in the seat beside him, and Mrs. Bronson and Annalee in the rear seat. The luggage was packed behind.

Halfway to town they saw three mounted men approaching. Silent turned to Andy with a smile.

"Maybe it would be better if you was driving," Andy suggested with a knowing look. "I'm not feeling any too well, you know."

Silent nodded, and they exchanged places.

The three riders proved to be Sheriff Moran and two others, plainly ill at ease, whom he had deputized for the occasion.

"Good afternoon, sheriff," called Silent cheerfully as he pulled up the team.

Sheriff Moran wore a deep scowl on his face and kept a hand inside his coat on his gun. He scanned the party quickly, noting the look of surprise on the girl's face, the mother's white features, and Andy's huddled figure.

"Going in to town?" he inquired gruffly.

"Just where we are goin'!" sang out Silent. He frowned, with a backward motion of his head, toward the women in the rear seat. "Taking the folks in. Two of 'em are a little under the weather."

"We'll drift along behind," the sheriff announced with a keen look at the girl. "It's got so now I know pretty well where to find you when the trail's at all fresh. You wouldn't have got away with it, if it hadn't been for the blizzard. I expected to find your body out here on the prairie somewheres."

"Sheriff," said Scott, his eyes gleaming dangerously, "I reckon you know how men can conduct business together. That's the way you an' I'll tend to our affairs. You can trail along behind if you want, but keep the conversation till we get to town."

He started the team, and they continued on their way, with the sheriff and his two men following. Silent kept looking to southward, and when the others glanced in that direction they saw a buggy journeying toward town. Silent kept the horses down to a walk and seemed much interested in the buggy. After a time it appeared to the others in the wagon that Silent was deliberately holding back so that they should not reach Brant ahead of the conveyance to the southward. When he pushed on at a smart pace behind the buggy after it had entered the lane, they were sure of this.

Annalee was worried at this new turn of affairs. Why

did the sheriff want Silent Scott again? Was the Lummox case to be revived? It seemed the only plausible explanation, and she accepted it. She remembered, though, that after everything was taken into consideration, she knew very little of Silent Scott. She felt a thrill as she realized that she didn't care what his past had been; she hardly cared what he might be now. The ideals and conventions which had always been a part of her existence seemed very far away from this snow-ridden, wind-swept land of desolation which was thawing in the warm Chinook wind. She believed Silent to be a man. Instinctively she reached forward and patted him on the shoulder. Then she shrank back and snuggled into her furs, avoiding his eyes as he turned round. Her eyelids drooped.

Scott drove directly to the hotel, where he superintended the unloading of the baggage. Annalee saw Capron in the lobby as she entered, and was surprised when he nodded to them pleasantly. But the sheriff also had followed at their heels. Another thing which attracted her attention when Silent took off his coat, was the absence of his gun, although the gun belt and holster were about his waist and thigh.

She saw him confront the sheriff; saw him motion to the official to go with him into the bar, away from the rest of the company.

"No!" snapped out the sheriff. "You're coming with me, Scott, right from this spot. You're charged with the robbery of the Choteau stage just before the blizzard!"

"A definite charge, sheriff?" drawled Silent as the girl's heart pounded in her throat.

"A definite, specific charge," said the sheriff loudly. "Are you coming along without making a fuss, or will I have to put these on you?"

He had drawn his gun with one hand and had taken a pair of handcuffs from a side pocket of his coat with the other.

Silent's face went white at the sight of the steel, and the girl cried out aloud. But before another word could be said or another move made, Capron stepped between them.

"I take it you've made a mistake, sheriff," he said sharply.

"No, I haven't," declared the official. "He was seen in the vicinity at the time of the holdup last spring, an' he was in town right after the stage was stopped this time. What's more, he was gambling. Some of the bills taken the last time was marked; they've been marked every trip since last spring. And those bills got onto the gambling tables in Brant, Capron!"

"That may all be," said Capron coolly; "but for this man to have stopped the stage he would have to be on the ground, sheriff. He'd have to be *there,* wouldn't he?"

"He was there, all right," said the sheriff grimly. "He'll have a chance to prove he was somewhere else—if he can."

"It isn't necessary for him to go to the county seat with you to prove that," said Capron. "He can prove it right here and have an end of this business."

Silent had stepped back and was calmly rolling a cigarette. He seemed to be the least of all present

240

interested in the proceedings.

The girl watched him for signs of guilt, but saw none.

"Yes, he can prove it!" sneered the sheriff sarcastically.

Capron's face grew dark. "You're going to be square in this, Moran," he barked out. "I'm going to tell you something, and then you're going to think over whether my word is good or not. I *know* Scott wasn't west of here at the time of the holdup."

"You—know?" said the sheriff in amazement. "How do you know?"

"Because he was at my ranch!" thundered Capron.

The sheriff stared at him in stupefaction. "I thought—you two—"

"What you *think* hasn't got a thing to do with it, Moran," said Capron sternly. "I'm stating the facts."

The sheriff considered this, smiled wryly, and held up a hand in a gesture of resignation. Only Annalee saw the look that flashed between the rancher and Silent Scott.

CHAPTER XXX
THE SHOW-DOWN

Annalee's feeling of relief at hearing that Silent Scott was not at the scene of this second holdup of the stage was only temporary. Although she did not intimate to her mother that she was worried, she feared that their entry into town might prove the signal for trouble—trouble which had been brewing ever since Silent Scott had first come to their aid.

She reflected that Silent had not been frank with her during his last visit. He had gone to the Capron ranch, had made no explanations, and now it had developed that he had been there before. Why? Neither had he told her that there had been a second holdup; that he was suspected of it. The tears came into her eyes as she realized that he might be concealing much from her.

But it wasn't these things so much as it was the undercurrent of mystery—a sinister foreboding—that seemed to be in the very air. Silent's look, the glance which had flashed between him and Capron, Andy's peculiar attitude of knowing more than he wished to tell—these coincidences gave her pause. And now she realized for the first time that it was for Silent Scott's own sake that she wished trouble avoided, as much as for any other reason.

She had a vague, intangible feeling that circumstances over which she had no control, and yet in whose molding she was concerned, were making for disaster and gradually setting the stage for a tragedy. It was all part of a code, perhaps, which she did not understand. It might be that a feud was ripening before her very eyes without her being aware of it. So much could happen in so short a space of time in this peculiar country, this new land where customs seemed ages old—old as the dim buffalo trails which Silent Scott had pointed out to her on that day of the great electrical storm.

Now the air again was charged with electricity—of a different kind. She felt it, and it maddened her to realize that she was helpless.

After she had made her mother comfortable in bed, she sent for the doctor. He came; a kindly soul, gray-haired, wise in the ways of the West and old-fashioned, homely medicines. He made her mother comfortable and did more by his words of quaint philosophy and reassurance and deliberate movements than he accomplished through the medium of his powders and pills.

"She needs rest," he said, shaking his ancient, gold-rimmed spectacles at Mrs. Bronson; "she needs rest and—company. I must send up my wife. Mrs. Brown is just the tonic that she needs. You haven't been in contact with any of our real women out here, except this Mrs. Clarendon you speak of, who has gone to California. You must get acquainted. People here are the same as anywhere else, except they may not seem quite so cultured on the—ah—exterior."

"But, Doctor Brown," the girl protested, "the men! They—they seem so secretive; so full of underlying purposes which they do not disclose!"

Doctor Brown coughed. "The men in this country, ma'am," he said impressively, "endeavor to keep their troubles from their womenfolks. But I must be going. You will be all right, Mrs. Bronson. A rest, sleep—I'll send Mrs. Brown up to see you. If you can survive her ministrations and gossip, you can survive my medicines!"

Both Annalee and her mother had to laugh at this. Mrs. Bronson felt better, but the girl was still fearfully worried.

After her mother had quieted down and was resting easily, Annalee stole out of the room and crept down the stairs. There was no one in the lobby whom she knew except the clerk. She went up to the desk and asked if he had seen Andy Sawtelle.

"Went to the barn to put up the horses, I believe," said the clerk with a queer smile that was not lost on the girl.

"How do I get to the barn through the rear?" she asked.

He directed her, and she went through the dining room and out of the kitchen door. But Andy was not in the barn. The horses had been taken care of and Andy had left without waiting to see that they were attended to after he had given the order to the barn man. No, the barn man did not know where he had gone.

Annalee was forced to give it up and went back to her mother's room, her thoughts in a turmoil.

Meanwhile, Silent Scott, Andy Sawtelle, and Capron were in the little office of Neeland's. The locator had not had time to escape when he saw them coming. Silent had seen to that. He had sent Capron and Andy around to the back door while he, himself, had entered by the front.

Neeland, fairly caught, was white and shaken, and sullen.

"Take your time," Silent counseled him; "an' remember we ain't goin' to forget whatever you say. You see, Neeland, you won't sneak out the back door this time—you'll talk."

"I know what you want," cried Neeland defiantly, "an' I'd have talked long ago, but Gruger threatened me. I ain't the first one that's backed down in front of Gruger. I ain't the only one that's afraid of him!"

Silent smiled in the face of the locator's words, which virtually constituted an accusation.

"You located Mrs. Bronson wrong an' kept quiet about it after you knew it?" he asked in a pleasant voice.

Neeland looked at him suspiciously. That voice sounded altogether too pleasant.

"It wasn't my fault altogether," he said lamely. "I forgot the township line was there, an' that the girl was in one township an' her mother in the other. In my—er—hurry, I put down the number of Miss Bronson's township the same as her mother's, in the description for filing."

"But you took their money, didn't you?" asked Silent. "You took their money, an' then when you realized that you'd made a bad mistake, you failed to tell 'em about it? Neeland—" Silent's voice suddenly became hard—"that's one thing the government won't stand for; you know that, don't you? Mislocation is fraud, Neeland, an' the government won't stand for fraud so far as this homesteadin' business is concerned. These people acted in good faith. They built their houses, an' Andy had no idea he wasn't building Miss Bronson's house on the right land. It was up to you to tell her a mistake had been made an' to fix it up."

"It can be fixed all right!"

"It was up to you to fix it long ago!" Silent thundered. "Now answer: Did Gruger tell you to keep still about it?"

Neeland, pale as death, nodded his head, his jaw wagging. His efforts at verbal answer were fruitless.

Silent Scott turned to Capron. "Neeland's out of it," he said quietly; "that is, he's out of it so far's you an' me are concerned. If the government men get up here before he can catch a train out—that's another thing, besides bein' *his* lookout. Now, let's get right down to cases. I took sides with these women first, because they were women. They didn't stand to get a square deal at Gruger's hands, nor at your hands, at first. You've heard what Neeland said; now you call it quits!"

"I called it quits some time ago when the bankers showed me that this land rush was going to boost prices of acreage," said Capron firmly. "As for the other—this mislocation business, I mean—I didn't know a thing about it."

Silent Scott rose with a smile. "There's another little thing," he drawled. "I hear you've sold part of your ranch and are goin' out of the stock business."

"What's that got to do with it?" growlingly inquired the rancher.

"I was thinkin' maybe you wouldn't be needin' Gruger's help any more," Silent Scott suggested.

Capron looked at him for a long time. Then he smiled broadly. "You have me on the hip, Silent; but I understand what you mean. You want Gruger out in the open where there isn't any influence a-rearin' up behind him. You ain't just lookin' for a man to lose his job."

"I want him clean an' clear away from the Bronsons," said Silent sternly.

Capron shrugged. "Have it your own way," he said. They parted outside Neeland's office. Silent and

Andy remained standing in the street for a few moments.

"It was your good work that showed up Neeland," said Silent to Andy. "I'm goin' to tell Annalee before I go."

"But, listen, Silent—you and Capron—what—"

"Nothing," said Silent, pushing him toward the hotel. "I'll see you in a little while."

Andy looked after him, startled. Silent Scott was proceeding across the railroad tracks! He was flinging Gruger's threat in his face! The poet started to run after him, but something turned him back. The entire affair seemed suddenly to have passed out of his partial grasp, leaving him helpless to interfere.

Silent Scott, however, did not proceed along the main street of the old town after he had crossed the tracks. Instead, he walked around to the rear of the buildings on the north side of the street and slipped past them until he was behind the Green Front resort. Here he climbed a flight of stairs outside the rear of the building leading to the two rooms above.

He entered the little hallway between the rooms noiselessly and listened. From the room on his left came the soft sound of hushed voices and the dull clicking of poker chips. He drew his gun from within his shirt, opened the door suddenly, and covered the men at the table.

His quick glance roved over the faces of the players until it rested on that of Myrle Capron. He motioned to the youth to come out, while the others stared at him in awed amazement.

"Cash in!" he ordered sharply as Myrle started toward him, leaving his checks on the table.

Myrle turned back, shoved the stacks to the dealer, and received a wad of bills in exchange.

Then he preceded Scott, who backed out, still keeping the players covered.

In the little hall Scott faced the frowning youth.

"Do you know where I was when the blizzard started?" he asked in a low voice.

"You was ridin' in from an all-night game in Conrad, from what I heard," the youth replied. "Why—how—"

"No, I wasn't!" Silent interrupted sharply. "That was when the Choteau stage was bein' held up, an' I was at your father's ranch. Your dad just told the sheriff that to prove an alibi for me."

"Dad—said that!" gasped out Myrle. "Why—why should he want to alibi you?"

"Because your dad has learned a few things," said Silent grimly.

The boy's face went white, and his lips trembled.

"An' he wants to see you privately," Silent continued. "I've come to get you an' take you to him." He motioned sternly toward the door.

Myrle stuffed the bills in his coat pocket and obeyed.

A few minutes later, Annalee, looking from the hotel window, saw two queer sights. She saw Silent Scott and Myrle Capron walking rapidly across the railroad tracks from the old town, and she saw a man, lugging two heavy suit cases, trudging across the tracks in the opposite direction.

It was Neeland hurrying to catch the train.

CHAPTER XXXI
THE MEDDLER

T he fact that Silent Scott had crossed into the old town despite Gruger's warning did not impress the girl particularly since he had returned without any evidences of there having been any trouble. But she could not understand his presence with Myrle Capron. It was another puzzling incident of a day which she never would forget. However, she breathed more easily. She was not particularly interested in Neeland's movements. Not being in possession of the facts, she attached no significance to the matter of his leaving town.

It was a glorious afternoon. The sun was shining brightly, and the snow was almost gone. The whole land was laved by the warm Chinook which blew steadily from the southwest. It seemed like spring, and she opened the windows. It was the weather as much as anything else that revived her spirits and sent her down to the street for a short walk.

She heard the whistle of the train in the south and decided to walk to the depot to witness its arrival and departure. As is the case with a small town where there is little excitement, the station platform was thronged. She saw Neeland standing close at the edge of the platform with his suit cases. She thought he looked startled when he glimpsed her in the crowd.

The train pulled in, and its few passengers alighted. Neeland swung his suit cases aboard and had one foot on the steps when a voice roared his name from the rear of the train.

Annalee, who was watching curiously, saw Gruger jump from the rear steps and come plunging through the crowd toward Neeland. The locator scrambled up the steps as the conductor cried, "All aboard."

The train, late and making up time, already was under way when Gruger leaped up the steps after Neeland, shouting to him at the top of his voice. The girl caught a fleeting glimpse of the locator's pallid features and staring eyes, of Gruger's look of intense rage and his purple lips. Then Gruger's right fist struck out, and Neeland was knocked backward into the car.

Trainmen surged toward Gruger on the coach platform, and for a moment he hesitated. Then he leaped from the train and stood on the edge of the platform, shaking a fist after it. He swung about and pushed his way through the crowd.

Annalee, unable to understand the purport of it all, walked rapidly back to the hotel. Gruger had not been in town, then, when Silent Scott had crossed the track into the old town. But now he was back, and his presence constituted a menace not only to her peace of mind but to the peace of the community. It had been plain to see that he was in a terrible rage about something. It was all more of the mystery which had been prevalent that day. She went back to the room in the hotel, determined to have a talk with Silent Scott or Andy Sawtelle at the first opportunity, when she would demand to be told everything.

• • •

Andy Sawtelle was standing at the bar of the hotel, talking with the patrons of the place about the drive through the blizzard. He could do this with unstinted praise of Silent Scott, for Silent was not there.

"And all this time," he was saying, "there was a bottle under the seat that Pat had put there a long time ago. That's one reason why I'm not taking any more drinks, boys; I didn't take one then, and I'm not going to take one now."

The attention of his audience was suddenly attracted to the door leading into the hotel lobby. Andy looked in the mirror behind the bar and saw Gruger entering. There was a silence in the place as the foreman advanced to the bar and ordered refreshment. He took absolutely no notice of Andy, yet Andy knew Gruger was aware of his presence.

Gruger downed his drink. Andy thought the man's fingers shook a bit. His lips, thick and purple, were trembling, too, and his face was dark. He seemed struggling to regain his composure. Suddenly he walked down the bar, thrust one of two men aside, and confronted Andy.

"I was down to the Falls," he said with a black scowl.

A weight seemed to fall from Andy's shoulders. He felt light—almost gay. He threw his head back and looked at Gruger quizzically.

"I expect it's your privilege to travel," he said, almost in a tone of insolence.

Gruger's eyes narrowed. "You've done some traveling yourself lately, eh?" he said harshly.

"That was also my privilege," replied Andy. "I have been known to flit hither and thither, from pillar to post; but this time, as you probably learned, I went straight to the post."

"You meddler!" cried Gruger with an oath. "You knew I was goin' to file myself on the quarter where that Bronson girl was located by mistake. Now, Sawtelle, what was the big idea?"

Andy frowned, but he was cool. The others in the place were watching breathlessly. Already something of Neeland's mistake, his departure, and the part Gruger had played in the affair had been rumored around. Impending trouble hung in the air like static electricity.

But this apparently did not affect Andy, whose eyes shone brilliantly. The poet appeared proud, defiant, coolly confident.

"You want to know what the big idea was, Gruger?" he asked in a quiet voice.

"You heard me!" snapped out Gruger.

"All right, Gruger, listen to me!" said Andy in a clear, vibrant voice. "I got wind of what was the matter out at the homesteads from Neeland, although he was too scared of you to tell me all about it. I went to the land office in the Falls and learned that Annalee Bronson was mislocated. Then I filed on that quarter section where she built her house to protect her interests. You understand, Gruger, I filed on that quarter to protect her interests!"

Andy's voice rang through the hotel. Upstairs, the door of her room open, Annalee Bronson heard the statement with a thrill. She ran to the top of the stairs to listen.

"You meddled!" exclaimed Gruger. "That's what you mean, you yellow little rat. You stepped in where you didn't belong an' meddled!"

Andy's laugh floated up to Annalee. "I wasn't going to let you pull a ringer on Miss Bronson, Gruger, if that's what you're getting at. You bluffed Neeland out of telling that girl that a mistake had been made. As soon as I got an inkling of it, the day I came in for the Thanksgiving turkey, I beat it to the Falls and put the kibosh on your scheme. It does me a whole lot of good to know that I did that, Gruger; I wish I had a chance to do something like that every day."

"It won't do you as much good as you think, you sneaking meddler!" roared Gruger. His face was nearly purple, and his eyes were darting red. "I know what's been goin' on out there. Ain't I seen Silent sneakin' out there every chance he got? It must be pretty soft when a man'll take a chance in a blizzard to get—home!"

Annalee put her hands to her face as she caught the sneering import of Gruger's words.

Then she heard Andy's voice, shaking with passion, but cold and menacing in its metallic tone.

"Gruger, *you're* the rat!"

Gruger, seeing that he had struck home, leered into Andy's white face. "If I am, I'm a pretty wise rat, eh, poet? Tell that to the man you've been hidin' behind. Tell him no fool would take a chance in a blizzard like the one we just had unless he had good reason. Get that in, poet—good reason!" Gruger's sneering laugh of scorn filled the hotel.

Andy started back; then his right hand swung up and outward with a quick motion, and Gruger's laugh was stopped by a slap on the mouth.

At first Gruger stood motionless, with a ludicrous look on his face, as if he could not bring his senses to realize what had happened. In that moment Andy's left followed his right and a second slap echoed through the place like the crack of a whiplash.

With a roar of rage, his face livid, Gruger made a dash for the poet. Andy sidestepped and caught a glancing blow on the shoulder. As Gruger whirled about, Andy's right fist caught him full on the jaw. Gruger leaned back against the bar. There was an almost imperceptible movement of his right hand and a crashing report from his hip.

A curl of smoke spiraled upward in the still air above the bar.

Andy raised a hand and pointed at Gruger, smiling painfully. "You—know now—you lied!" he said. Then he crumpled to the floor.

With a quick glance about, Gruger shoved his gun into its holster and, without speaking, walked out of the door to the street.

Annalee came running down the stairs, her heart in her throat, a great fear shining in her eyes. Then men ran forward to pick Andy Sawtelle up from the floor and bear him tenderly to a room upstairs.

CHAPTER XXXII
REVELATION

From the bed Andy smiled faintly at Annalee Bronson while they waited for the doctor. There was a crowd in the hall, and they could hear mutterings from the men. Annalee went to the door and pressed her fingers to her lips, a signal to them to be silent. But one of the men spoke to her in a low voice.

"We'll see that this thing is made right, ma'am." He made a motion under his chin, implying something about his throat.

"Oh—no!" said the girl, drawing back. "Not that— promise me. Please promise me. There has been so much trouble. Let the law take care of—of it. Andy would have it that way."

She heard Andy calling in a far-away voice and hastened back into the room.

"Tell them to let him alone!" he said hoarsely, trying to sit up in bed as she gently pushed him back on the covers.

"Tell them," he commanded. "Go tell them."

Annalee hurriedly conveyed the message.

"Please respect his wishes," she pleaded; "and send Silent Scott up here as quickly as you can find him."

She went back to Andy.

"Listen," said the poet in a stronger voice. The fact that he had something important to tell her showed in his burning eyes and seemed to revive him.

"Listen, Annalee, I'm hard hit, I guess—but I don't

care." For a moment he turned his face away. Then he looked back at her eagerly. "I want to tell you—when Silent found out Neeland had double crossed you and was scared of—of Gruger—he cornered him in his office to get the truth out of him. Neeland sneaked out the back way to old town where Gruger was. Silent wanted to go over there—and get him—make him talk. He didn't go because he knew it would mean trouble with Gruger, and—he'd—promised you. See? You see, Miss Anna? He had to keep his promise."

Annalee nodded, with tears in her eyes, and laved his temples with cold water. His face was very white, but his eyes were burning with the fever of his desire to speak.

"Please don't try to talk, Andy," she pleaded with him.

"No, no." He shook his head impatiently. "There's something to be cleared up, Miss Anna. I may be harder hit than we think for. You know why Silent went after Myrle Capron across the tracks? It was to get Myrle and his father together. Listen, Miss Anna, it was Myrle who held up the stage. That first time last spring Silent nearly caught him at it and got shot in the hand for his pains."

"He—took the blame?" asked the girl wonderingly.

Andy nodded eagerly. "And then later he held it as a threat over Capron's head. That's one reason why Capron was so decent lately, Annalee. He was afraid of what Silent knew and realized that Silent was your— our—friend. He had to be decent. Then, this last time, when Myrle went wrong and turned the trick again to give himself money to gamble with, he made Capron agree to lay off us and fire Gruger. There won't be any more trouble from the C-Bar bunch, Miss Anna." His voice was emphatic.

The girl sat with her hands in her lap, looking wonderingly at the glowing eyes of the poet.

"Are—are they going to arrest Myrle Capron?" asked Annalee.

Andy shook his head. "That's where Silent's been. He's been all the rest of the afternoon with Myrle and his father, bringing them together. Capron thinks everything of that kid. Silent told 'em to keep quiet and the sheriff never could get anything on the boy. He said to let 'em be suspicious of him—of Silent. That was doing them both a good turn, Annalee. Silent does those things and doesn't say anything about them. He's that kind."

Annalee was suddenly in tears again at this demonstration of the friendship of one man for another.

Then Doctor Brown came and set to work upon Andy, with the assistance of two other men.

The girl went out in the little front parlor and sat down alone. She knew now how Silent had protected them, even when he had been away. She knew why Neeland had taken the train out of town so suddenly, and why Gruger had attacked him on the coach platform. She knew, with a great sense of relief and joy, that Silent Scott was not guilty of the stage robberies, that he had even protected the culprit. She saw peace, ahead, in the prairie country to eastward. Then, as she thought of Andy, of his courage when facing Gruger, of his avenging of Gruger's insult, her eyes filled with tears.

After a time Doctor Brown came out and found her there. He shook his head gravely.

"Not—not *that,* doctor," she said brokenly.

The doctor nodded slowly. "I'm afraid he hasn't a chance. He's hit on the left—near the heart. The peculiar part of it is that he seems rather to welcome the—the end."

Annalee pushed past him into the room where Andy Sawtelle lay in the bed, his face white and drawn, his eyes closed. She dropped down beside the bed and buried her face in the covers.

The doctor touched her lightly on the shoulder. "It won't do any good, Miss Bronson, and—it won't help *him* any," he said gently.

She rose, walked to the window for a moment, then sat down in a chair. She did not dare call her mother in, for she feared the consequences of the shock.

The door opened softly and Silent Scott entered the room.

For some moments he stood, looking down upon Andy's face. Scott's own features were nearly as white as those of the dying man. In his eyes was a peculiar light which seemed to glow steel blue.

Annalee's hands flew to her breast as she saw that he again wore his gun.

Then Andy opened his eyes, looked up at Silent, and smiled. Silent took off his hat, sat down on the edge of the bed, and took one of Andy's hands.

"I told her—everything," Andy whispered, trying to nod his head.

Silent pressed the limp hand within his own.

Andy's lips moved again. "He—got me—but I made him show—he lied," he mumbled.

Silent smoothed the white brow. "If—if I'd been there, Andy. It was my fault," he said softly. "Andy, you're all man. Is there—anything?"

Andy managed to nod his head. "My inside coat pocket," he mumbled.

Silent rose and went to where Andy's clothes were lying on a couch. From the inside pocket of the coat he took some papers. These he took over to the bed.

"Look at them," said Andy.

Silent opened the first paper. It was Andy's location of the homestead on which Annalee's house had been built through a mistake.

Scott opened the second paper and saw a number of verses bearing the inscription: "To Annalee."

He looked at the girl and back at Andy. The dying man nodded with a smile, and Silent handed the papers to Annalee, who was now standing beside him.

The girl's eyes were swimming with tears as she read a verse:

> Winds of the wide prairie night,
> That begin their songs in the soft twilight,
> Sing only one song to the life of me—
> My joy in my love of Annalee.

It was not the poetry; it was the sudden realization of

what she had meant to the writer of the verses which caused the girl to fall down by the bedside and press her lips to his. The secret of Andy's walks on the starlit prairies was explained.

He was speaking faintly again, as one hand moved slowly up to stroke her hair. "It—wasn't—just a home to me—out there," she heard. "It was—a shrine."

He raised her hand and brought it to his lips, then suddenly released it with a surprised expression and a slight cough. The doctor hastily bent over him, but Andy smiled. His eyes again sought Annalee's. She kissed his cheeks. The eyes had closed.

Doctor Brown drew them gently away, Annalee unseeing through her tears, Silent Scott looking down at the still face with that awed, wondering look with which men regard death.

The doctor walked to the window and threw up the shade as far as it would go, letting in the crimson rays of the sunset.

CHAPTER XXXIII
A SCORE IS SETTLED

Silent drew Annalee out of the room and into the little front parlor. The girl clasped tightly in her hands the manuscript which Andy Sawtelle had worked over during the long evenings on the homesteads. Her eyes were wide and dry. The tragedy of it all was too great for tears.

"You must go in with your mother and rest," Silent said in a queer voice of authority.

She looked up at him quickly. Then she stood back from him, startled by the pallor of his face and the look in his eyes.

"Silent," she said, "you're not—oh, no—no!" She threw her arms about his neck.

Gently but firmly he pushed her away, while she stared at him, transfixed with horror, terror, and a feeling of utter hopelessness.

He looked out of the windows toward the crimson skies as he spoke slowly. "Andy Sawtelle was my friend—our friend," he said in a voice as soft as a vagrant breeze. "He was our friend, Annalee—*my* friend. And he was unarmed!"

She knew as she listened to his voice that whatever was about to take place would come to pass. She was powerless to prevent it. She suddenly felt very much alone.

Silent took her hands, rumpling the manuscript in his grasp, and for a moment he looked into her eyes. Then he turned and walked rapidly out.

She stood still and heard his footfalls on the stairs. She even counted—one, two, three, four; one, two, three, four—to herself as he descended. Funny that she should do that, funny that she should feel so calm in her sense of complete isolation, funny that the sun should be glowing red above the western mountains!

She thrust Andy Sawtelle's manuscript into the bosom of her dress and stepped to the window. The snow was gone from the prairies. People were moving in the street. Gradually she realized that most of them were moving in a given direction. They were walking slowly, talking casually in pairs—moving westward across the railroad tracks. Why, they were going over into Old town!

Then she saw Silent crossing the street. His hat was pulled low over his forehead, and he was walking slowly—alone. She saw him look quickly about now and then, and yet there was a deceiving quality in his alertness; he seemed to move so leisurely. He, too, turned toward the railroad tracks. Then he stopped and, taking papers and tobacco from his shirt pocket, rolled a cigarette. He struck a match, and a little curl of smoke rose above the broad brim of his high-crowned hat. He walked on. As he crossed the tracks a fitful gleam of the sunset shone red upon the black butt of the gun in the holster strapped to his right thigh.

Annalee stood at the window, breathless, fascinated, as he passed from view.

Men who met Silent Scott on that short journey from the hotel across the tracks into the old town still talk of the look in Silent's eyes. They nodded to him, but none thought of speaking. He proceeded slowly, his sharp glances darting about under the brim of his hat. Once he stopped and looked up into the sunset. Then, with a shrug, he continued on his way.

Men never knew the distance between the new and old sections of Brant was so long until that day. They whispered to each other in hushed, guarded voices, and they strolled on until they reached a point in the street near the Green Front resort. A few—a very few—went in.

Silent Scott approached the place at a tangent from across the street. He paused a moment before the entrance, then, with a quick motion, threw open the door with his left hand and stepped inside. His gaze swept the place in a flash as men scrambled away from the bar, overturning card tables in their haste, leaving a clear space between Gruger, at the bar, and Silent, at the door.

Silent strode toward Gruger as their eyes locked.

The big man leaned a bit backward, and his face became blue.

"Gruger, I'm on your range!" said Silent, in a ringing voice. "I kept off it because of a promise I'd made to keep away from you. But you broke that promise for me with your insults and your gun!"

He waited for a reply, but there was none.

Gruger's lips merely curled in a sneer.

"Andy Sawtelle was unarmed, Gruger," came Silent's voice again. "You shot him down like a dog. That's murder! Any man can take a murderer in to the law!"

Gruger's lips parted. "You mean he can *if* he can," he snarled.

"I'm here to take you, Gruger," said Silent clearly; "an' to tell you you're an out-an'-out coward with your hide on the fence where any man can see it. If you're not goin' to use that gun, *give it to me!*"

Gruger half turned with the rapidity of his draw, and, on the instant, the room rang with the reports of guns.

Silent Scott stood straight, smoke curling upward from the weapon at his hip. A steel-blue light flamed in his eyes as he watched Gruger's features twist into a look of surprise, then gradually grow blank, as a veil came over his eyes.

The foreman's gun rattled dully on the floor. He wet his lips with a dry tongue and raised his left hand upward—upward along the outside of his coat upward toward his heart—upward—

Suddenly he sank to the floor as Silent whirled on his heel and walked slowly out the door.

Annalee was still at the window. She had not been able to move. It seemed as if she felt something gripping at her heart, something intangible that she couldn't define. Then she saw Silent Scott coming back; back across the railroad track, his shoulders bent, his face turned down. In his right hand he still carried the gun. She wondered at that. She wondered that he should carry the gun that way, in plain sight. She saw him stop, look vaguely about, toss the gun to the ground, and walk on.

It seemed to her that she had ceased breathing. She saw him step into the street opposite the hotel. There were men crossing the tracks behind him now. They were talking excitedly and gesturing. She gathered from their actions that they approved of whatever it was that had happened.

Now Silent was crossing the street. He did not look up. He passed from her sight below the porch roof. In a few moments she heard his step upon the stairs. He was coming back to her! He was coming back—one, two, three, four; one, two, three, four—

He stood before her in the doorway, and she noted that the look in his eyes had changed. With a sob in her throat she knew everything.

"I—I had to do it, Annalee," he said in a low voice. "I had to do it. It was in the pictures. I'm sorry. I'm sorry, Annalee, and I'll have to leave you now—for good. I'll go back to the Musselshell, where I've been working, an' try—to forget."

He came toward her, took her in his arms, and kissed her forehead.

"It was a shrine for me as well as for Andy," he whispered softly.

He released her and turned toward the door. She stood motionless, her face white as death, an agony in her eyes, as he passed out.

Then she tried to speak, but it was only a sob. She reached out her hands and sank to the floor.

Her mother found her there.

CHAPTER XXXIV
SPRING

They buried Andy Sawtelle in Brant, with the whole town attending the funeral. As if in recognition of his love of the land, the sun shone warmly that day, and the Chinook wind blew gently from the southwest.

The shock of the poet's death, and the killing of Gruger, seemed to divert Mrs. Bronson's mind from her own troubles, and she gained rapidly. The doctor's wife proved to be a genial, hospitable, sympathetic woman and was soon a good friend of the Bronsons.

They met other women of the town and were quite content in Brant, living in two rooms in the hotel.

Myrle Capron came humbly with his apologies. The rancher himself visited them, and the feud was at an end. It was whispered that Myrle's father made good the amounts taken in the stage robberies, and there the matter was dropped by mutual consent of the authorities to give the young man a chance to make good.

The county attorney blamed the gambling tables in the old town and closed the lid down tightly on all gambling. Myrle, himself, contrite, gave promise of better things, and was on terms of perfect understanding with his father. He told Annalee how he had shot Silent Scott through the hand when almost discovered in the act of the first robbery, and how Silent had virtually handed him back his life. He was sorry Silent was not there to receive his thanks.

Silent Scott was exonerated in so far as the killing of Gruger was concerned. The whole countryside was roused over the brutal murder of Andy Sawtelle, and at the time Silent crossed the tracks into the old town, a sentiment in favor of lynching was rapidly gaining headway.

Capron explained that Gruger had been out to "get" Silent, and had caused the charge of killing Lummox to be withdrawn, so that Silent could be at liberty and he, Gruger, might have a chance at him sooner or later.

The long winter wore on. Blizzards—blinding, howling, snow-filled—swept down from the north with a ferocity that made Annalee and her mother shudder whenever they thought of the families battling through the winter on their lonely homesteads. They experienced degrees of cold so severe that they wondered how people could move about in the open—thirty, thirty-five, forty, and once, fifty-four degrees below zero.

Annalee often sat alone at the window, looking out over the vast plain of white, a yearning look in her eyes which gradually changed to hopelessness and resignation. Her mother knew, and was silent. She, too, had come to love the tall, blond man with the clear, blue eyes, almost as a son.

Spring came, almost in a day. The snow left the prairies, and river and streams were swollen. A new influx of homesteaders began, and hundreds arrived to take up residence on their claims. Annalee and her mother journeyed to Great Falls, where the error in Mrs. Bronson's location was corrected by the land office officials, after they had heard the facts in the case.

Then came the day when they went back to the homesteads. Pat, having returned from his winter in the "South"—which meant Great Falls—went with them. They found the houses and barn all right. There was a fine stand of winter wheat, although it could hardly be called a "stand." Nevertheless, it was well up, green and thick. It promised an excellent crop, providing the June rains did not fail them.

Annalee and her mother had decided to prove up in the fourteen months, if possible, and thus get title to their land, so that they could borrow on it if their funds became exhausted.

Homesteaders came into that section and located all about them. They received a visit from Capron, who was very cordial, and who told them that they could have a man from his place any time they wanted him. He intended to sell the balance of his ranch in the fall and move to California.

Pat began plowing, with the intention of sowing some spring wheat and oats, thus adding to the prospective crop. They bought some chickens and geese. Then Myrle Capron came, one day, leading a fine milch cow, and insisted that they accept it as a gift from him, in recognition of the favor their friend, Silent Scott, had done for him. His speech was so earnest, although embarrassed, that Annalee could not refuse; and the cow proved a most valuable acquisition.

The spring was full and overflowing, and they planted a garden on the ground watered by it. The garden flourished. They planted potatoes, too. Altogether the outlook was exceedingly favorable.

Annalee went about her work listlessly, although she did it well. The great, green stretches of prairie, the purple mountains and pink buttes, the green of the graceful cottonwoods along the river did not have the same lure for her; nor did they appear as beautiful.

This, until one evening in May, when she saw a lone rider coming from the southeast. She was interested in every rider, these days; and there were many of them, for homestead shacks were springing up all about them, and they had many neighbors.

But, for some reason which she could not define, this rider, even at that distance, seemed different. He did not sit his horse like a homesteader. For a moment the girl felt a wild thrill of hope, then she flushed, and the hopeless light came back into her eyes. But she could not take her gaze from the approaching horseman.

Then, suddenly, she turned and ran into the house. "Mother!" she exclaimed. "Mother!"

Mrs. Bronson, getting supper, looked at her daughter in astonishment. The girl pointed out of the door.

Then came the pound of hoofs. He was coming at a gallop!

Mrs. Bronson was on the little porch when he dismounted and swept his big, broad-brimmed hat close to the ground.

"Silent!" she cried in a tone of glad welcome. "Well, you've stayed away long enough!"

"I had to come back, Mrs. Bronson, to see how you were gettin' on," said Silent Scott.

"Is that all you came back for?" inquired Mrs. Bronson, extending her hand.

"Mother!" came Annalee's reproving voice from the kitchen. Then the girl, pale, but with a peculiar light in her eyes, came out of the door.

Silent looked up at her gravely as she held out her hand.

"You're just in time for supper," said Mrs. Bronson. "Put your horse up and come right in. Call Pat, Silent. I declare, it's good to see you again. Come and help me, Anna, dear. Hurry now."

At the supper table they told him about the winter, and he explained that he had been working with a large outfit in the Musselshell country.

"I couldn't leave the cattle, or I would have taken a run up to Brant to see how you all were, I guess," he said smilingly.

That evening he and Annalee walked on the prairie in the twilight.

"I reckon I ain't a man of my word any more," said Silent plaintively. "I said I couldn't ever come back, an' maybe I shouldn't have come, after—after everything that happened."

"I know now that it had to happen, Silent," said the girl softly.

"You know?" he said quickly. "You understand?"

"Yes, Silent—I understand."

The prairie wind whispered in the waving grasses. The first stars were peeping through the purple velvet of the deepening twilight. In the air was the scent of growing things.

"You—you forgive me, Annalee?"

She stopped and looked up into his eyes. "There isn't anything to forgive, Silent, except your staying away so long."

He put his hands on her shoulders. "Annalee," he said softly, "I came back to the shrine because I love you."

Then she was in his arms, and he was kissing her, holding her tightly, stroking her hair, muttering brokenly.

"Silent," she whispered from his shoulder, "there's something you haven't asked me."

"Girlie, mine, will you marry me?"

"Not that, Silent. You haven't asked me if I love

you." He could barely hear her voice.

"Do you, Annalee?" he whispered.

"Forever!" she said with shining eyes, as she drew his face down to hers.

In the east, beyond the painted buttes, across leagues of shadowy prairie, the silver disk of the moon rose above the rim of the horizon. The night wind freshened and sang in the billowing grasses. The heavens blossomed into stars.

Center Point Publishing
600 Brooks Road • PO Box 1
Thorndike ME 04986-0001 USA

(207) 568-3717

US & Canada:
1 800 929-9108